Necronomi-RomCom

What makes human hearts (and other parts) beat faster? For some, it's other humans. For others, it's tentacled creatures from beyond time and space. In this frightful Dark collection of Cthulhu Mythos-inspired romcom, nineteen stories and poems, part of a duology, we meet Cthulhu's wife and children, do some gardening with a wife at the end of the world, join a women's cult, honor the beloved dead, steal cursed furniture, hook up with Nyarlathotep, and get chased by some Dark Young in pursuit of true love. This Dark tome includes many beloved Mythos creatures and a host of new ones.

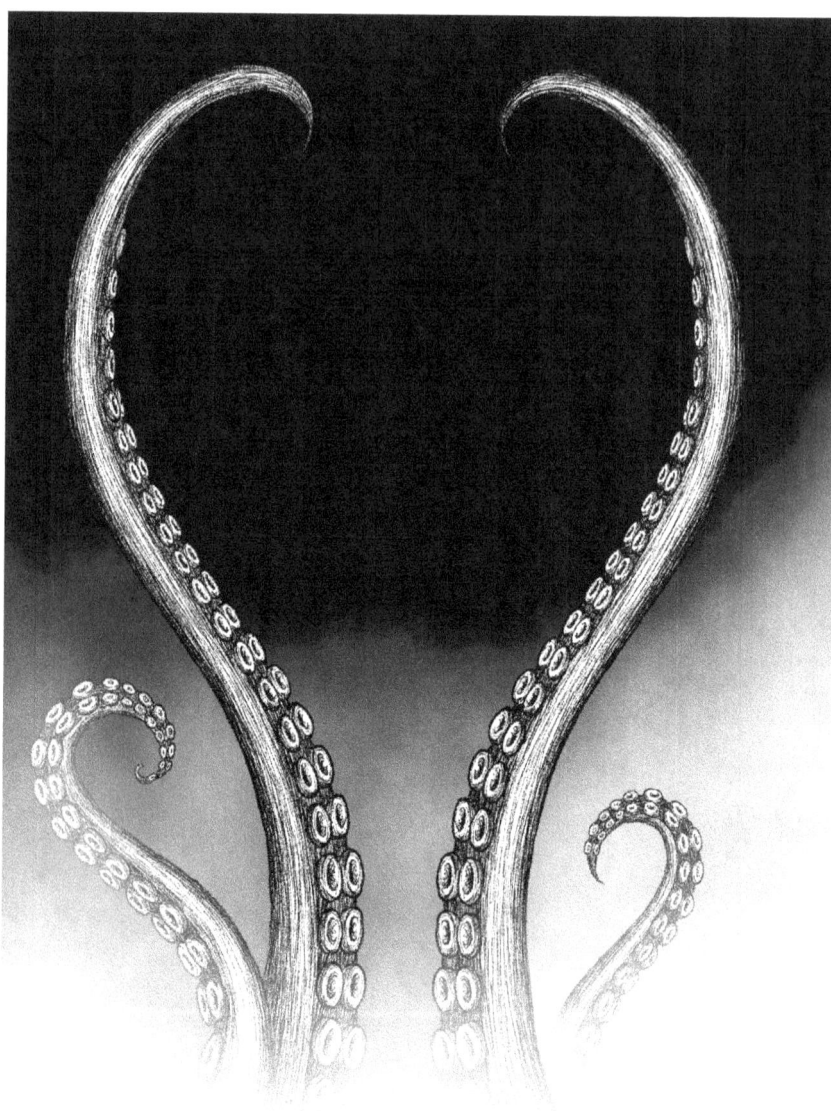

Table of Contents

Foreword:
Strange Bedfellows

Kristi Petersen Schoonover

Say "romantic comedy," and it immediately conjures images of films like *Mystic Pizza, 50 First Dates* and the structure of meet-cute followed by chaos and misunderstandings that result in a happy ending. But say "cosmic horror," and there's often a long beat. There could be mentions of "The Colour Out of Space," Dagon, ancient gods, secret societies, and madness. Those of us who know and celebrate cosmic horror appreciate that these are surface trappings; cosmic horror is *existential*. It's about the things we don't understand: why we exist, where we fit in the scheme of things, who or what is really in charge, and our impending decline and doom.

Romantic comedy and cosmic horror, then, might seem like strange bedfellows. But when we consider the undercurrents of romantic comedy on a deeper level, suddenly, cosmic horror becomes romcom's most eligible match. After all, that initial meet-cute can seem to be fatefully arranged by mysterious, unseen forces. Pursuing that special someone may end in the discovery that it's something we don't want after all. And falling in or out of love changes our perception of ourselves, impacts our priorities, and redefines the world and our place in it.

This *Necronomi-RomCom* double-volume is a glorious eavesdrop on their pillow talk. Using all the trimmings of cosmic horror—monsters, cults, the knowledge that should not be known, and, of course, sacrifices—these pieces show us that cosmic horror can be a potential language to explore the human condition in romantic relationships.

Some characters learn that beings from the beyond have other ideas about our destinies. In Derek Paterson's "I Summoned an Eldritch Horror (Without Even Trying!)" (Light volume), a young girl tries her hand at witchcraft—resulting in an exciting otherworldly first date that shifts the course of her life. In "James and the Dark Grimoire," by Kevin Lauderdale (Light volume), a nephew's attendance at a wedding leads to the discovery that there are larger, terrible powers behind the nuptials.

Others suffer the consequences of redefined perceptions and their roles in the

Foreword

world. T. L. Guthrie's "Cthulhu Family Dinner" (Dark volume) is a perfect example of the sacrifices we make for love—in the most extreme cases, losing ourselves in the process. And in Sarina Dorie's "Cthulhu's Girlfriend" (Light volume), the big guy's meet-cute is, at first, a refreshing surprise. Eventually, though, it changes his priorities, threatening his predestined plans and forcing him to make a tough choice. And in Joseph C. DiNallo's "My Marriage, or a Cult Dedicated to A Perverse Fertility Goddess" (Dark volume), a bored suburban housewife is driven to a dark act—but embraces it.

Finally, in a nod to the knowledge that should not be known, love isn't always what we expect, and may turn out to be the last thing we want. Andrew Leon Hudson's "The Birthday Party with a Thousand Young" (Dark volume) shows us that the dream of the perfect family life in suburbia might actually be a nightmare, while in Rob Smales's "Emissary of Love" (Dark volume), a secret society screwup finds the love he's been craving—possibly at the cost of his sanity. In "Lovecraft, Actually," by Jennifer Lee Rossman (Light volume), a woman falls for someone, only to find out that someone is a some*thing*—but maybe she doesn't actually care.

Romantic comedy and cosmic horror are about who we are and where we fit in the universe, what we know, what we don't, what we shouldn't. They're about taking blinders off. They're about pursuit, consequences, and self-awareness—or the loss of it.

Dr. Rebekah McKendry is a journalist and a professor at USC School of Cinematic Arts who's directed several cosmic horror–influenced films, including 2022's award-winning *Glorious*. She gave a presentation at the 2023 H. P. Lovecraft Film Festival called "Defining Cosmic Horror: How to Abandon Yourself to the Horrors of the Universe in the Most Fabulous Way Possible." In her opening, she described her relationship with the genre.

"It's the simultaneous love and being scared to death at the same time with the feeling that there is something much larger out there that I don't understand," she said.

Now, doesn't that just sound like falling in love?

Kristi Petersen Schoonover
Founding Editor, *34 Orchard*
January 15, 2024

Kristi Petersen Schoonover has been in an existential crisis since birth and was therefore overjoyed to discover cosmic horror. Her favorite piece of all time is Lovecraft's "Colour Out of Space." Her short stories have appeared in almost 150 publications, among them *Dead Stars and Stone Arches* and *Lovecraftian Microfiction* Volumes 6, 7, 8, and 9 (all from Timber Ghost Press). Her short story collection, *The Shadows Behind*, will be followed by a second collection, *Songs for a Dying World*, in 2024.

She holds an MFA from Goddard College, was awarded three Norman Mailer Writers Colony residencies, and is the founding editor of the dark literary journal *34 Orchard*. She also serves on the board of the New England Horror Writers. She lives in the Connecticut woods with her husband, Nathan, where she watches birds and still sleeps with the lights on. Follow her adventures at kristipetersenschoonover.com.

Introduction

Gevera Bert Piedmont

Necronomi-RomCom is an anthology of Cthulhu Mythos combined with comedy and romance. But do we really need another Cthulhu Mythos anthology? I think we always need another Cthulhu Mythos anthology! It's a world so rich and varied that we will never be done exploring the Mythos and expanding on it. But why *romcom*?

I was walking down my back hallway in the summer of 2022 when a little voice in the back of my head—the one that tells me to do things that I probably shouldn't—said, "Necronomi-RomCom." That was all. And I just kept thinking about that concept. I thought it would make a great themed anthology, but I didn't think that I was the person to do it. I mentioned it to a few writer friends who thought that I could do it. They encouraged me to do it, and so I did it. And here it is.

I don't think that I need to describe the Cthulhu Mythos in great detail. In a nutshell, it's cosmic horror encompassing the worlds, monsters, and concepts originating in the work of American writer H. P. Lovecraft and expanded on by others. Lovecraft created the famous occult tome called the *Necronomicon*.

Romcoms are romantic comedies. Usually, they have a happy ending. Sometimes whether the ending is happy or not depends on whose point of view the story is told from, hence how I ended up with both Light and Dark volumes.

Why two volumes? I received a vast outpouring of stories for the anthology. I realized I would have enough quality stories to make up two anthologies. Instead of a pedestrian "volume one" and "volume two," I decided to go with a light and dark theme. The "light" theme would be happy endings, sillier stories, the ones where the couples stay together. The "dark" theme would be the unhappy endings, where the lovers separate, the world ends, or the dog dies (spoiler alert). Both books are funny, romantic, and chock full of monsters.

Necronomi-RomCom was my first solo anthology call, and many of the authors I chose became a little family, huddling with me on a private Discord server and being patient and uplifting as we went through the process together. Although I had done the necessary steps with others on various anthology projects, I never did all of them

Introduction

all at once and by myself, and I often felt overwhelmed (going through two knee replacements as I was putting these volumes together), but my authors encouraged me and made me laugh.

This project, started almost on a whim, consumed my life for over a year. I read stories that made me laugh out loud and that made me snort tea up my nose. I fell in love with one based on its title and another on its shape. I posted amazing snippets into the Discord as I moved pieces into the "accept" pile.

Yes, the Cthulhu Mythos is dark and unknowable, but that doesn't mean it's unlovable. And humans will fall in love with anything, as you will find out in these pages.

You hold in your trembling hands the Dark volume. It's not *all* existential dread; light and laughter bubbles through the cracks.

Three authors featured my favorite Lovecraftian creatures, the amphibious humanoid Deep Ones, including John A. DeLaughter's "Crustaceous Wishes and Dungeness Dreams," where a young man finds an unusual lover on a remote Hawaiian beach and follows her deep below the waves.

Elizabeth Davis's visually stunning "Full Moon Siren Song, or The Harmonic Analysis of the Tides off an Unnamed Maine Coast" is a poetic song of longing and pain set to the tides. And in Robert Bose's "The Loveseat," a group of modern Miskatonic University students go on the hunt for the ultimate piece of fun-time furniture.

The tentacled, treelike Dark Young make their appearance in "I Lost You to the Summer Wind" by John Opalenik, where a college student working in a beachside New England bookstore meets the manic pixie cultist of his dreams. Ngo Binh Anh Khoa's poem "Mother's Blessings" posits what it's like to love one of Shub-Niggurath's Dark Young.

Shub-Niggurath herself, the Black Goat of the Woods, is worshipped in two stories as well. A woman's marriage falls apart as she discovers the odd truth about a neighborhood cult in Joseph C. DiNallo's "My Marriage, or A Cult Dedicated to a Perverse Fertility Goddess." Nora B. Peevy takes a different route in "Shub-Niggurath's Shindig" where someone has yarn-bombed Shub-Niggurath's goats just before the Summoning of the Scarlet Circle.

Nyarlathotep, the Outer God, creeps through a trio of stories in various guises, including J. L. Royce's "Theophany at Wall and Broad," where a greedy video game company using likenesses of the Great Old Ones gets what's coming to them. Rob Smales, in "Emissary of Love," describes an incompetent summoning that brings forth The Emissary of Nyarlathotep and inadvertently sets her free. Charles Montgomery's "Gnarly Love" tells of a modern Miskatonic University student who meets Nyarlathotep in a bar.

In the only appearance of Cthulhu Himself, T. L. Guthrie's "Cthulhu Family Dinner," offers a darkly comedic glimpse into Cthulhu's home life, complete with garlic bread and quarreling children.

The remainder of the stories feature original monsters that circle around the Mythos and cosmic horror. In Robert Dawson's "The Gift of the Calamari," an Elder God answers a woman's Christmas wish in a twist on a classic tale. David A.

Gevera Bert Piedmont

Kennedy's "Cyloptorus" tells of a forgetful boy who unleashes a lovelorn monster of his own creation.

M. Stern's "Hearts Synchronize" brings together avant-garde haircuts, interdimensional maggots, body horror, and experimental musical composition with good old-fashioned youthful love.

Andrew Leon Hudson's "The Birthday Party with a Thousand Young" was voted the GOAT by all the kids, but the parents found it kind of forgettable.

In Alec Lownes's "Brandy," a brash sailor learns the hard way not to hit on the aloof, pretty waitress at a seaside bar. Bill McCormick's "Twerking for Jesus" describes a widow spreading the Gospel through dance, opening the door to gods she could never have imagined.

Agrimmeer DeMolay's "Vuil Huis" features two old frenemies meeting in a crypto castle for a ritual that goes horribly wrong. In D. A. Salvatore's "You Can Still Have a Life," the end of the world is hysterical, full of gardening, tentacles, and snark.

I love all of these stories and poems, and I hope you will, too. The Light side also calls to you if your heart is soft enough to open the other volume.

Gevera Bert Piedmont

Cthulhu Family Dinner

T. L. Guthrie

"Mom, Ph'lu made worms come out of his mouth again after you told him not to," a little hellion shouted. "And then he made that *scree scree scree* noise like Daddy used on the delivery guy!"

With a weary sigh, Abigail turned to face the carnage of the dinner table where six blond children of varying sizes screeched at each other in such a din she could scarcely hear herself think, let alone decide what to do about it. Mgu'pha, the gleeful tattletale, knelt in her chair, peering down her lizard snout at her mother, clearly waiting for justice. Mgu'pha held up her hand, pointing a damning finger at her eldest brother Ph'lu, who screwed his boyish face up into the picture of innocence.

Heavily pregnant and exhausted, Abigail debated whether it was worth the fight. She glanced at the closed basement door where said delivery guy had disappeared earlier today. Another van she'd need to drive into the ocean once the kids finally settled down. She wasn't looking forward to trudging through the sand with her swollen feet. Cthulhu would carry her, if she asked, but she hated feeling like a burden.

"Ph'lu, no worms at the dinner table." She brought over a large pot of spaghetti. "But you managed your eldritch shriek? Good. You've been practicing for weeks."

"You brought worms," the boy protested, pointing his sharp, black talons at the noodles. "And shut *up*, Mgu'pha!"

"*Ph'lu*," Abigail scolded. "Kind language with our siblings. And you know it's spaghetti, not worms."

The little girl stuck out a victorious forked tongue at her older brother. Six years old and covered in thick, green scales, Mgu'pha loved winning and being right. She got it from her father, Abigail thought, ruffling her spawn's untidy hair as she moved past to take the bread from the oven.

Once Abigail's back was turned, Ph'lu unhinged his jaw and vomited a cascade of hissing beetles across the table at his sister. "Not worms," he screeched in ear-piercing victory before they pelted from the kitchen and tumbled into the den in a

Cthulhu Family Dinner

pile of scrabbling limbs. Three of their remaining siblings screamed with glee and poured after them, leaving only the baby at the dinner table—she'd have to make them all wash up *again*.

Abigail picked her headphones off the counter as the childish wails reached a dangerous pitch. Now was not the time to dissolve into a gibbering mess. The bread was ready.

She hummed to drown out the madness coming from the den and turned to remove the garlic bread. The oven opened to reveal a black abyss filled with needle teeth, dripping yellow-green venom, reeking of corpses. Abigail slammed it shut and closed her eyes.

"Give me the bread." After a count of five, she opened the oven to wet heat, animal shrieks, and the scent of heavy brimstone.

Abigail sighed. "The bread."

She closed and opened the oven door, this time finding fresh-baked garlic bread sitting peacefully on the rack. The appliance sulked in a fit of stainless-steel rage.

Something seized Abigail by the hair as she put the bread on the cooling rack. She shook off her oven mitts as she turned to see the baby wailing in his highchair, his little face full of tentacles opened in a tormented shriek that painted her vision red. Between her headphones and the other children, she hadn't heard him. Blood and centipedes wept down the wall, pooling around the highchair and congealing into quivering blobs. He was so upset that a wet appendage had burst from his chest to grab her by the head.

Abigail sighed as she dropped her headphones and tried to untangle the claw from her hair as she moved toward to him. "Don't pull," she complained.

He yanked her hair out with his infant-sized claw. It shoved the hank into the baby's tentacled maw, and he calmed immediately at his mother's scent and taste, chewing with gusto. His human arms waved with glee.

Abigail wrinkled her nose at him and rubbed her head. Her fingers came away clean: no blood. Six eldritch children—and a seventh on the way—had given her a remarkable tolerance for pain, and their father would take care of it later. The baby burbled as it slurped down the scalp snack, and the chest appendage sank into his rubbery flesh with a wet glop.

"Mommy's little monster," Abigail said fondly, bopping his nose before raising her voice to shout at the others. "Dinner! Everyone wash up!"

The house shuddered underneath her feet, and Abigail grabbed for the counter to keep herself upright. She'd have been all right if she wasn't so big. It was hard to keep her balance with her center of gravity all wrong. The structure moaned and shook, then went quiet. Even the chaos in the den was silent for a beat.

And then it began again with renewed purpose.

"DADDY!"

"Dad's coming up!"

"Dad—Look what I can do!"

The last was accompanied by a piercing noise like metal being torn apart as Ph'lu showed off his new talent that he *was not* supposed to be using at dinner. The baby added his squeals to the noise, and even the spawn in Abigail's belly twisted and heaved with excitement. Everyone ran to be the first to the sink.

The door to the basement blew open in a howl of black wind, spilling an endless wave of pimpled crustaceans with too many legs and not enough eyes across the kitchen floor. Some burst, splattering blood and gore all the way to the ceiling. The electricity flickered and buzzed, a light bulb shattering in the living room. Again. Did she have light bulbs on the grocery list? Heavy tentacles hauled themselves up the dark stairs, pulling a wet body behind them, a roughly humanoid horror.

Abigail didn't really know what he looked like. She couldn't look at him. But he was wearing the pants that she liked, and he'd broken in his new shoes during his ritual tonight. "You wore the Crocs," she said, smiling. "Did you dream well?"

She stiffened like a corpse as he reached out, her eyes rolling back in her head until only the whites were visible. His voice rasped out of her throat. **"I DREAM OF WHAT IS TO COME. THE RITUAL PROCEEDS. I REQUIRE GARLIC BREAD."**

Abigail came back to herself and gestured for him to take his spot at the head of the table, the baby between them. All the children piled into their seats, beaming at their father. Behind them, the robotic vacuum cleaner churned through the crustacean debris. "There's plenty. I know how you get after you take your company downstairs. You'll need to come with me to the beach tonight if you want me to get rid of the van. I don't think I can get out of the sand by myself."

"YOUR DEDICATION TO THE BROOD IS UNPARALLELED."

"Thank you." Abigail picked a rogue beetle from the spaghetti as she served him. "The children have missed you." This was enough to set the table into eruption once more, as all six competed to be the loudest one so that he'd pay attention to them first, though there was no need. Each would get their own turn of affection from their father. "Ph'lu has learned his eldritch shriek. I think tonight is the night." She glanced at her son, who lit up like a lighthouse beacon.

Ph'lu demonstrated, and six sets of eyes turned to see if their father approved. Abigail observed the children, taking note of the moment sunlight broke out across all their monstrous faces. He was pleased, just like he always was. They all adored him so.

"YOU WILL JOIN ME IN THE DEPTHS, CHILD?"

Excited whispers broke out among them, and Ph'lu did his very best to appear grown-up as he nodded. It was a big moment for them all. At ten, Ph'lu was the oldest of them, and would be the first to return to the sea. Many would be sad to think that their child was born to be a sacrifice, but Abigail smiled. They could only go away if their father wanted to keep them more than anything else; otherwise the ritual would be wasted. Once they shed their mortal coil, Cthulhu's children would live with him forever in the depths. Every child dreams of love like that. Her children would never know the pain of the world. Honestly, it was a mercy.

"But what about the movie, Daddy?" Ag'req asked, her pincered mandibles clacking together with excitement. "You promised that you'd show us how to trample a city!"

"TONIGHT IS PH'LU'S TIME. TOMORROW AFTER SCHOOL, YOU WILL BE THE ELDEST SPAWN THEN."

Cthulhu Family Dinner

All the children cheered, and even Abigail smiled. Sure, maybe their family wasn't quite what she'd envisioned when she was younger, but it was hers. She wouldn't trade it for the world. "I'll make caramel popcorn in the afternoon," she said. "Save me a seat."

"I get to go tonight?" Ph'lu shouted, so excited that he jumped from the table and knocked the whole thing backward. Abigail reached to steady her drink, and Ag'req made a disgusted noise.

"Watch it, lizard lips!" Ag'req sniped, making a face and clacking her mandibles.

"Dung beetle," Ph'lu replied, making a face back. A piece of garlic bread slapped him on the cheek, thrown by his brother Grib'nith. Although he was only four, Grib'nith was almost the same size as Ph'lu. A giant scorpion tail towered over his back. He had butter on his freckled cheeks, and his tentacles wriggled with his jealousy.

"Gross!"

"No fair!"

"Grib, don't throw!" Mgu'pha screeched. "Mom says not to throw!"

"FOOD IS FOR BIOLOGICAL SUSTENANCE, NOT VIOLENCE."

"That's not very good manners, Grib'nith," Abigail scolded. "We've talked about this. Polite boys and girls keep their hands and other appendages to themselves, don't they?"

"Yes, ma'am," Grib'nith said, his tail drooping sadly over his shoulder.

"Until when?" Abigail asked.

"Until there is consent," Mgu'pha announced like a smarmy know-it-all, when he took just a beat too long to answer. "Or ritual sacrifice."

"But do I really get to go tonight?" Ph'lu sat down, tossing the runaway garlic bread across Mgu'pha and back onto Grib'nith's plate. Abigail was pretty sure it was getting fed to the vacuum.

". . . I AM PREPARED." He didn't sound positive. Abigail delighted in this. It meant that he truly was ready. He did not want Ph'lu to go, so the time had come. She was so very proud of all of them.

"I should get to come see," Ag'req complained. "I am going to be the eldest tomorrow. If I got to come see, I could start practicing now."

"No, *I* should get to come see!" Vroc'luf said, his large wings raising behind their seats. Ag'req ducked and gave him a dirty look. He'd almost hit her. "I'm the third oldest, and I'm the oldest *boy*. I should get to see!"

The kitchen erupted into shrieks and wails.

"Who cares if you're a boy?"

"Parts have nothing to do with it!" Ab'req said, grabbing hold of his shirt. An unseen wind whipped her hair around, fog boiling up from the bottom of her chair at her anger.

"Consent!" Grib'nith reminded them around his mouthful of garlic bread.

"*Ritual sacrifice!*" Mgu'pha shot back, her eyes bottomless pits with fiery lanterns in their depths. Her jaw opened too wide in her anger, forked tongue flicking over pointed teeth. "Boy parts have nothing to do with it, or you'd be last, Vroc'luf!"

"You don't even fit on the school bus without walking sideways!" Ab'req said, but she'd released him and brought her hands back to herself.

"Enough," Abigail said. "This is family dinner time. Behave, or there will be no movie tomorrow, and no caramel popcorn. Everyone is staying here except for your father, Ph'lu, and me." She looked at their father across the table. "We'll need a sitter."

"I HAVE JUST THE THING."

←♥→←♥→←♥→

Half an hour later, the dishes were done, the gore cleaned from the ceiling, and the babysitter shuffled up the basement steps. They had filled his empty eye sockets with balls of blue painter's tape, and the same tape held his empty chest cavity closed as well, since the ritual had used his heart. It hadn't been easy to put him back together again. A pretty pink ribbon, splattered in blood, kept his disconnected head from flopping around.

"—all need to be bathed," Abigail finished. Only simple commands for the babysitter would work. "Bedtime at nine. Do not accept override commands unless we've been gone for twenty-four hours." She glanced significantly at Ab'req, who made that last part necessary. Abigail wasn't sad to miss bath time. It was always an unholy terror. They were Cthulhu's children, after all. The water brought out the best and the worst of them.

"Ag'req, Vroc'luf, Mgu'pha, Grib'nith." Abigail looked at each child. "Behave. And you." She smiled at the baby, depositing him into the delivery sitter's waiting arms. "You be good too, Hank." Hank cooed at her through his tentacles, gurgling with glee at his name.

"We will, Mom," Ag'req said.

"I'll tell you if anyone doesn't," Mgu'pha assured her.

"NO GLITTER."

Ph'lu could hardly contain himself as he vibrated with excitement in the foyer, waiting while his father fussed over his jacket. It would be the last one Ph'lu wore—it was important! He aimed for somber and adult as he gathered himself to listen to his siblings, but he broke out into an excited grin as they chorused their farewells.

"I've put a lot of thought into it," Ph'lu said, bouncing on his toes. "Ag'req should get my room. She's the eldest spawn now."

"Not for like another hour I'm not!" Ag'req protested. "But yeah, I want the room."

"And Vroc'luf should have the Hot Wheels," Ph'lu said. "You don't play with them."

"Fine."

"We'll be back soon," Abigail said. "Listen to the sitter and be good. I'll see you in the morning for breakfast."

"Bye, Ph'lu!" Another round of goodbyes as the sitter stiffly tried to herd them toward bath time. The remaining children scattered like cats, cackling with delight as the door closed behind them.

Abigail took her time hauling her bulk into the driver's seat of the delivery van, trying to adjust it so that her feet could reach the pedals without crushing her belly into the steering wheel. A tentacle curled affectionately around her waist as she buckled the seat belt, and she smiled over her shoulder at the monstrosity behind her, taking care not to see him.

"You're sitting in the back?"

"YOUR SAFETY IS MORE ASSURED IN THE FRONT."

He fussed over Ph'lu, unsatisfied with how the restraint fell across the boy's lap, before curling another tentacle across his son as well. He held Ph'lu just a little tighter than Abigail, because he knew he was going to have to let him go tonight. Abigail patted Cthulhu's tentacle as she checked her mirrors and cranked the engine.

Sunset painted the sky red as they headed toward the ocean cliffs where they usually rid themselves of any unwanted sacrificial components. No one would ever find the van once it was in the water, but Cthulhu needed Abigail to get it there. Even if he had been able to drive, the sight of him at the wheel would have driven all the other people on the road to madness, and while that might have been satisfying, it was terrible for getting anywhere with any speed. And the ensuing pile-up made getting back to the kids a real pain in the neck.

"DO YOU REMEMBER THE RITUAL, CHILD?"

Ph'lu rooted in his pocket until he located a worn piece of notebook paper, folded until it was the size of a deck of cards. "I wrote it down." He opened the note. "But it's simple. All I have to do is float, scream all my air out, and take a big breath when I get dragged under the waves. It should only take a couple of breaths, and it'll all happen really fast. Then we'll be together forever. Me and Ag'req have been practicing in the bathtub. I worked on my death shriek too; I have a great one!"

Abigail stifled a laugh. He did have a pretty good death shriek. She'd heard it too many times.

"Dad, do you think that one day I'll be able to come back?" Ph'lu asked. "Maybe if Mom has another baby? Like, get reborn? I bet I'd be twice as strong if I got to do it all over again."

"SPAWN ARE UNIQUE. YOU WILL NEVER BE REPLICATED, MY SON. BUT YOU WILL LIVE ETERNAL WITHIN THE HORRORS OF THE DEPTHS. WE WILL CRUSH MANY HUMANS FOR THEIR INSOLENCE."

"Except Mom?"

"EXCEPT MOM."

Abigail smiled. Times like this she couldn't help thinking back to when she had first met Cthulhu. She hadn't imagined that she'd ever find someone so horribly sweet. She was young—in her twenties, working a dead-end job as a tour guide on a glass-bottom boat. That day, everything had gone wrong. She'd overslept, and her car had a flat. When she'd finally made it to work, her boss yelled at her for a solid half hour before insinuating that if she wanted him to forget it, he could lock the office door and see what happened.

She'd been saved by the timely arrival of a tour group, and she'd leaped at the chance to get away from him. He'd followed her and spent the tour continuing his harassment. He wasn't supposed to be out on the water—he couldn't swim. When Cthulhu capsized their boat, Abigail had closed her eyes and given up, waiting for the depths to consume her. It wasn't her day, and she was ready for it to be over.

It wasn't until the screams stopped that Abigail opened her eyes, floating next to a piece of the boat. On it were her manager's glasses and a scrawled message: YOUR LIFE IS ALREADY MADNESS. HAVE A BETTER DAY OR PERISH. He must have thought she was crazy; how she'd laughed over that. Everyone in the world and it was Cthulhu who cared about her day. Now and then, they still joked about it: Have a good ritual today, dear, or perish. Have a good time at the grocery store, broodmother, or perish.

Abigail was still chuckling over this memory when she pulled off the road at the cliff path. It was a bumpy ride, but delivery vans were tough and made for inclement weather, and she had driven many of them along this route.

Ph'lu bounced in excitement, his wide, green eyes taking in everything around them as they wove through scraggly coastal trees and sandy loam. The boy made an appreciative noise as they broke through the brush at the edge of the cliff, where the ocean stretched in front of them in all directions. The horizon shone fiery red, fading away into blues and purples with the coming dusk.

"What a beautiful sunset." Abigail unbuckled her seat belt. "You'll need to unbuckle, dear. We have to roll the windows down. There's still a few minutes to sit, though. It's not quite time, right?" she asked the looming presence behind them.

"WHEN THE WAVES TURN BLACK, IT WILL BE TIME."

"Precisely. A few minutes more."

"It's so pretty." Ph'lu sighed, slumping down in his seat. "This is the best day ever. I can't believe I get to go into the water on such a great night."

The tentacle around Ph'lu held him a little tighter, and the boy wrapped his arms around it as they watched the sun fade away. Eventually, reluctantly, the tentacles slipped from around their waists.

"We have to go," Abigail said gently to Ph'lu. "Are you scared?"

"No," Ph'lu said, smiling. "It's going to be like Hot Wheels. And then nothing in the water can hurt me."

Except Dad. Who could, and would, and must.

Abigail smiled back at him. "All right." She turned the engine over and took a breath of her own. How many times had she driven vehicles off this cliff? Too many to count. It never stopped being exhilarating. She backed the van up a bit to give them more runway off the sheer cliff, and then double-checked the windows were down.

The engine roared as she floored the accelerator, and the van jerked forward, tires spinning before grabbing traction and shooting them ahead. For five heart-stopping seconds, they gained speed, the cliffside whipping by, and then they launched into open air, free and untethered.

Ph'lu whooped with glee, and Abigail laughed before joining his cheers. For just a moment, they hung suspended in the young evening sky, a new star sparkling in the gloom, bright against the black of the ocean. Gravity took hold of them, and they plummeted toward the water below—faster, harder, more exhilarating with every second. The fall was both eternal and terminally short.

There was one last chance for a breath. The van smashed into the waves so violently that the nose crumpled and the hood ripped away. As the vehicle plunged underwater, Cthulhu pulled Abigail and Ph'lu out of the shattered windshield into the inky black. The presence of Cthulhu was thick in the water, enveloping and enshrouding them like the tentacles coiled gently around their waists. Abigail felt the suck of the current as the van sank beneath them and the abyss claimed it completely.

She and Ph'lu surfaced to bob in the waves. This far out, and with his sheltering eyes watching over them, there was no danger. If it wasn't for the ritual that would complete him, Abigail wouldn't have believed that Ph'lu could drown. Like all his siblings, he'd been born here in the water, and it hadn't left his veins. It was a peaceful place, with the distant cry of the gulls and the roar of the waves against the cliffs. The few distant boats were visible only as lights against the horizon. She had come to love it. There was no reason to be afraid of what might be below, because it was here with her. She knew the terror of the depths better than anyone else in the entire world because she was his favorite eldritch whore.

"Come here." Abigail pulled Ph'lu to her. She wiped his wet hair from his face with one tender hand, smiling as she rubbed a thumb across the freckles splattered on his cheeks. "I'm going to miss you so much. Do you know that?"

Ph'lu grinned at her. "Yeah. But I'm not going anywhere, Mom. I'll be here with Dad, and you're here all the time. We knew this was the way it was going to be. We've been practicing."

"I know, sweetheart." Abigail hugged him. "You're going to do great. I'll be here the whole time."

"PERHAPS NOW IS NOT THE BEST TIME."

The voice of the abomination was so great here in the water that it thundered through their bodies almost painfully. In the beginning, it had knocked Abigail's breath from her lungs, but over the years she'd gotten used to it.

"It's time, darling," Abigail whispered. "You knew this would be the hardest part. They can't go until they are the most important, precious thing to you. We knew this when they were born."

"I want to go, Dad," Ph'lu said. "I can do it. We can both do it, you and me. We'll be together forever. You must be brave, like Mom says."

"THE BROODMOTHER IS WISE."

"I'm going to say the words," Abigail said. "Are we ready?"

Ph'lu wiggled with excitement as his mother chanted. The words had taken a long time to learn, but she'd had ten years. They came easily to her, whipping the sea around them into a frenzy. There had been no clouds when they left the cliff, but lightning arced across the sky, thunder cracking on its heels. Abigail felt horrible, invigorating power gather within her as the words rose to their apex. She brought Ph'lu close one last time and kissed his forehead, her lips leaving a glowing scarlet mark on his flesh.

The mark of the sacrifice.

"I love—" the boy said, cutting off in a sharp shriek as Cthulhu dragged him screaming down into the depths. She saw him for even less time than she'd seen the van before he was gone. Abigail knew he would never surface. But she waited in the too-still calm. She waited for a long time, until a great howl echoed across the water. She knew it well, because she felt it, too. Grief, as endless as the ocean beneath her.

T. L. Guthrie

The water frothed from smooth glass into a whipped, churning boil; waves as tall as a building crashed around her. Abigail bobbed under, choking and coughing when she surfaced again. She was not afraid. He was with her, even if their grief threatened to capsize them both. It was for the best. Ph'lu would never hurt. She knew this. They both knew this. It would only hurt them.

The distant boats crumbled and dropped beneath the waves as Cthulhu lashed a father's rage against the cliffs. The wail that came from the ocean chilled her more than the water ever could, his piteous cries for his loss and his awful gain tearing at her heart. Abigail comforted him as best she could, soothing his monstrous pain as only a partner truly could.

She was cold by the time the sea calmed. Abigail settled with the waves, gratitude overcoming her. Ph'lu never had a day in his life where he didn't feel his purpose. If all her children were that happy, she would die fulfilled. And if she was very lucky, one day when all the children were gone, Cthulhu would love her enough that it would be her turn. Until then . . . they had all this time to build something wonderful.

Abigail smiled, buoyed by her thoughts and by his tender embrace. "Let's go home, darling," she said. "The children are waiting."

←♥→←♥→←♥→

T. L. Guthrie is an invasive species located in the Oregon Willamette Valley in the Pacific Northwest of the United States. Originally discovered in the Appalachian mountains in the 1980s, Guthrie was transplanted to the Pacific Northwest in 2010 for reasons unknown and continues to thrive there unabated with family. They can be found focused primarily around short works and novels of strange science fiction, fantasy, and horror. If concerned, please report any sightings to your nearest Extension Office immediately. Follow Guthrie on X @tl_guthrie.

The Loveseat

Robert Bose

They say *necessity is the mother of invention*. As a proverb, it's a comfortable classic. Relatable. Inspirational. The sort English majors expound while transmuting mundane garbage into literary delight. So, in keeping with that grand tradition, drunk and delirious in the shadowed corners of disreputable Arkham flophouses, we expelled our own idiomatic maxims. Some nonsensical, some excessive. Most metaphysically impossible. One, though, one stuck with me.

Desperation is the father of the absurd, I thought, eyes locked on the stained stucco ceiling, contemplating love, life, and serious lack of furniture. The party of the semester dropped next week, here in this very dump, and due to a combination of impromptu Pnakotic evocations and accompanying frantic sexcapades, our stock of furnishings was sorely depleted. Sure, we could fit three to five danger-loving individuals on the beer-soaked faux-velvet recliner, and there was always the unfortunately maligned waterbed, though as previous parties still moaned, seasickness, heat stroke, and the bed's current batrachian resident were clear and present dangers.

It didn't help that our finances, or lack thereof, proved somewhat of a dilemma. We were students. We were destitute. Which, of course, meant all available cash went to potables and life-preserving caloric necessities consisting entirely of grilled-cheese sandwiches. We couldn't even afford cardboard-quality thrift store folding chairs.

I had a solution. A daring one. A desperate one. I want to say it came to me in a dream, the mythic sort where overeager supernatural investigators stumble through abandoned lighthouses in Kingsport, but my dreams were as insipid as I was. This party, a certain extravaganza, required a desperate solution, and fortuitously, desperate solutions were a time-honored tradition at Miskatonic University.

As it happens, scattered around campus were *Chairs*. Not just any chairs. No, these were unusual. Ancient and oversized, constructed from stained Brazilian rosewood and black rhino leather, with burns and graffiti and the engraved initials of hundreds of horny student couples and thruples. And the thing about these chairs, most pertinent to my solution, was that over time they had become infused with eldritch carnal essence, tending to become semi-sentient, and, if removed from the warded confines of the University, they became capable of transporting the amorous to alternate planes of existence. Oh, the *Chairs* themselves turned up again, used and abused and confused, but their occupants, if located, were forever altered in indescribable ways.

These attributes, of course, made the *Chairs* targets of larceny.

Campus security was all too aware, and the acquiring of these mystical erotic thrones became more difficult and perilous every year. First came the hideous orange stickers screaming *Miskatonic University Property—No Fornication—No Spatial Transposition*. That wasn't much of a deterrent and summarily ignored. This escalated to placing them in busy common areas where lack of privacy and constant surveillance would provide its own defense. Laughable. The latest initiative was to shackle them to the bones of the University itself, a formidable strategy requiring cunning and arcane power tools to overcome.

But . . . I wanted a *Chair*. I needed a *Chair*. And I was determined to obtain a *Chair* at any cost.

The subject of heist was broached during breakfast, an unnatural time when we cut our grilled cheese into quarters, giving our mornings a much-needed touch of class.

"I think we should pilfer a *Chair* from campus this evening," I said, leaking cardboard crumbs and getting straight to the point. "It's Saturday. There are no events. The only folks roaming the halls will be grubby game club cultists scavenging for dice and misplaced souls."

Shadrach was enthusiastic. "Grand larceny? I'm in." A recent escapee from Innsmouth, our resident waterbed dweller regarded the regal institution as one to be pillaged and despoiled, a product of his salientian robber baron heritage.

"What an absolutely terrible idea," said William, the third in our entangled trisection of $407-a-month basement suite rent. He was often counted on for sober second thoughts, though he was rarely, if ever, sober.

"Oh," I said, sipping the weakest coffee still considered coffee. "Do tell."

He held up three fingers. "One, they're hideous. Two, they weigh a ton, and we don't have a lift. Three, they won't fit down the stairs and through the door. Four, they have the tendency to spirit people away in the throes of passion at the most inconvenient moments. Which, realistically, I don't have a problem with, but I invited a lot of potential organ donors, and the last thing we need is for them to end up tainted or tentacle probed on Aldebaran."

Shadrach squeezed Will's shirtless bicep. "Love is in the air. Think of what we could do with such an . . . erotic carriage."

"It's an epic quest," I exclaimed, "of the best sort. Our glory days lay strewn behind us, the putrid rubbish of our sordid youth, but we have a party to furnish, and unless you have a better idea on how to accomplish that—I'm looking at you, Will—I say we cast off, get roaring drunk, and pull an Ocean's Three sure to etch us into the annals of University Mythology."

Will sniffed. "Whatever, I'm bored. What's the worst that could happen?"

A proper question with a plenitude of answers, this being curse-infested old Arkham.

The Loveseat

If one means to pull a heist like this, one needs to do it solidly. So, after *borrowing* a sigil-inscribed, dubiously sourced hacksaw from Milton, the annoying degenerate who inhabited the upper reaches of our French Hill heritage house, we hit the campus watering hole. And I mean *hole* in the fondest, most sordid sense. A dank pit of abysmal pizza, trays of happy hour pilsner, and listless gloom. It was there we discovered to my, though apparently no one else's surprise, a critical element missing from our intrepid trio: brains.

"Hello, Jane," we said, sausaging our way into her back corner booth.

"Hmm." She sipped a murky highball and didn't take her eyes off the micro-documentary on the constellation Taurus projected against the dance-floor wall.

We ordered a round and pounded them back in a volley of primal grunts and explosive belches. Our ferocity did not impress Jane. It never did. A bio-chemistry/astrophysics major by day, a liver-destroying super-vixen by night, she was rarely impressed. What she saw in me, I can't possibly guess. Yet here we were. Once the show ended, she bit my earlobe hard enough to draw blood and narrowed her eyes at my unfortunate choice in roommates.

"Jesus," said Jane. "Let me guess, you wanted to go on a waterfront bender, but you only have six dollars, so you're slumming until you can find someone willing to take pity on you?"

"Not quite." I shushed the guys when they opened their mouths.

"Right . . . I know your MO. Remember last month? When they had Monkey's Lunches for a buck, and you had to be de-milked for three days?"

"Not our finest moment, I'll grant you. But—"

"Your dorky boyfriend wants to pinch a *Chair* for our party next week. Apparently, the recliner and my waterbed won't cut it." Shadrach wiggled out of the booth and stumbled off, chortling.

"Get me a Hendrick's Cucumber Lemonade," yelled Will. "A double." When Shadrach veered toward the bathroom instead of the bar, Will growled. "Big feet, tiny bladder. Is there a bio-chem term for that?"

"Troglodyte." Jane sipped her drink. "A *Chair* heist, eh? Tricky these days. They've been anchoring them with hardened, ensorcelled three-eighth cold iron bolts and chains. I hope you have a metaphysical power grinder, the kind they use to cut reality with."

"Uh, short notice. But we have this." I tossed the hacksaw onto the table.

Jane ran a finger across the blade and examined the resulting rust smear. "Nice, last century blood. Where'd you get this? The ghost of Wilbur Whateley?"

"Dammit," wailed Will. "Old Milt was holding out on us; I knew he was a creep. Corpse bride wife and peeping Tom kids."

"Relax, she's joking. You are joking, right?"

"It would cut through bone like butter, if that's what you're asking."

Shadrach returned, sans drinks. "Who has cash?"

While Jane laughed, I tucked the last of my life savings into his damp, webbed fingers. "Another round. Jane, want anything?"

"Freedom from the patriarchy."

"Apparently, as many tequila shooters as that'll take, then," I said.

Robert Bose

"Don't take this the wrong way, but your . . . tool isn't going to cut it," said straight-faced Jane.

"Then I'll just have to use the rest of God's gifts," I said, sliding my hand up the back of her shirt.

An indeterminate amount of time later, the four of us stumbled, lubricated, oozing bottom-shelf booze, between quiet, shadow-infested buildings. We searched far and wide, scouring every *Chair* location on our mental map. The acrid corridors of the Science Hall: nothing. The labyrinthian stacks of The Library: a single candidate which, on close examination, proved firmly in the possession of an amorous, nontransportable, and exceedingly malevolent threesome. The stuffy study nooks of Liberal Arts: an ancient "proto" Chair so desiccated one could peer through missing leather and bent springs into a void of unquestionable longing.

Thirsty yet undeterred, we circled the graduate residence lounge, affectionately known as the Black Lung, historically a warehouse of *Chairs*, albeit ones deliquesced by decades of smoke, beer, and sin. We found it closed. Barred. Chained. Padlocked. I looked forlornly at my hacksaw.

"What about upstairs in Locksley Hall, the fourth floor?" Jane deftly hopped over a splash of pizza spew.

I'd been to the third floor, where those aforementioned weird-ass game cultists lurked in their magic stairwell.

"There's a fourth floor?"

"Student Union offices."

We crowded into the service elevator and pushed the glowing IV. The door closed with a swish, and away we went, rocketing upward on the wings of angels.

The fourth floor was unimpressive. Dim pot lights cast long shadows across a small, empty hallway containing identical doors adorned by glowing yellow sigils of the most familiar, yet unnerving, sort. When they throbbed, we crept beneath them, huddled together in mutual terror, testing each knob.

Locked. Locked. Locked.

Jane pushed me against the wall and pressed her lips to mine, the heat of her breath, her body like a flamethrower against my bones.

"Screw this; it's two in the goddamn morning. Let's go to my place and break the bed. I'm tired of worshipping the unspeakable god of lost causes. I'll lend you the back seat we ripped out of Grandpa's old Plymouth if you're that desperate. It's impervious to all known fluids, and some unknown."

She had a point. A damn good one. For a moment, I was honestly tempted. The time of the *Chair* had passed. I could see that now within this tiny cocoon of clarity. I'd be an idiot to say no to her. Her eyes glittered mischievously. Her face glowed. Her grail beacon face.

"One last door," said Shadrach.

"Yeah, one last door," said Will.

"One last door," said I, tearing away from her.

"Jesus," said Jane.

One last door. I held my breath, turned brushed steel. Pushed. Gasped. The hallway illumination revealed an expansive room, undoubtedly the student's union executive lounge. Opulent. Pristine. Distinctive new car smell. We tiptoed in, cased the joint.

And saw it. An immaculate and totally free-range loveseat. The black rhino leather glowed. The polished rosewood glistened. Not a *Chair*, but a *Loveseat*. It was glorious.

"Wow," said Jane, diving in. "Virgin furniture. Unsullied by degenerate asses."

"Untouched," growled Shadrach, looking at Will.

"Unexploited," hiccuped Will, looking at Shadrach.

"Unavailable," barked I. "I'm calling dibs. Once it's touched and exploited, you two can have your turn, but if anyone is going to sully this beauty, it's going to be me."

A cough.

"And Jane."

Without further word, we hoisted it, glanced both ways, and booked. I told myself we were borrowing, intending a return by end of term. There was no wrongdoing here, no crime. We had a moral obligation to give this *Loveseat* the love it would never get from pretentious executive asses. Infuse it with the spark it desperately required to become something truly special. Shadrach and Will carried, the only reason I'd brought them honestly, while Jane and I stumbled ahead to the elevator. I pushed the down button.

Now, back to every heist movie ever made. The plan is proceeding like clockwork. Ticks in the spreadsheet. Timing to the second. But there's a hitch. There's always a hitch. Oh, afterward you discover the hitch was part of the plan all along, so it's just for dramatic effect, but at the time you're twisted into a theater chair, shoveling overpriced popcorn down your salt-lined gullet, not actually worried.

Our hitch was definitely unplanned.

We heard a ding, watched the door open, and scattered like roaches when a tall form in a black robe stepped out, clenching a flashlight with sinuous gloved fingers. A two-foot-long baton-shaped torch, the kind trolls beat people to death with when a tree trunk wasn't handy.

Time stretched.

The figure tilted its hooded face at us, at the beautiful, pristine *Loveseat*, back at us. A hiss escaped what I assume were drawn-back lips, and an impenetrable shadow crawled out and up the elevator door frame, projected edges writhing, looming above us, slithering around us, gnawing our minds. A silence descended, stealing the hum of the elevator and our harrowed breaths.

Time stopped.

The piping of flutes, from a great distance, broke the silence. The figure hissed again, flipped back its hood to reveal a handsome face of pitch-black skin, hair, and eyes.

"Noble questers, let me give you a hand with that . . . contrivance." He stepped out of the elevator, oozing indescribable menace and charm, and used his light to keep the door from closing.

A trick? A trap? It didn't matter. We were committed. We played along, waiting for him to disclose his little joke, to banish us to Leng or someplace equally abysmal. Or rip off and devour our limbs, one by one, and when gorged, have our torsos blacklisted from the building for all time. But he didn't. He just, with a knowing half smile and eerie piping, helped us load the loveseat into the elevator.

"Main floor?"

We nodded, shaking hard enough for our rattling bones to produce orchestral harmony, as he pushed the down button and bid us farewell and good night, slipping his phone number into the front of Shadrach's tattered sailcloth trousers.

"Don't disappoint it." His final words echoed in our heads as the door slid shut and we plummeted, stomachs yanked through our esophagi, brains, and skull tops.

"Oh my," croaked Shadrach.

There wasn't much else to say until the *Loveseat* was outside under the mosquito- and moth-crowded lights.

"You are the luckiest idiots on the planet, have I mentioned that recently?" said Jane. "If I didn't know better, I'd guess we dozed off somewhere and took the seventy steps to lighter slumber into the Dreamlands."

"Now what?" asked Will from where he'd flopped on the grass. "I told you we needed a lift."

Jane and I snuggled on the *Loveseat*, leather growling.

"It's thirsty," she said, nuzzling my neck and slipping a hand into my pocket. "Wanna?"

"What, here? Now?"

"Well," she pointed to a couch-sized patch of shadow beneath the shrubbery, "we can drag it over there. We've talked about this. I recall you insisting you were always up . . . for an adventure. Plus, you owe me. I'm calling in a marker."

Shadrach cleared his throat. "Look, who am I to say what is or isn't meant to be, but I'm not hanging around watching you fumble for . . . two minutes? There's a waterbed grilled cheese calling my name." He grinned at Will. "And stuff. So, let's get this puppy home, and you can tan that leather to your heart's desire."

"Yeah," Will wobbled to his feet.

"Cowards," she sighed. "Fine. Home it is, then. Chop. Chop."

"I got an idea about that." Shadrach had ridden his mountain bike, a hideous purple thing he claimed to have purchased for nine dollars at the factory surplus auction, and he retrieved it from the racks and hurried back. "Will, sit on my handlebars. You two, bring it here and lift it as high as you can."

We grunted and heaved it up, straining, while Shadrach and Will wiggled underneath, still on the bike. They half balanced it on their heads, half balanced with a single arm each, and rolled ten feet before flopping over with a crash.

"No!" I bounced over, knelt down, and ran a hand over the scuffed wood.

Jane tousled my hair. "Rough love. It'll be okay, adds character. Like a spanking. Or a brand. You didn't expect it to stay pristine for long, did you?"

Once untangled, we tried again. More wobbling. Crazy serious wobbling. But they found the balance and somehow made it work. Like they always did.

"See you at home, losers," laughed Shadrach. "We'll cut through the cemetery."

Jane and I watched them shrink into the distance and darkness, and followed down Lich Street, hand in hand.

"I always wanted to do it in the cemetery," she said, walking fast enough to

The Loveseat

pull me along. "The atmosphere. The spooky fear. The taboo. The thrill of getting caught. Number three on my sex bucket list; how about you?"

"I have an irrational fear of the dead. They lurk. They watch. They tend to critique."

She squeezed my hand. "You say the most romantic things."

The campus ended, spitting us out into the surrounding community where parties smoldered, embers of music and conversation flaring whenever a drunk poked a fire with a stick. We wandered by a frat house, waved at some naked guy sprawling on the upper edge of a gambrel roof. Not technically naked, I suppose; he had a flat of Coors balanced across his groin, and a featureless pallid mask.

"Classy," yelled Jane.

"Free beer!" yelled the nude frat cultist. "Nearly free; pay with the love of your patron god!"

Cheap at half the price.

Before long, we reached an arch of weeping red brick flanked by thorny hedges and capped by tarnished brass signage. The back entrance to a cemetery, the one used by maintenance staff and slothful university students. An iron gate blocked the way, chained shut, but there was a gap in the hedge where it bent around a decorative storm drain. Our shoes squelching in the clammy, trimmed grass, we let our eyes adjust to the pale moonlight and hurried to the cobblestone path meandering through the clustered grave sites and past a mausoleum infested with leering gargoyles.

"You implied a certain carnage, a cacophony of carnivorous corpses," Jane said, voice floating among the marble. "Not sure if I'm disappointed."

"Suspicious." I strained to see or hear anything, anything at all. Silence pervaded the mist-choked air.

Jane slipped her arms around my chest and incised a mouthful of flesh from my shoulder. Her hair fluttered in my face, hints of pomegranate and cherry Jell-O forcing ravenous thoughts. I hungered. For many things. For all the things. And whether this was or wasn't appropriate on corpse-ridden ground fled my mind. Our lips brushed, electrified. Our eyes met, smoldering. Fingers fumbled, tugging on buttons and zippers. Seduced by the inevitable, who was I to reject my lover's bucket list top three?

Someone moaned. And it wasn't either of us.

"Told you," I said, tearing myself from her grip and struggling not to faint. "Ghouls."

"Jesus," said Jane.

"Flesh-eating ghouls."

"Or Shadrach and Will."

"They wouldn't . . ."

"Five bucks says they would. And are."

Instead of running away, like any sane person would in this situation, we traversed the path toward the erotic wailing, entered a memorial forest, and slammed to a stop. Shadrach's purple conveyor blocked the way, discarded in haste. Nearby were two empty boots and two empty shoes. Three socks. Two pairs of pants. And one shirt. When I stopped to kick the bike, Jane pulled me along to where we'd heard the last echoes of passion, a small clearing where we found the *Loveseat* tucked between two intertwined birch trees. There were no signs of the guys.

"Guys?" I whispered.

"GUYS?" Jane yelled.

More silky silence.

Jane sat down on the *Loveseat*, patted the greasy, bloodstained leather next to her.

"Damn," I said. "Fiends. Despoilers. How could they? They've stolen our thunder!"

"Does it matter?" asked Jane, "Come here. Now."

I eased in beside her. Felt the *Loveseat* take us into its embrace. Wrapping around us as we wrapped ourselves around each other. We worshipped at its altar, and it blessed us. What we gave, we received manyfold. The sky grew clear, the stars brightened, the glow of the Milky Way, as if seen from the other side of the galaxy, infused our bare skin.

"Blessed Aldebaran," she moaned in my ear as tentacles caressed my body. "Number two on the list."

Robert Bose grew up on a farm in southern Alberta, Canada, spending every free moment reading Fritz Leiber, Karl Edward Wagner, Michael Shea and whatever pulp and weird fiction he could get his hands on. He's the editor of a variety of books and anthologies for Coffin Hop Press and The Seventh Terrace, the author of myriad short stories including the fiendish collection *Fishing with the Devil* (The Seventh Terrace), and the co-curator/  coauthor (with Sarah L. Pratt) of *Terrace VII: Wall of Fire*, *Terrace VI: Forbidden Fruit*, *Terrace V: Penitent's Gold*, and the forthcoming *Solstice in Purgatory*, all from The Seventh Terrace.

He is currently researching and writing a prairie gothic novel about spirits trapped in a coal seam with an accompanying series of short stories set around a haunted prairie lake. When not writing, publishing, and running ultramarathons, he spends his free time working as a software architect for a small economic forecasting software company. Find out more by visiting robertbose.com.

Crustaceous Wishes and Dungeness Dreams

John A. DeLaughter

In the dead of night, I walked alone on a hidden Kauai beach.

Across the shimmering, chaotic face of the ocean stood Ni'ihau, the forbidden Hawaiian island, set aside to preserve Hawaiian traditions and culture. No public eyes could make a spectacle of the private lives of those who lived there.

I was barely a man, more of an overgrown teenager. Ni'ihau, though full of mysteries to an outsider, wasn't the only puzzle hidden in the emerald depths of the sea. As I treaded the thick sands of that lost Kauai beach, I was alone not only in my person but also in my thoughts. I was trying to finish school at Hawaii's premiere college, on Oahu, an island long ago given over to tourism, a true melting pot of decadence and decay, far away from the other countries that swarmed its carrion waste, feasting on the carcasses of lives ruined there.

It was the height of the Cold War. A peanut farmer was president of the United States. The USSR—Union of Soviet Socialist Republics—in the West stretched an Iron Curtain across Europe and its environs. Red China stretched its Bamboo Curtain across the East. A countdown clock ticked inexorably toward zero and a nuclear apocalypse, defining our lives, always lurking in the background, a monster under the bed, not only of kids but of every adult.

Even the isolation achieved by the native Hawaiians of Ni'ihau could not prevent such an Armageddon from reaching its shores.

Why was I alone on such a night? I was an introvert by chance, not by choice. And awkward. Such was the lot of children raised in a military family, moving every few years, always the outsider in a new school, in a new community, always the bullied one, because being from elsewhere brought out the differences bullies loved to expose and exploit.

I made my happiness the best I could, always hoping for a different future than my less-than-promising present.

The bright moonlight swam and swarmed in the moving face of the ocean, among classic sounds such as the crashing waves. Still other sounds, shrouded in

John A. DeLaughter

the darkness, made me think of the God Emperor of the Oceans.

Hawaii had plenty of surfer guys and surfer girls, children of the sea. Native kanes and wahines knelt in the sand and played out each party's part in the rituals of romance and fantasy fulfillment. The Dionysian drama played out at the better-known beaches throughout the islands, men and women kissed by the sun, novice worshippers of Apollo, the sun, Neptune, the sea, and Venus, their passions.

Even in the evening, when I strolled the vacant beach, the sand remained warm from the day's heat. I walked with no set goal, as it was a means to empty my head of the day's events and ponder the barren loneliness of my solitary heartbeat.

I had no twin echo to share my life with.

Ahead, a great wave washed up a tangled pile of kelp and seaweed. Several coils of kelp hung like underway cables amid blades of seaweed fronds stretched across a sand spit and rocks jutting out from the beach.

The colors of the sea forest were spectacular in the spectral moonlight.

I spied on it for a moment, out of curiosity. Since I didn't major in beaches, as did some of my fellow students—hey, we were attending a school in Hawaii—I hardly gave it a thought, much less a second thought.

I was about to wander off when I noticed something flopping and a flash of silver tangled in the seaweed coils. My immediate thought was *dolphin*, although its colors were wrong for such a beast. Dolphins beached themselves for undisclosed reasons. Reporters using such incidents to fill vacancies in TV news broadcasts called these beachings *suicide*. It wasn't like such purveyors of sensationalism took the time officially to confer with someone from the Oceanographic Department at the University.

Should I get involved? was my next thought. I was alone; it was dark except for the moonlight. The irony hit me as I stood there, going back and forth in my mind. Here I was in a terribly romantic spot: the moon beckoning, the sand warm, the sounds of the surf suggestive of the rhythm of life and following the instincts a man and woman entertained in such love-inviting locales.

But I was alone with a beached dolphin flopping around, trapped in seaweed.

I gave in to my curiosity and moved closer. The water lapped at the wet shore about fifteen feet away. Perhaps I could roll the thing back into the sea.

I stopped. Something about the thing's form . . . it wasn't flopping, but it rippled, it "undulated," I think is the word for what I saw. I glanced around to see if anyone else had stumbled onto my situation while I stood here gawking at the sea beast.

Whatever the thing in the moonlight was, the closer I crept, the odder its outlines became. It was freeing itself from the coils of the kelp. Its life force was far from dwindling. It was not in its death throes, as I initially believed.

My heart beat rapidly; was this fear of the unknown or something else? Did my animal instincts recognize some elemental shapes in what my apish mind saw, one that predated cognition and the higher facilities that surfaced in Cro-Magnon man?

It turned onto its side and emitted a soft, dare I say, sound, a cross between a serpent's hiss and a feline's purr. The emanation bore none of the timbres of desperation or urgency, if one could recognize such primal emotions in this cross-species interaction.

Maurice Ravel's *Boléro* played in my mind, and I hummed it aloud. Why this sudden reference to *Boléro*? What was my subconscious mind trying to tell me? Was I so hard up that I started to imagine Bo Derek wrapped up in kelp wrappings like a surprise package?

I looked around me again, half expecting a movie crew and director, or the face of Allen Funt popping out of the darkness yelling, "Smile, you're on *Candid Camera*!"

Nothing happened.

Nothing except an unmistakable cooing hiss. A cross between a vulpine, a hominid, and a Komodo dragon's head arose on scaly shoulders, aimed in my direction. Its red eyes glowed with intelligence. Kelp-like dreadlocks spilled down its shoulders and framed its face. Canine ears jutted out from its head prominently beyond its dreadlocks.

The head shifted as it shook off water, and then its eyes met mine.

I backed away. I should have run, but my feet and legs felt like lead.

A muskiness lingered around the thing, not fishlike, not an oily smell that sticks to whatever it touches, not an excremental smell, or one of rotting flesh; no, none of those.

I inexorably got hard and excited. Why, in God's name, why?

I knelt, my senses overwhelmed. My mind filled with a sense of impending danger and doom, but at the same time, perplexed by an unmistakable sense of animalistic attraction.

What was going on here? What gives? Who goes there?

As I sat there, the sound of the night surf against the beach, the heartbeat of the sea, matched the pounding of my heart.

The thing sat up. Dammit, it had its own alien version of curves, an hourglass out of time and place, the jutting out of the iridescent half-moons of shimmering breasts, opaque nipples that glittered like gemstones.

Lost in a momentary confusion of conflicting sensations, I failed to notice its inextricably long arms, surmounted with two long talon-tipped fingers and an opposable, taloned thumb, reaching out to me, as the thing, I swear to God, hissed with pleasure.

It grabbed me by the temples as I screamed out obscenities, dragging me effortlessly to its side and looking me square in the eyes, its irises glowing a hue between yellow and red.

Then, instead of tumbling intertwined into a bed, we tumbled into the sea.

←♥→←♥→←♥→

I was immediately translated to another place, a bewildering aquatic locale, a world apart from that lonely beach on a lost Hawaiian night.

I no longer knelt before a siren of the sea, a daughter of Poseidon. *No*, she corrected me, *a daughter of Dagon*.

Who the hell is Dagon?

As I swam beside her, she put a mighty clawed finger to my lips, as if to silence my inane babbling. She touched my forehead as a thought, her thought, entered my head. *Listen to what you see—*

"Listen to what I see?" What the hell does that mean? Listen with my eyes? No, you listen with your ears.

I guess they communicate—whoever they are—by some kind of mind-melding, sharing their thoughts, maybe augmented by some type of sign language I hadn't seen yet. If there was an Atlantean sign language, would it be an English translation of that sign language? There were at least twenty-five documented sign languages in Africa alone; what if a greater number existed in this undersea world?

What if our destination was R'lyeh and not fabled Atlantis, fabulous Lemuria, or fantastic Mu?

The only words from that sunken city and its dead language I remember were:

Ph'nglui mglw'nafh Cthulhu R'lyeh wgah'nagl fhtagn.

Don't ask me where I heard that language before, perhaps in a dream.

←♥→←♥→←♥→

Somehow, I could keep up with her/it—whatever the hell the fish-thing was—who initiated this first contact. Who the hell was I kidding? For centuries, lonely sailors and lighthouse masters had shady encounters with sea sirens and mermaids, essentially mail-order brides from down under.

Sorry, Australia, there's a new Down Under—

I might be hard up, but not that hard up for companionship.

She noticed I was dawdling as if I couldn't swim and think at the same time.

Hey lady, I'm swimming, not as I've never swum before. I was no Olympian—Mark Spitz, your record is safe from me—but I didn't struggle so much that others recognized my awkwardness. Every style of swimming I tried to emulate—the breaststroke, the backstroke, the Australian crawl, the sidestroke—eventually turned into a dog paddle.

Luckily, bubblegum chewing wasn't added to the mix—I had enough problems walking and chewing that stuff at the same time. She urged me onward with a slap to my ass—hey lady, how did I suddenly start skinny-dipping?

"Can you do it again? I've been a bad boy—"

Darkness is the word for the sea depths. According to all those Jacques Cousteau specials aboard the *Calypso*—I can still hear John Denver singing about that ship, I can't get that song out of my head now—the ocean is a spellbinding place of colorful reefs and equally dazzling schools of fishes.

So what's with all this darkness?

Oh, it was nighttime when we hooked up.

I wonder where she lives; God, what's her name? Something unpronounceable in any known Earth language, probably. I swear if she says her name is "Zontara," how coincidental could that be?

Did her people originally filter down from the stars, specifically Venus, after its own nuclear Armageddon turned that planet into a raging, inhospitable inferno?

Why is she taking me where she's taking me? To meet her parents? I just met her and we're already doing that? Isn't it a bit premature? I mean, I was never one

Crustaceous Wishes and Dungeness Dreams

who could hold my breath for very long.

Come to think of it, how could I have held my breath for this long?

Or instead, is she inviting me to dinner with them, because they like my kind *fresh*?

Speaking of food, I was getting hungry.

I lost track of how long we had been swimming.

I followed her trailing, luminescent form, an undulating, shimmering turbulence; she was something hard to miss, even in the dark waters. I wondered whether she glowed for the same reasons as those sea beasts from the deep trenches, the death valleys that crisscrossed the ocean floors near subduction zones, where plate tectonics ruled, sound evidence of the continental drift theory.

How romantic, all this talk of plate tectonics.

Yet down here she was my light in this world, one way or another. She was also my path; hell, I didn't know where I was going.

Mind you, not that I knew where I was going before she entered my life.

Oh yeah, enough overthinking this thing. My stomach was growling, though it was more of a sensation of emptiness in the depths.

She looked back at me and smiled.

Her smile contained not just four pointed canine teeth; all hers were pointed and serrated, like a shark's mouth! I could lose my tongue in a moment of passion with her.

Where were all the molars for grinding one's daily bread? Didn't anyone cook their meals down here?

A word formed in my head, with a feline fishy sound. Thoughts with sounds.

Silly, or *idiot*, or *ninny*, getting lost in translation.

So, what does one eat down here, and when does one eat?

Fish. One goes fishing to satisfy one's palate. That's what she says, err, thinks on the subject.

What, no catch and release? Where's the sport in that? What are you people down here, barbarians?

We approached a distant, glowing mountain. Its cliffs stood illuminated against the otherwise pitch-black depths. How far down had we traveled and how far out to sea, I had no idea. Time lost all meaning in this abyss as we traversed the undersea void.

Come on in, the void—err—the water's fine.

We passed through shimmering currents, the outer layers of shoals of iridescent fish, their collective radiance reflecting the glory of the mountain below. I thought, *Here's an undersea volcano.*

Yet that idea didn't match the hot-spot theory of how the Hawaiian archipelago was formed; that is, the first undersea volcano formed Kauai, the oldest island in the chain, with the Big Island of Hawaii being the youngest. The active hot spot remained underneath the Big Island, adding land mass through the Kilauea and Mauna Loa volcanoes.

I had taken a geography class last semester, and despite my having slept through much of his lectures, the professor's words still rang in my ears down here.

How had the scientists missed *this* volcano? And why was my sea babe taking me there? Was I to be sacrificed to the volcanic goddess of the islands, Madame Pele? Appeasing an Almighty with human sacrifices; why didn't they use one of their own? Were none of them virginal?

The mountain wasn't simply a weeping volcano. The glow came from ruins hanging like a crumbling, lustrous lei around its undersea slopes.

Ramshackle towers of white stone teetered at odd angles, burnt and pocked like buildings in devastated European cities at the end of World War II. Once-great arenas, scalable to the size of the grand remnants of the Roman Colosseum, lay broken like eggshells, scattered masonry-strewn heaps nearby.

Had the Gods fought over this derelict of a city during a time when it had stood young, shining, and glorious?

Bannered pavilions crumbled everywhere, their ragged pennants fluttering in the shifting currents. Like in India, small temples randomly dotted the mountain, aglow with offerings of incense and other things. Strange statues of white marble, gray granites, some gold and silver gilded, reeled this way and that. Many were human in rough outline, but the coincidental likeness to human beings ended there.

Others bore no such resemblance to anything normal or sane. They were extremely life-like and extraordinarily inhuman, however.

A group of statues personified ridged, barrel-shaped monsters bearing thin horizontal arms issuing spindle-like from a central halo, with vertical knobs or bulbs projecting from the head and foot of the barrel. Each upper and lower knob was the hub of five lengthy, flat, triangularly tapering arms that hung around it like the arms of a giant starfish—almost horizontal, but curving slightly outbound from the central drum.

These were not the stylized renderings of a hereditary god or tribal deity whose likeness in stone had been approved by a ruling priestly class. Each bore deformities and strange jewelry, individualized to each monstrous bearer.

As we swam through the city, I recollected, from a terror-filled night, images from the damnable *Necronomicon*. One witching hour, my drunk buds and I had attempted to use it as an interdimensional Ouija board, trying to access those from the outside.

My mind was forever stained that night by blasphemy after blasphemy, first rendered in bloody ink, then given brief, spectral life arising from its odious pages.

This was the ruins of one of their undersea cities—the star-headed Elder Things—abandoned since the dawn of time.

Was this entire episode, including my marvelous Mer-lyn Monroe, with an emphasis on the "roe," like an LSD flashback from the otherworldly trauma I experienced that unforgettable night?

Was that why the star-headed sky spawn was common to both experiences?

I had no option but to plow ahead.

Plow? Too nautical, no, I had too much water on the brain.

Rough roads of white and red cobblestones crisscrossed the city, though why they needed such undersea, I hadn't a clue. Black obelisks stood next to

Crustaceous Wishes and Dungeness Dreams

those curving, crumbling courses, carved with alien hieroglyphs and blasphemous images of demiurgic orgies, indecent and inhuman.

We swam toward a polished, white pyramid that dominated one side of the sunken ruins. An enormous single eye, with three independent pupils, floated atop the temple to the dead; its eyelid fluttered in the currents.

I hesitated.

Extreme paranoia and anxiety seized me. How might my destiny be linked to that all-seeing, cycloptic eye and its attendant, cyclopean ruins?

Why hadn't I felt this way before, during the bipolar extremes of my experience? Perhaps I felt it was but a dream. Maybe a passing flight of fancy. Possibly someone had handed me a brownie laced with a potent street drug that opened one up to other vistas, exits from the commonplace reality that deadened our senses to anything and everything that swarmed as schools of fish in the unseen beyond.

I half expected Albert Einstein to swim from the shadows, towed by his own aquatic gal pal—he was a lady's man, despite his iconic mantle of science. Would I find his face and form transfigured, yet still recognizable? He could swim alongside me, as our merwives exchanged the gossip. He could share his formidable thoughts on this experience, and through that impartation, calm my concerns and cool what confounded me.

This all proved a fantasy within a fabrication. I was trying to come to terms with what was proving to be more bizarre and alien at every turn.

She turned on me again, the expression upon her aquatic face akin to dismay. That she had some sort of affection for me was unmistakable, though was it as for a pet, over a curiosity, or of infatuation.

She touched my forehead with her enormous taloned hand.

Quiet—One thought passed between us. It was not chastisement, a mother scolding her child over an unlearned lesson. No, it was an infusion, a powerful transmission of her own state of mind, to give tranquility and order to the jumble and chaos that raged deep within me.

Though there was much to be afraid of, I felt she would be with me all the way.

All the way through what? Was I an initiate, a neophyte who must face a series of tests to prove my worthiness? Worthy of what? What did I stand to gain? What did I stand to lose?

She was taking me to a temple; what temple, whose temple? Did it matter, because in the world above, hadn't there been thousands of temples over tens of thousands of years? Every letter in the alphabet had a god behind it, either in English or simply anglicized. Above, while images of a singular god, or its consorts, or the gods of its lineage crowded such temples, they mostly felt devoid of dignitaries and deities.

Would the undersea temples be any different? Or did their gods hold court in such places? Did they operate as throne rooms where one held audience with an attendant god?

The Palace of the Presence—that's what she named it, though no clever wordplay captured her shared thoughts. The sanctuary was tall, pyramidal, less ruined than the surrounding facades. It vibrated with light and life. Don't ask me to explain. It's not like schools of fish or other sea entities poured through its seven gates, in through the front, out through the back.

The local flora and fauna didn't treat the place like a man-made reef, where the fish mindlessly and instinctively followed the current.

Dark, serpentine feral faces, their eyes red and aglow, hovered in place, forming a path for my merwife to pass through, myself in tow. I do not know whether they eyed me as a prize, as one to be envied, or out of ravishing hunger. I had terrifying mind-glimpses of taloned and webbed hands, striking from the assembled predators, slicing skin, fat, and muscle from me, hoping none of my succulent form would be missed in the massed pawing that was sure to come.

Weaponless, I did not stop for fear they would start on me with talons and teeth, a swarm of tearing, ripping fiends.

But act, they did not; something about my aquatic gal pal, something in her standing among the hierarchy of the seas, prevented their instincts from overcoming their better judgments.

Was I projecting human sentiments on instinctive brutes who operated under no such civilized sentimentalities? Was I seized with a nostalgia that bordered on delusion? Or was I sitting in a padded cell in a forgotten mental asylum, dreaming this nightmare while wide awake?

Impelled by motivations I did not understand, I soldiered onward.

My cetaceous, curvaceous companion looked less like a monster and more like a mate in the light of the sanctuary. Alabaster skin instead of silver scales showed on parts of the scintillating, subtle sweeps of her body. The strange webbings and surprising fins here and there on her person were less frightening.

Instead of staring in fear, I flowed forward, seeing things from behind her, looking ahead of her.

I felt a change in the water, a heat different from what I had felt before.

Until now, I hadn't noticed the differences in temperatures through the depths I had penetrated with my tetrapod temptress, my batrachian and bodacious blind date.

Was the source of the heat volcanic? There were simmering lights ahead. The distance across the base of the pyramid's base, the lower chamber we transversed, was immense. Something like balconies in a theater filled niches in the walls, holding what I assumed to be higher-ups in this kingdom.

A low, subtle music, some Mephistophelian variation of a Mozart medley, played brazenly in the background.

May I have this dance, milady?

How could one hear music beneath the waves?

Here lay the bejeweled thrones of Mother Hydra and Father Dagon, where we all came from, she shared.

Steps, gilded in platinum and gold, led to the thrones. Each otherworldly aquatic deity bore stony crowns and odd bicep bracelets on their many arms. They had fashioned their adornments from a material that seemed to be predominantly

Crustaceous Wishes and Dungeness Dreams

gold, of a weird light lustrousness that hinted at some strange alloy with a beautiful and scarcely identifiable metal. No feet touched the ground beneath their glittering presences; instead, there undulated the broad, vertical tails of fish, pierced with platinum ringlets, bedecked with symbols whose meaning was known only to their bearers.

A pillar of radiance flowed around each brutish, exoskeletal form. As lesser fish floated mindlessly by, fingers of flame sprang from the pillars, consuming the offerings.

Legions of enormous centaur-like seahorses with golden cutlasses enacted endless saber dances before the sparkling thrones. Throngs of drummers, their inhuman faces hidden behind yellow silken masks, pounded obtuse rhythms with swarms of Shiva-like arms and hands. Rogue beasts, indistinguishable beneath their robes of rough barnacles, danced odd gyrations, seemingly possessed by dark demons from the upper world, the inner world's hellish core, and the empty voids of time and space.

Other unknown musicians played in the shadows, their dissonant riffs carried on the drummers' writhing rhythms.

The water around the pair of Leviathans rumbled deeply; here was the source of the vibrations I felt outside the edifice, palatable, much like the soundings and calls of the great whales, present in the moment and cosmic in proportions.

Were there alien intelligences from elsewhere, traveling the backwaters of the universe, seeking out these sounds, ancient remnants of a universe-wide hive-mind of similar sentients, hoping to reunite with the timeless undersea denizens that lurked behind them?

Two lesser thrones of platinum and ivory stood vacant to either side of the massive, flaring, central presences. Fiery chandeliers swayed above each of the lesser daises, ready to entomb and empower their occupants.

Before all these wonders, in the common grounds leading up to this underwater Olympus, amid the chaos of worshippers, sat an elongated crystalline box analogous to a clear casket. Its occupant was a massive Poseidon-like figure, a faltering glow outlining its titan, recumbent frame.

I waited as my aquatic accomplice left my side. Upon a motion of one of the Leviathan's bejeweled fists, my she-maid swam forward. She knelt—if such a thing were possible.

She arose at another gesture of the same fist. A storm of swarming waters, bright and intense, swam forth to embrace her, an undersea dust devil. Her eyes glowed as an expression of satisfaction crossed her strange face.

A similar stream of consciousness—I made an educated guess as to what it was—flowed toward me from the Leviathans. The swirling funnel of water engulfed me, trapping me in a web of waves, the water taking on a sticky, steely consistency.

Alien ideas and assailing images filled me with strange visions. I beheld the congealing and coalescing thoughts of those on the thrones.

A dark, distant, dying world where curtains of volcanic cones and their vomiting calderas filled the heavens with ash, brimstone, and destruction. Those

John A. DeLaughter

surviving Deep Ones—a new word detailing who the skeletal, scaled beasts were—formed giant, living wicker men and swarming shoals, cube-like in their swelling appearance. By some means, lost to their ancestral consciousness, certain of those convulsing wicker men and undulating cubes swept into space, beginning an uncountable aeons-long journey away from the burning death that turned their home world to ashes.

Father Dagon conveyed in a moment the momentous migration of their kind to this world and the events, wars, and geological cataclysms that shaped the face of their new world, my world. My hands went to my head to prevent it from bursting.

She swam to my side and put her palm against my forehead. The scenes of carnage, cataclysm, and courage blinked like a series of transmitted images. They shrank to a white dot as my inner vision became a blank, black-and-white screen.

I shrieked, and though it made no noise, she was visibly taken aback by my strong, silent emotions.

Her hand slipped off my forehead for a time.

She allowed me a moment to gather myself.

When I again dared to look at her square in the eyes—do you know what it's like to find affection staring back at you from a set of phosphorus-yellow eyes?

No, I guess you don't.

She placed her palm on my forehead, and new words and sensory impacts filled my mind.

My chosen, my mer-mate lies dying in yonder crystal bed. Our kind is nearly eternal, but even among the strong like he, the radiations of your world lack the potency of our former home to prolong his life forever—

I'm not sure I understood everything, but that she called me *her chosen* made me feel better.

His personhood cannot be prolonged. Neither can we keep you alive for much longer—
Me? What has his death got to do with my life?
I will show you, for doesn't your kind say, "A picture is worth a thousand words?"

A new vision fills my head.

We're swimming.

She's ahead of me, the shimmering ghost of the depths that I'm following on our first blind date. She seems awfully quiet. Has she forgotten me? All the glowing mystery of being with such an exotic creature has worn off. The sounds of songs such as "Brandy (You're a Fine Girl)" are no longer rocking in my head.

Maybe this mirrored my friend Maury's experience. Someone at school slipped him LSD, and he was there, yet not there for three days. It was on a weekend, after a concert. Fleetwood Mac rocked the Blaisdell Arena to the ground. Maury's body was there, but Maury wasn't. I don't know how else to explain it.

Was I lying on a beach, the victim of a drug-induced prank, while my celestial being was surfing the astral plane? Surfing under the sea; who ever heard of such a thing?

For an instant, I feel something solid and wet beneath my back. A hot Hawaiian sun burns above me, and the surf pounds my ears. I blink; the sun's that

Crustaceous Wishes and Dungeness Dreams

bright. There are no shadows nearby, so it must be near noon overhead.

The concerned faces of strangers hove into sight. I feel pressure on my chest, as someone's leaning over my face, too close, too intimate.

Lips are on mine; someone's shaking me; what the hell is going on?

Back down below, the sea wife has stopped and she's appeared through the veil of her own churning wake. Her long arms and talon-tipped fingers snake toward my head, digging into my temples at the last moment, her mermaidish face filled with concern. The sun and surf at the beach, where I am . . . no, now that scene is fading, my essence being drawn from there to here, back under the waves, back with the scaly goddess of the deep hovering in the water before me. I feel intense warmth flowing like an electrical arc between her grappling fingers. The surge pierces my temples.

Oh, the pain is intense. Am I dying?

Where am I? Which is real, here or there?

←♥→←♥→←♥→

See, your life hangs by the thinnest of threads. Your kind are so fragile. I found you half-drowned, almost dead. You tried to stop your bitter loneliness by ending your life in the sea—

That was me on the beach? Is that really me back there, up there? I asked.

Yes, my chosen. I offer you life, in the form of my dying mer-mate. I can sustain you in an in-between place, but only for a short season, a harbor between your death above and his death below. You will assume his form and learn to live, love, and reign beside me, consort to the daughter of Dagon, Lord of the Deep Ones—

And the choice is mine? I asked. *A death up there or new life down here? Why me?* I pressed her.

Only the Great High Priest knows why from his sunken city, for He sees all. It is said of Him and His kind: They could only lie awake in the dark and think whilst uncounted millions of years rolled by. They knew all that was occurring in the universe, but Their mode of speech was transmitted thought.

I felt boxed in. Was any of this real?

Given the choices, death up there or life down here—she offered.

I chose you and the life ahead of me rather than the death behind me—

Her smile, though exceedingly toothy, like a shark's all-consuming grin, spoke of her pleasure at my words.

Amid the protozoan pomp and planktonic pageantry, my sea-seductress leaned over, put her taloned hand on my forehead, and whispered the thought, *Memento mori—*

What?

←♥→←♥→←♥→

Uniformed officials crowded the beach; civilian and military law enforcement officers conferred and shared their notes.

The grieving parents of the young man held each other tightly nearby.

A lone running enthusiast—the military was full of them—had found the young fellow, drowned by a noose of sea kelp during a moonlight swim in the ocean off the Kauai coast, trying to get to the distant shores of forbidden Ni'ihau.

←♥→←♥→←♥→

John A. DeLaughter

John A. DeLaughter, MDiv, MS, is a data security analyst. His nonfiction work has recently appeared in the vampire anthology *The Vampiricon* (Mind's Eye Publications) and the 2023 Candlemas edition of *Lovecraftiana*.

John's fiction has or will appear in the novella anthology *Eldritch Prisoners* (Macabre Ink), the horror detective anthology *The CultureCult Casebook* (CultureCult), Eerie River Publishing's *From Beyond the Threshold: Cosmic Horror Anthology*, the 2023 Halloween anthology of *Lovecraftiana*, Innsmouth Gold's Lovecraftian anthology *The Pickman Papers*, Nordic Press's *Eldritch Investigations: Lovecraftian Tales of Occult Detection* anthology, Skywatcher Press's *The Depths: Unleashed, Book 2* anthology, Horrorsmith Publishing's campfire horror anthology *Fear Forge: Summer Quarter 2023 Edition*, and Rogue Planet Press's *Dickensian SteamFantasy: A Very Different 1800*, an urban fantasy/horror/sci-fi anthology.

John lives with his wife, Heidi, and two dogs in Pennsylvania.

Twerking for Jesus

Bill McCormick

Amanda Johnson stood at the edge of the grave and smiled. She wasn't happy that her husband of fifty-four years was gone. Far from it. She had loved him more with each passing day until he'd finally shrugged off this mortal coil. He had been a good husband, father, grandfather, and lover. Especially the lover part. No, she smiled at the memories. They were all wonderful.

She ignored the rain pissing on her, rebalanced her cane, and peered from under her umbrella. Their four children waited there with their eleven grandchildren and two great-grandchildren. They were sad, but Amanda hoped they would remember the good times as she was. Thomas had been a font of happiness, and that should be his legacy.

Occasional shafts of sunlight broke through the clouds and moved across the lawn like alien beams from some cheap sci-fi flick. Thomas would have liked that. He'd loved sci-fi, said it provided hope for the future. He prayed every day but was no fool; his belief in God was based on his love of science. He'd refused to believe he was the most evolved being in the universe. Science said he was, most likely, not the most evolved, and that, somehow, made him happy.

Science said cancer had killed him, and also said it was his fault. Thomas ignored symptoms for years. Had he not, he would, most likely, still be alive. But not even that saddened Amanda. Thomas made his decisions and lived with them. He'd never played the "poor, pitiful me" card. He'd faced his impending mortality directly and with humor, joking that science would introduce him to God, albeit a tad sooner than he might have wished.

As the casket was being lowered into the ground, a rogue shaft of sunlight touched it, making it appear as if his soul was being beamed into the hereafter. That made Amanda smile all the more. Her smile widened further when she heard a couple of her kids—even though they were all around fifty, they were still her kids, talking about the same thing.

Thomas's legacy would be a good one.

She clutched her umbrella tighter as the wind kicked up. She headed back to the town car her son had rented. The driver opened the door, and she sat in the rear as the rest of her family piled in.

Amanda was pleased to hear laughter. The final shaft of sunlight had broken the somber mood. They all joked and talked on the ride back to her house.

Their house.

Thomas's house.

She'd already decided to sell it. She didn't want to live out her days in a mausoleum. Thomas would approve. Before she did that, however, there were a million details to take care of. Those would keep her busy for a while.

Then she would decide what the next stage of her life would entail.

←♥→←♥→←♥→

Oxyl floated above the bottom of the Mariana Trench. He didn't know it was called that. To him, it was just home—a place of shelter and food.

He sensed upwards and smiled as the New Gods began playing with the weather. They had been brought into this firmament to complete one single task. They were to rid the planet of the disease called humans.

The Old Gods had created the New Gods when they realized their long-game scenarios could not deal with the vermin's rapid evolution.

The New Gods' plan was insidious and glorious. They used the humans' planet-killing inability to care for their world as the means of their eradication. Given how quickly the Earth was heating up, they figured the humans would all be gone in a hundred years.

A mere blink to any such as Oxyl.

Or it would be if any of them had eyes.

He let his senses revel as the New Gods used existing wind and weather patterns to create storms larger than any seen before. Those would kill many humans, to be sure, but that was just a bonus. The end game for the New Gods was to disrupt the weather patterns enough to allow the planet to heat even faster than humans could compensate. In some places, they were past that tipping point already.

In less than a blink, the polar ice caps would melt enough to release their megatons of carbon dioxide into the atmosphere and envelop the planet in a shell of heat. That would be enough to trigger continent-sized deserts, and the resulting famine should do the rest.

Oxyl and his kin could then go above and finish any that got missed.

He would know it was time to leave his home when he heard the Dance of the New Gods.

He longed to, once again, feel the rhythm of the universe.

←♥→←♥→←♥→

A whirlwind of paperwork had filled the three months since Thomas had died. Today was Amanda's seventy-ninth birthday. The time for paperwork was done.

She set aside the final papers for the insurance company and began prepping for family and friends' arrival.

Amanda smiled when she passed the *Star Trek* shrine in the living room. Thomas had never been one for toys, one of his many reasons for dismissing anything related to *Star Wars* out of hand, but he'd grabbed small things through the years and assembled them. The top shelf was devoted to inventions that *Star Trek's* writers inspired. From cell phones to tablet computers, to translation devices, to a virtual reality simulator (as close as we're going to get to a holodeck in our lifetimes), to a copy of Miguel Alcubierre Moya's papers proving a Warp Drive was possible. He even had a model of the ship, proposed by Dr. Harold "Sonny" White from NASA, that showed how such a vessel should look.

When Amanda got to her room, she set her simple brown cane to the side and pulled out her black one with the silver tip and Klingon grip, wanting to be festive. She chose her outfit in the same manner, eschewing drab colors for bright.

She finished dressing just as the doorbell rang and smiled as she let in the caterer. This was going to be a fun day.

Several hours later, the backyard was jumping to the sounds of the latest hip-hop track, and her grandchildren were happily doing the latest dance. On a whim, she asked them to teach it to her. After being told she was too old to twerk, Amanda was more determined than ever to learn.

She planted her cane in the grass, bent forward, and began emulating the moves she'd seen.

Left butt cheek twitched? Done.

Right butt cheek twitched? Done.

Both butt cheeks twitched? Success!

To the cheers of "Go, Grandma, go, Grandma," Amanda began to twerk.

Left, left, right.

Right, right, left.

Both, both, both.

Left, right, both.

Soon enough, she was a booty-shaking commando, her ass pulsing precisely to the rhythm of the song. Her grandchildren joined in and soon had a conga line of undulating derrières.

After a while, Amanda tired and went to sit under the umbrella near the buffet. She was greeted by friends and family, all laughing and joking that she should take her act on the road.

"You know something," she said as she sipped her favorite bourbon, "That's one heck of a good idea."

←♥→←♥→←♥→

Oxyl was confused. He'd felt the tingle, savored in the call, but the New Gods were adamant they'd done nothing. The time was not yet. They knew not where the dance had emanated but were sure it hadn't been their doing. The sound was too distant, too feeble to be their doing.

The Old Gods pled ignorance. Oxyl knew none of the gods could lie, so he drifted back down to his home.

To make him and his kin feel a little better, the New Gods pointed out where humans were being swept into the seas. While the time for the large storms had passed, there was still enough heat in the air to allow them to push smaller, still lethal, ones ashore.

They kept stirring the pot, and Oxyl got to dine on fine human flesh.

He couldn't wait to go above and get it before it was waterlogged. Since it was something that would only happen once, he relished it all the more. After all, once he was freed, there would be no more humans to feast on.

He thought of asking the New Gods if they could keep some humans alive to breed them for food but decided against it. These creatures evolved erratically. There was no way of knowing what harm they might cause if left alive.

Nope. Better to eat them all and savor the memories.

←♥→←♥→←♥→

Amanda had been touring, sharing her unusual take on the dance, for nine months now. Her act, a combination of twerking, liberal-ish agenda checkpoints, safe Bible quotes, and an entourage of young ladies called the Bootyquakettes, had provided the kind of fun the world had forgotten it was missing. Amanda never took any of it too seriously, nor did anyone else.

The random troupe—no one joined, and no one left, they were just there or not—traversed the country and was soon to appear on an episode of *Ellen*. Amanda loved Ellen and couldn't wait to meet her. She had T-shirts made up for the dancers with "BOOTYQUAKETTE" emblazoned on the front and one of four Bible verses featured on the back.

Ecclesiastes 3:4
A time to weep and a time to laugh; A time to mourn, and a time to dance.
Psalm 30:11
You have turned for me my mourning into dancing; You have loosed my sackcloth and girded me with gladness.
Psalm 149:3
Let them praise His name with dancing; Let them sing praises to Him with timbrel and lyre.
Psalm 150:4
Praise Him with timbrel and dancing; Praise Him with stringed instruments and pipe.

Given that many of the young ladies were unencumbered by body modesty, one could honestly be pleased to note they were, at least, girded in gladness. If not much else.

The production staff from Ellen's show had sent a retinue of buses to pick them up in Phoenix and take them to LA for the taping.

Amanda was convinced the show would be, in the words of those hipper than her, epic.

←♥→←♥→←♥→

Oxyl was apoplectic. The tingling grew with each passing day and had nothing to do with the New Gods. The call was becoming too strong to avoid. Something had to give.

The New Gods had an idea. They would loose the volcanoes from under the tundra at the North Pole, thus releasing megatons of carbon dioxide to kick-start the apocalypse. There were fault lines and other planetary weaknesses they felt sure they could also exploit.

Then Oxyl and his ilk could be released to fulfill their destinies.

It meant more work for the under-beings, but none minded. The Old Gods would, once again, be free to balance the world, and the New Gods would retire until the next threat arose.

Oxyl, as much as he could, smiled.

He began his leisurely ascent and mapped his path to the nearest coast.

He would wait for his cue from the New Gods, but freedom was coming.

Along with food. Lots of tasty, fresh, human-tasting food.

←♥→←♥→←♥→

Ellen lived up to her reputation. The buses were opulent, the accommodations state-of-the-art, the audience packed with family and friends, and Ellen herself—can you believe it?—had learned to twerk like Amanda so she could join the crew.

Amanda got her a shirt.

They arrived at the studio at the appointed time. No way not to. They were herded from the hotel like cattle.

Amanda loved all of it.

Team Ellen had pulled out all the stops. Dr. Dre, not a real doctor, Amanda was bummed to discover, and Nikki Minaj provided the music. There were also many prominent feminists there to join the "Werk It & Twerk It" episode, as it was being billed.

About an hour after they arrived, a cute production assistant named Derrick came to their room and ran down the day's schedule for them. Square jaw, well muscled, with a deep, kind voice. He reminded Amanda of a young Thomas.

The thought of Thomas made her wince a little. She had been so busy Twerking for Jesus all over the country she hadn't thought much about him. Then she shrugged. She didn't need to think of him to have him in her heart. He was always there. His lessons, his laugh, just him, imbued all she was.

The next hour was a blur. Cameras flashing, celebrities dancing, people asking for autographs, charities asking her to host twerking events on their behalf, and so on.

When the show aired later that day, Amanda was sitting in her hotel room, sipping a well-deserved bourbon, watching intently. She couldn't believe how many people were spiritually helped by her elderly, bouncing ass.

The cameras showed people gleefully dancing in the aisles and singing along with each song. There were even cutaway shots of various politicians joining in on the fun.

Amanda thought science might be dry, but God sure had a lively sense of humor.

Near the end of the show, a crawling chyron informed her there had been a series of massive volcanic explosions near the North Pole. Scientists said it would take decades to assess the damage.

She refilled her glass, her good mood gone.

Shortly after the Ellen show ended, the apocalypse began.

Earthquakes were being reported globally. Two had already caused the beginnings of tsunamis. Amanda watched hopelessly as news show after news show showed giant beings, multi-tentacled and multi-mouthed, emerging from the seas to swallow humans like snacks.

Bill McCormick

Several, small by recent standards, hurricanes popped up in the Atlantic Ocean and headed directly toward the US.

Other beings, vaguely humanoid and larger than the monsters, performed some sort of ritual above the seas, moving from crest to crest. One station managed to get a helicopter close enough so the cameraman could zoom in on the aliens. The reporters on TV figured it out just after Amanda did. They were dancing.

Her dance.

Her special twerk.

Her twerk for Jesus.

The twerk that Ellen, and countless others, had so recently celebrated.

Left, left, right.

Right, right, left.

Both, both, both.

Left, right, both.

The dance which had brought so much joy also seemed to be the bringer of Armageddon.

People were dying by the millions while monsters danced.

Amanda pushed her glass aside and grabbed the bottle, glad Thomas was dead. He would have been so disappointed to discover science was wrong and hope was a lie.

Bill McCormick is an award-winning and critically acclaimed author of several novels, graphic novels, and comic book series, and has appeared in numerous anthologies. He began writing professionally in 1986 for the *Chicago Rocker Magazine* in conjunction with his radio show on Z-95 (ABC-FM) and went on to write for several other magazines and blogs. He writes a twisted news and science blog at WorldNewsCenter.org. It  provided source material for his weekly radio show on WBIG 1280 AM, FOX!, which aired from October 2010 to August 2022. Bill is a big fan of music and this rainbow-haired goddess who keeps waking up in his bed. You can find out more about him at BillMcSciFi.com.

Gnarly Love

Charles Montgomery

When a certain T'Orack-o'Far'k intimated, in the sibilant syllables of his native tongue, that he had documents pertaining to chthonic research, I purchased them sight unseen. When they arrived at my padded suite at the Arkham Harborhouse, I eagerly tore into them.

They were not what I expected—not ancient at all. Their story was not of ice-cold abysses, endless torments and madness, nor souls wrenched from mortal bodies. It featured no peculiar and antigeometric architectures inside an antagonistic universe full of incomprehensible creatures who, when they comprehend us, only do so to torture and destroy us. There wasn't even the beating of savage drums or keening of tuneless pipes.

The story was about a different kind of soul-rending ice-cold abyss.

It was a love story.

←♥→←♥→←♥→

Dawn was sitting at the Welcome Innsmouth Bar, across the street from Miskatonic Community College—motto: "Our Tentacles Reach Everywhere"—drinking beer with her friend Aurora. Onstage, a comedian was bombing.

"Knock knock," he bellowed.

"Who's there?" a bored drunk answered.

"Ca-thule," the comedian responded, wide-eyed.

The drunk answered in slow, single syllables, "Ca-thule who?"

The ecstatic comedian hollered, "Cthulhu! Now you've done it; you've called up the ancient, sleeping, evil Old Ones!"

Dawn and Aurora groaned.

Dawn tuned out the comic when *he* entered the room from the back. She could not see him; she *felt* him enter the bar.

"Psst." She elbowed Aurora. "Who is that?" She nodded at the back of the bar, where a tall, slim, dark man had just entered and slid into a booth, his conservatively bejeweled tentacles gracefully arching.

50

Aurora turned. "No idea, but he's kind of cute."

The comedian riffed on deviled eggs and recipes, ending with a joke about a cookbook called the *Nom-Nomicon*.

Dawn glared at the comic, shuddering at the callous evil humans could wittingly inflict upon their fellows. She returned her attention to the attractive fellow in the back booth. He was still alone, and with a boldness she didn't feel, she walked to his table and sat down. "My name is Dawn. Who are you?"

He looked Dawn over. "My name is Nyarlathotep, but friends call me Gnarly T. You can just call me Gnarly." He smiled, revealing perfectly white, nearly pointed teeth. "I hope you will be my friend." His tentacles undulated.

They chatted, but Aurora had to leave, and Dawn had promised her a ride. Dawn and Gnarly exchanged phone numbers, and Dawn promised him she would call soon, leaving reluctantly.

Dawn called two days later. They dated several times and quickly became a couple.

Her friends, out of jealousy, Dawn thought, made disparaging remarks about Gnarly's appearance, saying he looked a little . . . well . . . inhuman. He was maybe a bit fishlike about the head and eyes, or lizard-like, particularly regarding his tongue. That first night she learned that a lizard's tongue and a fish's lack of need to surface for breath made Gnarly, as she conveyed to her friends with an arched brow, *skilled*.

She also learned, to her surprise, that it wasn't just the length of the tentacle but also the circumference of the sucker-pad.

Dawn's diary revealed how deeply she had fallen. She wrote Gnarly's name dozens of times on each page, surrounded with hearts and flowers. She wrote a verse intended to be part of a rap:

> He's Gnarly T and he's original G!
> He's down with R'lyeh, deep in the Sea,
> Evil is how society portray him to be
> But in truth . . .

Dawn could not find another rhyme, so fortunately this is where the stanza ended.

After a few weeks, with things going well, Dawn introduced Gnarly to her family. That did *not* go well. As they entered her parents' living room, Dawn's dad had his back turned, watching TV. He swore spectacularly at *FOX News* reporting on the US–Mexico border. He barely turned to acknowledge the couple. Dawn's mom sat at the table, poking at a dispirited flower bouquet that seemed to wilt even more when Gnarly got near. Neither talked to Gnarly, instead routing their questions through Dawn.

The conversation was tense. Her parents asked Dawn questions about Gnarly, and Dad pecked relentlessly on his Chromebook at each response. Gnarly, reading the tension in the room, made an excuse to leave, citing unspecified "clean up" in "realms beyond time and space," and borrowed a bottle of stain remover on his way out. Upset as he left, his tentacles writhed and conjured up thunder, lightning, and a downpour of poisonous toads.

This left an awful mess in the living room.

Gnarly Love

Dawn's parents turned toward her and attacked.

"He says he's 'immortal'?" Mom hissed. "375 billion years old?" She made a bitter line with her mouth. "Don't think I didn't see that Just For Men in his hair. Don't think that at all." She paused. "He's 400 billion if he's a day!"

Dad jumped in. "And where is he even from? 'Realms Beyond Time'? What kind of bullshit is that? He's a foreigner! Does he have a green card? Is he an illegal immigrant?" Dad adjusted his MAGA hat. "You know, they don't send their best."

Dawn responded, "He's from Egypt, I think. He said it's the Outer Worlds and . . ."

Her father pointed at her. "I Googled him. He claims to be from a lot of places. You going to move to his 'home country'?" Dad made air-quotation marks to emphasize his anger. "Which one? What the hell, you like deserts? You like mountains? You like the dark recesses of icy-cold and distant space? Do you like oxygen? Because he also says he's from outer space. The dude is a lunatic!" He paused. "An illegal one."

Dawn, mentally making a note to have Gnarly switch his Facebook page to private, was heartbroken. "You just don't know him like I do."

She left, weeping, and texted Aurora: *My parents don't understand me and Gnarly! They were so mean. I left their house crying.* But I told them . . . I . . . *well, I told them that our love was forever and he would always have a piece of my heart!*

Dawn called Gnarly to pick her up. Seeing how upset she was, he promised her some time alone. They would go on a vacation and relax from the stress her parents had put them under.

Dawn reported the hunt for a perfect vacation in her diary: *Vacation planning is complicated! We visited Algol Enterprises, a tour company recommended by Gnarly's friend Mynoghra. (He says to call her "Minnie" and claims that she is just a friend.) We picked up a bunch of brochures. But everything was kind of dark. We got brochures for Nameless Hells; Deep Sepulchres; Nameless Mists; Vast, Terrifying Abysses; and Mind-Shattering Emptinesses.*

The Dark Young of Shub-Niggurath Tour seemed interesting (at least it had "young" in its name), but Gnarly had some friends who were already going and I wanted a couples vacation. It was kind of our first fight.

They settled on a trip to Disney World. Dawn loved festival food and rides, and it would allow Gnarly to immerse himself in the nameless, faceless evil of the Disney Corporation. As a bonus, Gnarly was friends with Ron DeSantis and cackled at the idea of visiting him.

Traveling to Florida was uneventful, with Gnarly, in good humor, joking that they should set their watches back fifty years. They enjoyed a week of line-cutting, drinking excessively on the monorail from the hotel, smoking on the gondola, and scaring unattended children. On the last day, Gnarly put a cherry on the top of the vacation by dressing Dawn in a wide-brimmed hat, over-the-knee boots, a jumpsuit, moto-jacket, and a small statement purse. Unfortunately, he did not have enough time to find a dog miniature enough to carry in the purse. Gnarly slicked his hair back, donned super-thick framed lensless glasses, Prada dungarees, and a hoodie with a neck scarf. He accessorized with combat boots and a man purse. Attaching their cameras to selfie sticks, they spent their last afternoon in Disney World pretending to be TikTok influencers. Gnarly found the selfie stick useful for "accidentally" poking people. They photobombed any family photo they could and ignored every warning sign as they took increasingly dangerous selfie opportunities.

It was, they agreed, the vacation of a lifetime.

That last night, Dawn walked in on Gnarly FaceTiming with Mynogrha. She flew into a jealous rage, screaming, "I gave you my heart; she didn't!" And "What's that bitch to you, anyway?"

Gnarly attempted to calm her down, but Dawn stormed out of the hotel room, flew back home alone, and moved back in with her parents.

But true love always finds a way.

In her diary, Dawn reported: *I've been lonely, but Gnarly is creeping back into my DMs. Well, not DMs. He's all about mindfulness and computers do their evil automatically. Anyway, he's been sending me cute little gifts—sulfur-scented perfume, a cute little octopus pendant (well, something* like *an octopus), cloven patent-leather high heels, and an* Idiot's Guide to the Necronomicon. *Something every day.*

Gnarly continued his charm offensive, and eventually Dawn's heart softened, particularly when Gnarly made a grand romantic gesture, which Dawn related to Aurora in the following text exchange: *I was at Mom and Dad's, sulking on my bed, and I heard music outside. It got louder 'til I recognized it. It was "Creeping Death" by Metallica! I went to look and it was Gnarly! He was walking up to my window in a long trench coat. Not just that, he was carrying a . . .*

Aurora (interrupting): *LOL. Let me guess . . . a boombox on his head?*

Dawn (amazed): *How did you know?*

Aurora: *LOL, it's from an old movie.*

Dawn: *Well, it was cute! Anyway, I let him in, and we had a great talk. I think we're an item again!*

Aurora: *Well, I hope it works out.*

To Aurora's surprise, the reunion went splendidly.

Dawn and Gnarly, once again exchanging heartfelt vows, settled into a comfortable routine. At home, they sipped absinthe and adrenochrome cocktails, bathed in virgin blood, purchased a Tesla, and refused to tip delivery drivers. They watched the complete run of the *Jerry Springer Show* and contemplated engineering a reunion of Hootie and the Blowfish.

If there was a chthonic "scene" to make, Gnarly and Dawn made it, from clubbing seals in Antarctica, purchasing T-shirts directly from Chinese factories, enjoying tea with Vladimir Putin, exchanging dick pics with Marjorie Taylor Greene, and visiting Burning Man. At Burning Man, Gnarly's tentacles helped him win a juggling contest and an arm-wrestling match and collect several sexual harassment complaints that eventually got the couple booted from the playa.

"They have minds of their own," he shrugged to Dawn as they drove away.

The couple traveled to every hideous place they could think of, including Bumpass Hell in California, which they found underwhelming, although Gnarly found it amusing to push children toward fumaroles with one tentacle while restraining them with another. They enjoyed The Gates of Hell in Turkmenistan and Batagaika crater in Russia. As Gnarly noted, in a rare philosophical mood, "Mother

Gnarly Love

Nature *is* a bitch. Just as she should be." Returning to the United States, they attended several shows in Branson, Missouri, at one of which Gnarly nearly had a stroke due to uncontrollable laughter.

Back home, cuddled in Gnarly's home theater, they watched the complete works of Steven Seagal, select Nicholas Cage movies, and the director's cut of *The Adventures of Pluto Nash*.

It was the best of times.

But, as summer took hold and the sun spent more time in the sky, Gnarly sank into seasonal affective disorder, retreating to his basement, drinking and bathing himself in black light to soothe his symptoms. He slid deeper into depression, drinking and lashing out at Dawn.

Depressed herself, Dawn poured her heart out to Aurora using direct messages on Twitter.

Gnarly is grumpy and boring—he constantly rattles on about the "Good Old Days." He sits around on his couch, pounding 40s of Shoggoth's Old Peculiar, cursing and swearing that "Someday, someday the universe will cower in its tracks and I will arise, arise and resume my savage rule over the pathetic mammals of Earth!" Aurora, I don't even know what that means! And doesn't he know I'm a mammal?

When he's drunk, the Deep Ones come over and all they do is sit around and bitch and moan. Last night they were pissed off about some "Noodly Appendage" thing. I think they call it Pastafarianism? Said they're nothing but copyright infringers. They bitch and bitch, but nothing ever comes of it. Then, when he's hungover, he blames me for everything and picks fights over the smallest things!

Aurora, I just don't know what to do!

Using Twitter DMs for this exchange turned out to be a mistake. Gnarly, like most hideous creatures from the evil reaches of icy, dark space, was close friends with Elon Musk. Dawn's rant to Aurora got back to Gnarly.

He stormed up from the basement to confront Dawn. The argument turned ugly. Dawn brought up her old complaints about Mynoghra. Gnarly raged about the small minds of mortals. The failed holiday to Disney was recapitulated. Dawn called Gnarly "cheesy" for his *Say Anything* movie stunt. Just when it seemed that things couldn't get more heated, Dawn made a disparaging remark about Gnarly's tentacles.

And. He. Snapped.

Gnarly thrust a tentacle into her chest, tearing her heart from its nest of blood vessels and triumphantly waving it.

Had Dawn not expired immediately, twitching in a puddle of blood, she would have been pleased Gnarly had been serious when he vowed he would *always* have her heart. After watching the last blood ooze from Dawn's chest, Gnarly padded to his basement and engaged a hidden switch, revealing a fireplace. Its mantel held a row of jars, each containing a heart.

Gnarly removed an empty jar from a cabinet, placed Dawn's heart in it, filled the jar with a clear liquid, sealed the jar, and placed it on the mantel.

He whispered sadly, "I'm such a sentimental fool." One bitter tear trickled down his face, thinking, *tomorrow is another day*.

He returned upstairs for a drink and to find that bottle of stain remover. After

Charles Montgomery

all, Dawn could no longer clean up after herself.

The love story of Dawn and Gnarly ends here, with one last document—a text from Gnarly to Mynoghra:

Yo, Mynoghra! How are things in Oregon? I trust you still can't pump your own gas, the racism is strong, and the weather still sucks? Man, I miss that place! Anyway, just dropping you a line from the Welcome Innsmouth. It's freshmen week. I'm chilling in a back booth, checking out the new batch of coeds. After the last few years, I'm a bit gun-shy, but . . . you know?

Oh, hey, get back to you later, dudette! Some chick at a front table just turned around and checked me out. Gonna see where I can go with this one.

Wish me luck!

Love kind of is eternal!

Charles Montgomery is a retired professor from the Translation Department at Dongguk University in Seoul. He now lives in Spokane with his wife/editor Yvonne Dominguez and several lesser (maybe?) mammals. He has been published academically, in travel magazines, and in fiction anthologies. You can find his embryonic publishing effort at descendingcat.com, which also has links to many of his publications. If you have a cool project or are looking for submissions, feel free to reach out.

Theophany at Wall and Broad

J. L. Royce

A chill breeze caused Gloria to glance up from her book. The stranger blew into the lobby as though borne by a west wind. Tall, lean, and dark of mien, impeccably dressed in a simply cut suit, he parted the bustling corporate minions, crisscrossing the space like prairie grass.

When the visitor bore down upon Gloria's reception desk, she quickly lowered the book and grew interested in her screen.

"I have a meeting with Eldritch Endeavors," he declared.

He slipped his business card from a silver case. Her nostrils flared at the smell of gin. She sighed and dropped her book into the desk drawer.

He removed his sunglasses, revealing eyes as black as his long raven hair, restrained by a thong.

The receptionist cleared her throat and studied the proffered card. Its heavy linen stock was embossed on one side with the visitor's name; the scripts of many languages, some wholly unfamiliar, covered the obverse.

"Mister $N \ldots N \ldots$"

His smile revealed perfect, white teeth. "Just call me Daniel."

"Thank you." She turned to the on-screen calendar and tapped an appointment. "I'll let them know you're here."

The printer chuffed and ejected a visitor pass. "You'll need to wear this." She passed him the adhesive label.

Daniel frowned. "On my suit? *Really?*"

"Oh—" Gloria rummaged in her drawer. "Here—a lanyard." Their fingers grazed as he accepted it.

He tossed the cord around his neck and attached the pass, smiling. "You're too kind."

She examined his face: angular and curiously ageless, as though his ancient eyes were daily placed in a freshly minted mask.

"Are you all right?" he asked. Concern, genuine concern—so rare in the city—crossed that face.

Gloria blinked and laughed, a little cough in her throat, and remarked, "That's a lovely tie."

He touched the cabochon at the clasp of his bolo tie. "Do you like it?" His manicured fingers stroked the ancient silver frame. "Turquoise; for protection. It's Indian."

She was about to correct his expression but caught herself: Who was she to tell someone their proper title? A thought rose unbidden: *Don't we all have many names?*

"I thought you might be Egyptian—your surname."

"Full blood Diné—Navajo, to you."

"How fascinating!" Her console pinged, and Gloria tore her eyes away from the visitor to consult her screen. "Seems they're not quite ready . . . it will just be a few minutes. Would you like to take a seat?"

Daniel tracked her gesture to the lounge across the lobby. "I'm fine standing here, if you don't mind. Unless I'd disturb your work?"

"No, not at all."

He rested his valise on the edge of her desk as his gaze wandered the room, taking in the corporate art on display. "All these . . . monsters. They've done very well, with their games and books and motion pictures. . . ."

"Yes, the company's very successful." Gloria admired his suit. "This firm you represent—" she stroked the inscrutable card on her desk "—do you own it?"

"Own it?" Daniel chuckled. "I'm merely the messenger. My clients—" his eyes darted to a poster featuring a tentacle-faced being, and away "—the *entities* I represent feel they have suffered grave harm because of your company's actions. Misappropriation of intellectual property. They're angry, *furious*."

Gloria's eyes went wide. "I wouldn't know anything about that!" Her hands, clasped on the desk, stirred uneasily.

"Haven't you played the games?"

"No . . ." She feigned interest in her screen. "They're expensive, and after working here all day, I prefer to do other things."

Daniel nodded, a slight smile curving his full lips. "Sadly, the innocent often suffer with the guilty when judgment arrives." He resumed studying the artwork, fingers drumming in a syncopated beat on the fine leather case.

Gloria, fascinated by his hands, was startled when he asked, "The book—what were you reading?"

She retrieved the thin volume from below the desk and slid it toward Daniel.

"Rich. A fine poetess."

"You've read her?"

"Of course." Daniel flipped through the pages, reading.

"Sometimes, at the end of the day, I think that poetry is all I have . . ." Daniel closed the book and stared at the author's picture on the back. "I knew another poet, before the war, before I became an attorney." He smiled at Gloria. "She was beautiful, too. And a blonde. Like you."

Before she could react, his smile changed to ineffable solemnity, staring into a memory.

"What happened to her?" Gloria asked in a small voice.

His expression cleared. "She went home, back to her people. I never saw her again."

Theophany at Wall and Broad

"You said, 'before the war'—would that be Ukraine? Or the Middle East?"

"Before that. Which war?" Daniel shrugged. "So many wars—it's hard to track them all."

Gloria couldn't resist. "And since?"

"My work." He sighed. It was answer enough. Daniel checked his gleaming wristwatch, frowning. "At this rate, it will be lunch by the time my meeting ends. I don't suppose you'd have a recommendation, someplace nearby?"

"Ah . . ." she shuffled through her drawer and produced a printed sheet. "We have some wonderful spots right here in the financial district, if—"

"Would you consider joining me? For lunch? It might be best for you to step out when I'm through . . . negotiating. There might be, ah, fallout." Daniel's eyes settled on her hands. Outstretched on the desk, they reached toward him like kittens eager to play. "But I see you're wed."

Gloria started. "That?" She yanked the cheap ring from her finger and dropped it to rattle at the bottom of the drawer. "Just to keep the visitors at bay." She laughed. "Present company excepted."

"Then it's settled." He slapped the side of his briefcase.

Gloria cleared her throat. "I write a little, too—poetry. If you'd like—"

Her desk console pinged. "It appears they're ready for you, Daniel—just down this hallway and to the right."

He arched an eyebrow rakishly. "Are they, though? *Ready* for me?" He laughed, a baritone echoing around the room, and Gloria joined him.

Daniel straightened. "How do I look?"

"Perfect," said Gloria. "Oh—would you like a breath mint?"

"What for?"

"Your breath . . ." Gloria paused. "I thought you'd been drinking."

He reached into his jacket and drew out a necklace from an inside pocket. "Juniper. For protection."

"Why do you need so much protection?" Gloria spoke in jest.

Her visitor fingered the dried berries. "Why indeed? Here." Daniel handed over the necklace. "For you." He grinned. "Well, then—to war. See you soon."

Gloria waited until he was out of sight before releasing her breath. She sniffed the juniper and smiled.

Such an elegant man. So . . . compelling.

←♥→←♥→←♥→

J. L. Royce is an author of science fiction, the macabre, and whatever else strikes him. He lives in the northern reaches of the American Midwest, exploring the wilderness without and within. His work appears in *Allegory*, *Cosmic Horror Monthly*, *The Fifth Di*, *Fireside Magazine*, *Ghostlight*, the Visiter Award–winning anthology *Love Letters to Poe: A Toast to Edgar Allan Poe* (Fun, Fiction, Fandom), *Lovecraftiana*, *Mysterion*, *parABnormal Magazine*, *Sci Phi Journal*, *Strange Aeons*, *Utopia Science Fiction Magazine*, *Wyldblood Magazine*, etc. He is a member of the Horror Writers Association and Great Lakes Association of Horror Writers. Some of his anthologized stories may be found at jlroyce.com.

Full Moon Siren Song, or The Harmonic Analysis of the Tides Off an Unnamed Maine Coast

Elizabeth Davis

Please see next page.

Elizabeth Davis is a second-generation writer living in Dayton, Ohio. They live there with their spouse and two cats—neither of which have been lost to ravenous corn mazes or sleeping serpent gods. They can be found at deadfishbooks.com when they aren't busy creating beautiful nightmares and bizarre adventures. Their work can be found in the anthologies *The Initialization of Briar Rose: A Speculative Fiction Anthology*, *From the Yonder Volume IV* (War Monkey Publications), and *Yay! They're Here!: An Anthology of Short SF*.

Full Moon Siren Song

Civilizations   *to be spared*

Washed   *The fell*   *pleas*   *for*

Of sea   *not with*   *murmuring*   *this moment*

Elegies   *screams*   *closer*   *to never end*

Tides rise up with our voices. All of us pulled with the moon, Earth's dreamladen twin. It's

But of   *embraces*   *that the*

Broken   *pulls*   *stone goblet*

heart   *that*   *of*

sorrow

Only to us

That belongs   *the same*

eternity   *shared on*

no coincidence they call the motions harmonic, when your scientists map them out in

Dripping   *this moment of*   *gossamer wings*

Of endless   *will overlook*   *sailing the stars*

Unforgiving time   *reflected in our*

Sheen waters   *are sound*

Dark   *we trace*   *and waves*   *and that's how*

curves and straight lines, even as they scrabble for understanding that has always been in

their movements   *makes waves*   *we learn*

For motion

Their far-flung songs   *that strips away that fails*

their bones. For everywhere has been touched by our seas, and those all rise in tide and all

Of cold mathematical precision   *leaving only*

Beating heart

Drawn with   *The flushes*

Elizabeth Davis

Of summoning circles   *the cheek*

hear our song in oceans of wheat, sand, and concrete. Those deafened by jealousy claim we

Their love   *before any*

       Touch is made   *not found in*

         Runes from lost pages

       Rhymes and faded photos

In notebooks with tortured   *are inscribed with*

    Pressed along with flowers   *shaking hands*

    Harlequins of aging yellow   *before the chant*

lure only with pale gold, even as they strap themselves to the mast. Yet we sing love-deeply

    But caught between

   By severe guard librarians

  Studies or imprisoned

Serious leather-lined   *Explores with smiles*

         For the first time   *giggles*

        Giving shape   *shudders*

    For both   *form*   *and*

   Of loneliness   *as the veil*   *breaks*   *moans*

  Moment   *strains and*   *just a*

On this night, no prophecies or histories touch us, as Mother Hydra and Lord Dagon court

   somber

  Last

The

    But only a smile for the summoner

   Of magic and witchcraft   *for they know*   *flute*

  Neighbors gossiping   *that the universe is mad*   *universe to his*

anew, and this small planet spins to their song, their heartbeat, our song, our song for you.

  Bites and bruises   *but so is love*   *Azathoth set the*

   burning   *and that's why*

That leaves

Vuil Huis

Agrimmeer DeMolay

Greg and Pascal gazed through the bug-dotted windshield at the flowing road—curving left then right—leading the car further into the mountain's flank. Roaming clouds multiplied above the scrolling canopy till they were countless, merging into an overcast expanse sporting a minty hue. A rogue wind buffeted the car into the oncoming lane for a second before Greg corrected. With three fingers he brushed his auburn hair out of his eyes as if flicking away a tickling fly, his mirrored sunglasses askew.

He ought to pay more attention, but he couldn't. He kept retracing the facts that led him and his canine to this moment. Ronald Modesto had invited Greg to his recently purchased "crypto castle" built near or on top of an old ruin on the edge of Appalachia. He instructed Greg to meet up by the walkway tunnel. Was Ron himself meeting him there? Oh, no. On the phone, Ron had said to meet his assistant at precisely noon.

He has a servant now. How nice.

Well, it was already 12:20 p.m., so things weren't going according to plan.

The open windows roared with the winds of motion and the mountain air, as if the ridge breathed dinosaur-breaths. Pascal, very undoglike, ignored the flow and the window's openness.

Greg still pondered. Despite being friends, there had always been an undercurrent of competition, a constant, slight tension. Thinking back, he wondered whether that sense arose in both of them.

Ron had stressed, "Don't bring anybody. Just you." He clearly meant humans, and it was thus perfectly acceptable to bring a chocolate lab. Pascal could be incognito, being at once a person and not. *I'm bringing MY assistant.*

And why an assistant meeting Greg? Why not the host himself? Was he still angry about the old dynamic? Back then, Greggy enjoyed Ron's company, but it was often because whiny Ron always made average Greggy appear collected by comparison, and maybe more outgoing. In those days, sitting at the counter, the diner's washed-out lighting granted Greggy's skin a hint of a false tan, especially next to Ron's somewhat jaundiced visage. They were an apt pair, but that arrangement faded over the years.

After the next curve, Greg eyed a patch of dirt on the roadside, wide enough to fit a car, and aimed for it, stopping barely on top of it. He pulled out his cell phone, counting two reasons to call Ron: *Why aren't you greeting me in person?* and *I'm a tad late.*

He dialed, waiting for the tone, but nothing happened. He had no signal. *Goddammit.*

He eyed the darkened sky while Pascal tried to get his master's attention, as he endeavored to give the man's cheek a single lick but tagged his beard instead. Greggy said to the dog, "What's that greenish hue mean?"

Pascal simmered with mild concern.

Could all this be a high-tech prank? With all Ron's newfound wealth, could he have purchased some new klieg light to taint the clouds?

After high school, Ron's life seemed to have improved, while Greg's stayed static. Ron stopped indulging in the diner, and that haunt simply wasn't the same for Greggy without Ron. Still, Greg kept going for a few more months, the food and social life both growing staler.

He switched the transmission back into drive, angling the car off the dirt patch, kicking up a cloud, which entered the interior with a smell of rubber and soil. He continued on the road, with its gradual climb in elevation, a shrill engine pulling them along.

It would be grand to escape the dampness and mud of the common world. Mountaintops are rocky. Are they not? I've decided that this is my vacation.

Following directions, Greggy barely found what used to be a parking lot, an old jigsaw of pavement pieces. Stepping out of the car, the human and canine saw no hint of any tunnel or assistant, just a dense half-dead copse and vines.

Pascal focused on a single point in the verdant wall and huffed at it.

Greg asked, "Hello?"

A woman's voice replied, "Are you Greg Stolman?"

Greg gave Pascal's back a light tag. "Yes. Aumbry?"

A woman in jeans and green flannel stepped out as if being beamed there a la Star Trek transporter, presumably Ron's assistant. Greg studied her mussed blond hair, her boxy frame, and realized that she wasn't who he was expecting. There was nothing corporate about her.

"I thought Ron said there was a tunnel here."

Aumbry replied, "And I thought Ron said noon."

Greg ignored her tone and studied the craggy cliff towering above the parking patch. He gestured vaguely about.

Aumbry sighed. "Follow me." She disappeared much the same way she had appeared.

Great, now we're bushwhacking. Pascal hesitated, too. Once Greg took steps, his feet sank into an inch of mud. *Yuck.* He quickened until he could spot the marching green flannel back and caught up to it on a dirt path, a branch tugging at his collar.

Vuil Huis

Despite the dense brush, Greg heard only their sloshing footfalls, not one bird.

A tunnel appeared in a cliff face, cluttered with rotting crates, a tire, a wheelbarrow, and built of brick, much taller than wide, with an arched ceiling. Aumbry weaved around such debris familiarly. Greg paused at its opening, which suddenly breathed outward with one long blast of air, which made a sound like *hhhhuuuuueeeee*.

It smelled like damp mud and mushrooms. Pascal's tail hooked backward between his legs.

"It's okay." Greg gave a reassuring pat to the dog's warm head.

Greg set foot within, feet scraping with an echo, Pascal inching after him.

Aumbry didn't glance back.

As Greg plodded, stepping over a broken shovel, he wondered again if this was all some prank. There was nothing affluent about this place. While they were inside that stony esophagus, it luckily chose not to intone its long wind-sound again.

Once they emerged from the other side, Greg saw a structure within the trees, built into the hillside, resembling a Dutch Colonial enlarged to be three stories, counting its basement, with a grand porch and a side door to that basement. The foundation comprised interlocking stones that blended with the hill behind the house. Thick trees, too close to its facade, towered over its roof, and the mountain loomed larger than those treetops. There was no yard, just shorter brush. Between the steep hill behind the house and the dense vegetation, the grounds appeared muted in eternal shade, like an old photo.

Aumbry said, "Welcome to Vail Huey," as she produced a key.

Greg noticed a second hillside sloping down away from the tunnel's entrance and from the front of the house, down to where the remains of another structure seemed to sink into the earth as vines half hid columns that held up nothing.

Aumbry turned back, noticing Greg's attention on the older remnants. "That's the foundation of the first Vail Huey, but that name's anglicized. It was really called Vuil Huis. Ron explained the history of the place when it was Dutch."

Greg turned back to the porch while he kicked a root. "He called it his crypto castle."

Aumbry seemed to remember something. "He called you Eggy Greggy."

He waved that off. "Just Greg, please."

Their footfalls seemed unnaturally loud on the wooden steps up to the front door. *This Aumbry is solid; is she also Ron's bodyguard?*

In the even darker foyer, clouded by musty curtains and faded paintings, Greg looked back to be certain Pascal made it inside, his tail no longer rigid. The dog sniffed the bottom of the wooden staircase before trundling past the threshold. A fleck of peeled paint remained stuck to the end of his nose. Greg removed his sunglasses to his shirt pocket.

Stairs creaked rhythmically, from a pair of legs in black slacks descending out of stark shadow, the whole man coming into the light as he stepped. Greg absorbed the fact that his friend was no longer brunet. He had bleached hair and a mustache, a blazer, and fine shoes. *Like a celeb.* He stepped deliberately, accentuating the creaking.

Once Ron reached the bottom step near Aumbry and Greg, nodding to both, the stairs creaked again, and a figure like an animated mannequin with a flowing, blood-red blouse and wide glasses appeared at the shadowy upper steps. Her rouged cheeks seemed to warm the room even from the shadowy staircase, bringing a wake of scents—watermelon, honeysuckle, and newness.

Ron grabbed Greg's attention and his shoulders. "My friend! You made it!"

Greg mumbled, "Well, your guide here . . ." He tried to gesture toward where he thought Aumbry stood but saw no one there.

Ron continued, "Greg, meet Lena. Lena, Greg."

As Lena reached the bottom step, Ron placed his hand on her lower back as if to present her. She extended her hand. When Greg shook her fingers, they dug nails into his palm.

Ron announced, "Your arrival is a welcomed distraction for me. Thank you for coming."

Lena agreed, "And for me."

Greg inquired, "Distraction from what?"

"From my dreaded self," Ron amended as he waved them all to the next room, which turned out to be either a storage room or a dining room, with chairs and boxes but no table.

Greg gazed at each of their faces, trying to decide how formal this moment was supposed to be. Lena glanced back at him in a way that was not formal. All but Aumbry sat.

Ron cleared his throat. "Trouble finding the place?"

"A little, it's not on any map app. And there's no cell signal," Greg complained.

"I said 'rustic ruin.'"

No, you didn't. Greg tried to be the conversationalist. "Are we in New York or Pennsylvania?" Dots on maps, absolute truths, were the facts that filled their heads and fascinated them in years past.

Ron replied, "Yes."

Greg switched topics. "So, crypto trading has been a win, and it helped you buy this place outright?"

Ron rounded his shoulders. "Guilty as charged."

Greg realized that he maybe had to readapt to Ron, who now owned a more precise voice and a firmer gaze, which seemed to be not an act. Not the old Ron. "And a historical site?"

Lena replied before Ron could say a syllable. "Home sweet home." Her accent was difficult to place. Where was she from?

Ron said, as if reading Greg's mind, "Lena grew up not far from here."

How much can Ron read in my face? I'd better watch it.

Ron was staring out the window—despite its being utterly veiled in thick drapes—as he continued, "You know, the Iroquois used to have strict rules about who was considered native and who was not. Two full seasons and speaking an accepted tongue, those were their thresholds. That would make both of us natives." He gazed purposefully at Lena, who briefly returned a glance with a slight nod.

Aumbry, lurking in the foyer, leaned in to ask, "Would anyone like a drink?"

Ron and Lena raised their hands.

Greg replied, "I'll wait until dinner."

Vuil Huis

Lena replied, "Poo."

Ron agreed, "Yeah, poo."

Greg ventured, "Pascal says he'll have one."

Ron furrowed his eyebrows but said nothing.

Greg inquired, "What finally caused you to get back in touch?"

"I need your help," Ron leaned his forehead over his knee as he accepted a glass of whiskey. "I can't always follow the market, and I need to moderate my focus." Lena sat upright and alert as Ron explained, "I've been indulging in a hobby. Some would call it the occult."

Oh, would that be some in-crowd club of rich dudes? "How demanding is that stuff?" Greg tried not to draw conclusions but was already there.

Ron rattled rounded ice cubes at the bottom of his glass, turned toward Lena, but addressed Greg. "I'll explain more at dinner."

"I can't wait," Greg replied, honestly curious. *How does "the occult" fit in with me? Jeez, how many stories start exactly like this?*

Aumbry showed Greg to his room, where he unpacked his gym bag. He passed Pascal a treat while they both deflated on a made bed.

He considered the present moment. Maybe he and his canine ought to slink out now—out the front door and down through the howling tunnel. *Hm, but the car's tank was only a quarter-full; the gas stations all close early around here*, so he'd better decide soon. On the other hand, he felt a slight stinging in his palm where Lena had gripped his flesh, and that nagging remnant brewed an itch in him, an urge to find out more. He could stay for dinner.

←♥→←♥→←♥→

A fully decorated dining table had appeared in the room where they had gathered beforehand. A plate held a dry steak and potato below Greg's chin, just like what Lena's and Ron's held. Whiskeys and Manhattans flowed.

Ron described his habits. "I check the value of ether first thing and then again in five minutes and then again in fifteen, and that lets me know whether to make a fractional sale. I should watch it only so much. If I'm too tuned in, I baby it and end up with a loss. I need other pursuits. That's why I'm up here."

Lena grinned warmly for a moment at Ron while he didn't notice. A second later, her grin dissolved.

Greg ventured, "Ether ended up being real after all, unlike the Michelson-Morley experiment."

Ron fumbled his potato over his plate's end and returned it. "Oh, I think that the other ether is real too. When one has time to dig below the surface, one finds things. One collects juicy tidbits."

"Like in a museum," Lena proposed.

Greg recalled Ron's earlier promise. "You'd mentioned you could explain more about occult matters."

"Yes, I ought to lay it out in an explainable way, shouldn't I?" Ron drained his glass. "Allow me to elucidate the elusive, after so much labor and patience it took me to puzzle together the genuine history. It takes years in the now to clearly see years gone by, those true forces of the universe stubbornly veiled for centuries. Not so, for those who have gone before. A native had a high understanding of stars and planets and observed them from this very mountain. They understood harmony and wove it throughout their spoken language, belying an understanding of sonics and physics." He plucked up his knife. "And to them, sonics-physics and metaphysics were the same, both solidly real despite being unseen, both kinds of sounds. Sounds and zounds. What lurks far above is also exactly what sleeps below. They had knowledge beyond us and around the edges of what human minds capture, ancient cosmic concepts having to do with . . . wonders and dangers that they knew better than we." He sliced his potato into halves, which rocked in place. "They tracked a wholly different entity that intersected with different peoples up and down the East Coast. I believe it had to do with the mass disappearance at Roanoke, but that's a tangent. They knew what could get the attention of that otherness. The ritual they sleuthed out, they gifted it to the early Euro folk to get them to either be more rooted in this land or to *banish* them resoundingly! They had such understanding. And the most daring, their own outcasts, they enacted their understanding! They did it right here. The control-wheel of the valve of it lies unused, and close by." Ron stared with satisfaction at the potato halves on his plate.

Through the swinging door to the kitchen, Greg spotted Aumbry standing at attention.

Greg complained, "Oh, fishhooks, Ron, that has nothing to do with me, especially these days. For example, I'm just off a regular light-industrial gig."

Ron pointed his knife at Greg's face and, with a confident grin, replied, "I need someone to provide distraction and also ideas, a consultant of inconsistency, a sounding board to not be bored."

Lena appeared flushed, maybe perturbed.

Aumbry grew sullen.

Ron's face was bright by comparison. He proposed, "And I need an assistant with the ritual."

Didn't he already have an assistant, one who's an official employee? Greg's eyebrows raised. "Like in *D&D*?" He waved his empty glass in the air to get Aumbry's attention. She lunged past the swinging door, bottle in hand, and filled the aloft glass.

Ron rolled his eyes. "No, I mean real life, more like voodoo, the kabbalah, shamanism, and a little something else I found."

Greg grew leery, wondering if a prank was indeed in the works. "How involved would that be?" He looked around the room for a small camera but found nothing remotely modern.

"The refrain of the world's religions is the concept of sacrifice. In one way or another, thinking beings must give up some piece of themselves to open the door. And I found it truly means giving up life that is connected to the land. The more connected, the more the sacrifice."

This Edgar-Allan shit ought to chase me out this minute.

Greggy shifted his weight in his chair, his fork probing the cooling steak. *This whole trip's a wash.* He noticed Lena glancing his way, as if to try to communicate something without Ron noticing. *There's some other mystery here, not just Ron's.* The urge to run was countered by a curiosity to learn Lena's untold tale.

Vuil Huis

Ron continued, "Do you understand? The West gets the meaning of sacrifice all wrong."

Greg's discomfort arose from the newfound confidence in Ron. It seemed to cast a shadow over everyone else, including Greg himself, unexpectedly. Greg turned back to Ron. "So says you and who else?"

Ron bowed his head, laughing. "Think on what I've said, hm?"

←♥→←♥→←♥→

After the empty plates were cleared, Greg stepped onto the porch and sat on its upper step. He placed his sunglasses on, sliding their nosepiece to the midpoint between his eyes, and gazed at the vine-covered cliff, defaced with its dark opening inward toward its own darkness. Pascal reclined by the door.

Lena appeared and sat next to him.

Greg ventured, "Great meal, wasn't it?"

Lena tilted her head. "The food—no. The conversation—yes."

Did she refer to "the meaning of sacrifice"? "Really? I hope you don't mind my saying, but you didn't seem happy with it. The conversation, I mean."

Lena remained quiet for long seconds but replied, "Is it your business?"

Greg tried not to be obvious when studying her bare, stretched-out legs. He turned to scan his own, his mud-caked shoes, and said somewhat distastefully, "I suppose not."

She added almost apologetically, "How'd you know Ron?"

"We're friends forever, from high school. And you?"

She exhaled audibly, her breath whiskey scented. "This is all one endless date. Been here for days."

"He won't let you leave?"

"I feel that he won't. It never works out that I can. It doesn't help that I'm afraid of that tunnel. I've only been in it once—to get here."

Was that true? Greg tried to compare that depiction with anything else he'd ever heard, but came up short. He stared skyward, at its low chunky clouds, a hint of ocher where they were darkest. He continued, as if with an epiphany, "You're a prisoner." He removed his sunglasses and said with an elevated voice, "Wait, do you recall what he'd said about sacrifice—being glued to the land. He's made you the perfect candidate. He's going to sacrifice *you*!"

Lena and Pascal both snapped upright as if listening for something.

Her shoulders rolled back, like at a job interview, facing a trick question. With a mix of mockery and fear she said, "Come on. He's not like that. What movies have you been watching?"

Greg said, "He's not the guy I used to know. Listen. I'll not allow his craziness to swallow you up. We have to get you through that tunnel." He gestured toward the stony opening.

She inched closer, gave a slow kiss to his cheek, a gaze, a promise of much more.

Was this true attraction or some wanton desperation? Whichever, it felt good.

They sighed again, this time in unison. He replaced his sunglasses, nesting them on his skull.

"Something else weird," he added. "Why's the sky greenish here?"

Lena snickered, "It's not. Not to me. It's your glasses."

They chuckled at his misperception.

The tunnel interrupted with one long note: *wwwwwwhhhooooooo.*

Pascal's tail tucked under his body, hair raising.

Lena announced, "Oh, hell no."

Greggy asked himself what he had just heard. *An illusion, a trick, a sonic effect, like with a huge wind instrument.* He forced a smile and recited, "*That* is our road. I suggest you take some rest and recover your strength."

"The *Fellowship of the Ring*, really? Aragorn?" Lena stood and stepped over Pascal.

"Hey. It applies."

←— ♥ —→←— ♥ —→←— ♥ —→

Alone in his room with Pascal, Greg heard a knock. He expected Lena, but when he opened his door, Aumbry stood in the hallway, vaguely annoyed. "You are to attend the ritual in fifteen."

Here we go. "Okay, fine, bye." He kept his hand on the knob.

Aumbry continued, "In the ruins of the first house." *Of course.* "You noticed them when you first walked up."

Greg said, "Thanks," automatically.

Aumbry added, "Wear purple and black. Do you have those colors with you?"

The only purple shirt with him was a T-shirt that read "Rutland Roofs Rescue" with a vaguely Scooby Doo-looking dog face sporting a hat like an A-frame roof. It would have to do.

Soon they gathered on the porch and then waded through the knee-high brush, the broken columns barely visible in the night, starless in the tentlike shadow of the cliff. Smaller shadows danced around Greg's legs like imps' limbs, cast by an electric lantern in Aumbrey's roving hand.

Greg couldn't see anyone's feet, including his. Despite the chill, a vague dampness appeared across his back, sweat or humidity. He wanted to gaze upon Lena's silhouette as she marched in front of him, to enjoy her wending edges, but he became conscious of his feet sinking into inches of pudding. He hoped to sniff her watermelon and honeysuckle, only to catch a whiff of old garbage, inexplicably, not recalling seeing a dumpster anywhere at Vail Huey.

Pascal didn't seem to notice the scent.

They descended into an oversized bowl of earth crowded with brush, plus their shadows cast from the marching lantern. At the first column, Ron picked up a claw hammer and drove a rusty nail into the old stones, a horizontal crack appearing. He hung a leather bag on the nail, orating in a language Greg didn't know.

Ron dropped the hammer and opened his arms wide as if soaking up invisible sunlight.

Greg shifted into a clearer patch to examine his shoes. They were covered in goo, presumably mud.

He scanned his companions, seeking Lena, but didn't spot her.

Ron spoke to the sky, wonder or awe filling his half-lit face, with vibrato more like a tropical bird's calls. The dog maneuvered to lodge himself between Greg's legs. *I can't figure out what's going on with Pascal pestering me like this.*

Anxiously, he took two giant steps away from the dog, gazing about. He spotted Lena behind a column, flask in hand. She glanced back at him with a toast, swirling her drink.

Near the stone wall, two shadows moved in opposite directions, baffling Greg. *How? What cast those?*

On high alert, seeking evidence of some light-show prank, he gazed all around, but all the shadows seemed to behave as if independent of whatever originally cast them, some hose-like, others wavelike, an inky pond of agitation that Greg waded through.

One smoky strand reached under Pascal, coiling and fattening between his legs. *If this isn't a prank, he's in trouble.* Greg wanted to reach for his dog, but couldn't, his feet glued to the earth.

Lena dropped her flask as she lunged toward Pascal. On her knees, she grabbed at his collar to pull him away from the ashen tendril, but a second smoky limb appeared behind her too and pulled, crane-like, on her hair. She fell backward.

Pascal writhed to face Greg, to gaze in appeal, while his fur turned gray with coils of evanescent ropes. Greg stared back into the dog's dark eyes for half a heartbeat before the canine lids closed. Pascal slumped over.

People yelled. The electric lamp flew over their heads. Greg wasn't paying attention. His senses frayed.

Instincts in Greg shifted—from paralysis to flight—and he tried to run, but could only tread sloppily over marshy ground, out of the vine-clustered bowl of earth.

Aumbrey picked up Pascal.

Lena's shoes scraped the edge of a step up the porch, Greg and Aumbrey not far behind.

Back in the dining room, Aumbrey laid Pascal on the table.

Greg waited for Pascal's chest to expand. "Is he—?"

"Gone," Aumbrey reported.

Ron appeared more annoyed than scared as he stomped up the stairs.

Greg ignored his friend's exit, gazing at Pascal's dormant form stretched across the table with two different colored muds on Pascal's paws, patches of wet and dry cake-like substance. It smelled like something rotting.

Is he really gone? Here? In this goddamned place?

Soon he stood alone. Perhaps the others meant to grant solitude, allowing him to mourn.

I'll sleep in this room, as a kind of vigil. He ripped off his shoes, covered in the same two-tone mud as Pascal's paws. He smeared his hands across his Rutland Roofs shirt, tried to lie on the carpet, to close his eyes, but nothing seemed to make sense. Greg could feel his own pulse in his neck.

Time passed; minutes, hours, he didn't really know.

Why am I even here? What could I possibly gain from this day or even the next?

Greg stood, petted Pascal's already cold neck.

Agrimmeer DeMolay

He began searching the house for Lena. Slinking from room to room, silent in his socks, he found no one, the ground floor somehow deserted, until he rounded the storeroom corner to see Aumbrey rummaging among some rectangular tins.

Without turning, Aumbrey said, "She's on the porch."

How'd she know who I was looking for?

Greg dismissed that question and considered grander matters. *I've lost my best friend—my real best friend. It's a sign that I ought to get to take Lena away from Vail Huey. I'm owed.*

He found her sitting on the steps, pondering the tunnel, its opening darker than the surrounding night. *Is it still night, or early morning?*

He stood over her. "You see? This place is just a madhouse. You can't stay, and neither can I."

Lena remained motionless. "What happened?"

Was she unsure? Really? He studied her for evidence that her earlier heroic efforts weren't imaginary, and he counted dark smudges on her skirt and covering her bare knees. "You saw. You, uh, tussled with it."

She felt around. "I lost my purse."

He glanced around and didn't see anything resembling a purse. "It's still down there."

She mumbled, "No. I didn't bring my purse to that . . . event."

Greg clarified, "Sacrifice."

She stood, stretching her legs. "What? It was a magic show gone wrong."

"Ron took Pascal. He was *sac-ri-ficed*. As Ron's dark offering." Greg noted that neither he nor Lena had changed their clothes since the incident. In a less serious tone, he said, "Neither of us changed."

She commented, "I kept my favorite lucky top on. It helped me make a friend yesterday."

He stared at her bare feet while she remained just inches away in front of him.

Her hand gently cradled his forearm. His breath sought the scent of honeysuckle and watermelon, found remnants of both, and he closed his eyes to absorb the sense of her.

She kissed his mouth while her grip on his arm strengthened. Tension faded, as lava surrounds and drowns a rock, melting it into more lava, to combine with the flow that melted it. During their kiss, his forked finger roamed through her hair, cleaning the skin of his fingers, replacing caked mud with dried mousse. A measureless moment in that one kiss, they remained just so, their lava lips alive.

From the center of the cliff, from its gaping opening, a long note arose, sounding like, *hhhuuuummmmmmmmmaaaannnnnnnnnnnnnnn.*

Tension returned. Lena tried to pull away, but Greg held her hand as she tugged, leash-like. "This is too much."

Greg replied, "Exactly."

He continued to hold on, feeling the bones in her hand, while they both looked toward the tunnel, its sound fading. Greg could hardly tell if he imagined the sound now, or if the tunnel hummed barely audibly. He heard the door open behind him.

Ron's exasperated voice asked, "What's this!?" Lena and Greg swirled toward

Vuil Huis

Ron as he gestured vaguely at them as if they were one creature. "This just takes the cake." Ron grabbed Greg's sleeve with one hand and drew back his other into a fist.

Greg let go of Lena and raised his hands to block a blow that was never thrown.

Ron turned away.

Greg wanted to challenge Ron, but he felt like the odds would be better if the confrontation played out in front of Pascal's corpse. *Let's have it out, with a prime example of your stupidity right in front of you—the perfect sacrifice you wanted so badly, asshole.*

Just as he desired, Ron stomped through the front door, retreating through the foyer and to the dining room. Greg followed. They stood on opposite sides of the table, Pascal's corpse between them.

Greg pointed from Ron to the dead canine. "You sacrificed him."

Ron appeared genuinely surprised. "Eggy Greggy!" His brow angled downward. "What a load of filth! Pascal died of old age or something. The craziest thing we saw tonight was your hysteria. And I told you not to bring him. You think I planned it? And, and, and you think that gives you license to move in on my girl?"

Greg was just getting warmed up. "All this, you've used your resources to enact a grand scheme of revenge for how I treated you over the years. Nicely done."

Ron's face darkened, insulted and disgusted. "So not true. In fact, I wish I'd never invited you."

"Then why did you? Why really? What could I do for you, anyway, at this point?"

Ron mumbled something that sounded like, "To hurt better" or "To serve your betters."

Neither of those options sounded good to Greg. *I didn't agree to any of this.* "Then we'll just go." Greg plucked up his left shoe, covered in foul-smelling slime. *I'll just put my shoes on, find my sunglasses, and . . .* But the shoe cradled in his hands felt too disgusting to touch, let alone wear. It seemed dangerous, like an isotope.

Ron giggled. "You can't go. I need you, despite your being such an ass."

"I don't care. I'm not helping you do whatever it is you want to."

"I have no choice. Last night was the last night to do it. My money's gone. My bank crashed. They're seizing my assets—likely today, except for here. This place is off the books. For now. But I'm locked in. I won't have another chance after tonight. And I need someone with your traits, to finish it."

"'It?' You've lost—'it.'"

"Yeah, true. But now I'm stuck with a partner who hates me. The worst of straits. Yeah, you've cornered me into the worst possible position. The last insult." Ron seemed to stop breathing, gazed at Greg's feet. "And so I curse you." He raised his chin. Eyes met eyes. "To never again see the sun with living eyes, to dwell in this valley, to contemplate loss." But to Greg, Ron was the one who felt deadened, reciting from a script like some chatbot.

Greg felt ire, resentment, and nausea overcome him, sickness expanding inside, from the center of his chest outward. "Right back at you, scumbag!" He flung the slimy shoe, striking Ron's chest, leaving an oozing mark, as if Ron had vomited sludge on himself.

All sound withered, as if something absorbed it, canceled it, or a droning roar

Agrimmeer DeMolay

drowned it all around them—it was impossible to discern which. The lights flickered like a doused campfire.

No one spoke. Emotion returned to Ron's face, in force, agape as if he had just realized something horrible. Shadows in two corners of the room raved while he raged, yelling—but as if from far away—"You son of a bitch!" He produced his hammer from under the table, cocking it back to throw it at Greg, but a ghostly, smoky vine as thick as a firehose found Ron's throat, tugging his body into the left corner where more shadows crossed his torso, darkened his face, and stole his breath.

He dropped the hammer, which soundlessly fell out of reach. As Lena and Greg stood paralyzed, Ron's body slumped. The writhing ghost-hose discarded Ron's listless body, his skin white, his open eyes aimed toward the ceiling, all emotion gone from him.

The roving shadow grew opaque, rhythmic.

A mass stepped into the room, as if through the wall behind where Ron had stood, its bulbous knobs knocking the chandelier aside, its sixteen limbs gripping the walls, casually breaking boxes, windows, doors, while its insectile eyes gazed in two different directions—one toward Greg and the other toward Lena.

The beast leaned forward, collapsing the dining table—as sounds again filled the air, that of wooden things cracking and breaking all around them—Pascal disappeared below the creature's shiny, black carapace.

Lena and Greg jumped toward each other. Each clutched the other, tightly, but not as tight as the greasy tentacles wrapping around them both. They closed their eyes as their bones snapped and mixed with one another.

←♥→←♥→←♥→

Daylight crept around the mountain.

Aumbry watched a tongue of fire lick the porch and grow vine-like along the walls.

She said, "To hell with you. You've had your fill, but you're done—I hope for a very long time. No house. No habitants. Nothing for your appetite. Done."

She turned away from the conflagration, trudging toward the passageway.

That opening said, *yyyyoooouuuuuuuuuuuu.*

She froze, staring into that titanic gap.

She paused to find out what would claim her. While she lingered, smoke soaked her clothes and hair. Still, she stood, unassailed. She waited for an inner strength to rise up, in order to step forward, to walk right into that yawning passage.

Once the burned walls collapsed into their foundation, when the fire finished its feasting on the passing of the second Vuil Huis, she took one step forward, as if taking her very first, with Greg's car keys in her fist.

←♥→←♥→←♥→

Agrimmeer DeMolay's days fill up with sauntering, building things, or making mistakes, since his background is in physics and his day job is the legal profession. Outside of all that, he'd rather be writing. His poetry has appeared in *RHINO Poetry*, *The Collidescope*, and *Chronogram*. His novel, *Alien of Acid*, is available from Amazon.

My Marriage, or A Cult Dedicated to a Perverse Fertility Goddess

Joseph C. DiNallo

Midge stopped pretending to be in love with her husband once he lost his job. It was surprisingly easy.

"It's just that you're so boring and unattractive," she told him over Thanksgiving dinner.

"I'm sorry you feel that way." Stan carved a thick slice of turkey breast and draped it across his plate. "Pass the gravy?"

"Do you think you'll be able to find a new job soon? Maybe I could pretend to love you again if you did."

"In this economy?"

Midge felt like she was the only one trying anymore, but she had promised herself that she would do anything—short of aggravated manslaughter while attempting to elude a law enforcement officer—to keep her house a home.

Stan, meanwhile, seemed unwilling to commit even a class-four felony to make their marriage work.

"Anyway, how's the stuffing?" Midge asked.

"Not bad!"

"I tried a different recipe this year. I was worried how it'd turn out."

"It turned out fine."

There was a silence as the soon-to-be-broken household chewed stuffing. "You know," Stan started, "they always need guys over at the factory. I could become a blue-collar family man—"

Midge slammed her fork on the table. "I want a divorce!" she wailed, and she fled out through the kitchen into the cold November night.

←♥→←♥→←♥→

"Doris?" Midge knocked several times, trying to give her neighbor some time to get herself together. "Are you home?"

There was no car in the driveway, but that didn't mean Doris was away. Her military husband often traveled, and all four of her children were communist agitators

74

who roamed the streets at night.

"Poor Doris," Midge thought. "Always spending the holidays alone."

Of course, that was Midge's life now, too. Or it would be if Stan didn't find work. Midge glanced across the street at her slice of the American dream: a three-bedroom ranch with attached garage. "It could all be gone soon," she murmured. The thought made her want to collapse right there on her neighbor's doorstep.

Instead, she straightened, smoothed her dinner dress, and fluffed her perm. "Doris? I'm coming in! I hope you're decent!"

Doris Rhodes was not decent. Midge found her passed out in bed, naked, surrounded by empty bottles of cough syrup.

"What a shame," Midge thought, shaking her head at the sight of Doris's bedraggled blond hair. "Such a beautiful, natural color, yet she never does anything with it."

Before marrying, Doris was a singer at a nightclub. She had the voice, personality, and hair; beautiful golden locks she wore like her namesake, Doris Day. "If I had hair like that, I could've attracted a husband with better job security," Midge thought. Even now, staring at the drunken wretch Doris had become, Midge couldn't help but fantasize about using a kitchen knife to scalp her, taking the scalp to the sink to rinse the blood off, storing the scalp in a Tupperware bowl in the fridge, using a different kitchen knife to remove her own scalp, then using hot glue to graft Doris's hair onto her own skull.

"Oh, but that would never work. My immune system would recognize her scalp as foreign and produce antibodies to reject it." Midge paused and cocked her head thoughtfully. "I'd need to take some kind of immunosuppressant, and then it would turn into a whole thing."

"Midge?" Doris groaned. "Is that you?"

"Well, it certainly isn't your husband. When was the last time he was home, and are you sure he even loves you anymore?"

"It is you, Midge. I can tell by the outline of your enormous hair."

Midge flipped on the bedside lamp, then took a few seconds to enjoy watching Doris shrivel away from the light.

"Get dressed, Doris. Stan and I are getting a divorce!"

←♥→←♥→←♥→

"I'm staying with Doris until you get your act together," Midge said into the phone, using her sternest possible tone of voice. "I'll get my things tomorrow while you're looking for a new job."

"I'm sorry you feel that way," said Stan. There was a pause as he chewed and swallowed. "Did you put chili powder in the stuffing? It's got a little bit of a kick to it."

"That's the paprika. I told you I used a new recipe."

"Paprika! I knew it was something."

"I was worried it would make it too spicy."

"Not at all. It goes really well with the sweetness of the bread."

Doris entered the living room with two bottles of Arestin Extra-Strength Nighttime Formula cough syrup.

My Marriage, or A Cult Dedicated to a Perverse Fertility Goddess

"I have to go now, Stan. I hope my dramatic display at the dinner table tonight opened your eyes to all your failures as a man."

"Oh, it certainly did," Stan chuckled.

Midge shook her head. She just couldn't seem to get through to him. "Good night, Stan. Make sure you put the food away before going to bed." She slammed the phone on the hook before he could respond.

"That's a real shame about your husband," Doris said in a sympathetic tone. "Mine was never home, but at least he always had a job," she added in a not-so-sympathetic tone.

Midge flopped onto the couch. Paisley upholstery covered all of Doris's furniture. It matched the floral-patterned rug and curtains. "I love what you've done with this room, Doris. It makes me feel better about my own home decor."

"Thank you, Midge. I like the way you do your makeup and hair for the same reason."

"How was your Thanksgiving? How are the kids?" Midge knew Doris had likely spent not just Thanksgiving, but also the past few days, drunk and alone.

"You know teenagers. Always going on about the plight of the proletariat."

Midge smirked. "Those godless, pinko bastards. I guess it's easy to be brainwashed by immoral ideologies when you grow up without a father."

"Are you sure about this divorce, Midge? What will you do for money?"

Midge let herself sink deeper into the couch. "We don't have any savings, and the house payment is due soon."

A lecherous, vaguely homicidal, not-at-all-attractive expression spread across Doris's face. "I may know of a way you could support yourself. But you'll have to be willing to consume human organs as part of an initiation ritual into the cult of a perverse fertility goddess, if you know what I mean."

Midge's eyes widened. "What do you mean, Doris?"

The lecherous, vaguely homicidal look on Doris's face became more homicidal. "I have two words for you, Midge: Shub-Niggurath, the Black Goat of the Woods with a Thousand Young."

←♥→←♥→←♥→

Midge spent the rest of that night thinking about what Doris had told her. Apparently, the cult of Shub-Niggurath was hosting weekly orgies after the normal Lutheran service at the local church. The pastor's wife, Beverly Johnston, was their high priestess, and she was offering financial support to new initiates.

"Worshipping Shub-Niggurath is a lot more fun than being a Lutheran," Doris promised. "Every week, the orgy has a different hunter- and quarry-based theme. This week's theme is 'big-game hunters of the savanna.'"

Orgies, cannibalism, bloodthirsty perverts crossbreeding with satyrs and other monsters that drink their goddess's maternal secretions containing mutagenic properties . . .

It was a lot to take in, but Midge already had an anteater costume that would be perfect for the theme of this week's orgy. She promised Doris she'd think about it.

The next day, Midge kept herself busy around the house. "Home . . ." she found herself muttering as she walked between rooms. "But not for much longer.

Unless . . ."

When Stan returned, he revealed that he hadn't landed an interview. They ate Thanksgiving leftovers together in silence, and later that night, Midge lay in her marital bed and wept. "Stan? Wake up, Stan!"

Stan rolled over. "Is something wrong?"

"I want to make one last attempt to shame you into being a better man," Midge started. She paused so that she could choose her next words carefully. "The fact that you don't have a job makes you a failure as a husband and as a man. I know we've already been over that, but I want to really drive the point home."

Stan nodded solemnly.

"You no longer provide for me," Midge continued, "which was the only thing making up for your inadequacies in all other areas of desirability."

Stan took his wife's hand and patted it gently. "I'm sorry you feel that way. Also, I'm sorry that I forgot to tell you earlier that we're almost out of toilet paper."

"Already? I knew I should've gotten an extra couple of rolls."

Stan indicated his stomach. "All that Thanksgiving stuffing," he said with a chuckle.

"Oh," said Midge. "That makes sense."

"There's enough toilet paper for another day or two, so it's okay if you don't feel like going to the store tomorrow."

"No, I'll go. I just wish I'd listened to myself and gotten extra."

Stan patted Midge's hand again, brought it to his lips for a kiss, then rolled over. Midge rolled the other way.

"I can't seem to do anything right these days. I've lost the ability to pretend to be in love with my husband, I got blackout drunk on cough syrup with the neighborhood communist, and now I'm considering joining a cult." Midge pulled the sheets up over her head and mulled the state of things. "I wonder to what extent my misery is related to my own actions, decisions, and worldview?"

The thought lingered in her head, threatening to spark the irritatingly bright light of an epiphany, but Midge shook it away and replaced it with a mental note to buy condoms while she was at the store tomorrow. "I don't want to *catch* anything at this orgy," she said without thinking.

Stan stirred. "What's that, honey? Are you attending the orgy tomorrow, too?"

←♥→←♥→←♥→

The Garkowskis spent Sunday morning getting ready for the big-game hunters of the savanna-themed orgy together. "This is an unexpected turn of events," Midge remarked as she stepped into her anteater costume.

"Life is occasionally marked by such things," Stan remarked back as he adjusted his safari hat in the mirror.

Midge shook her head as she pulled her costume up over her shoulders. "I can't believe Doris went behind my back to invite my husband to this thing. She's supposed to be my friend."

"She invited you to an orgy. That sounds like a good friend to me."

"Can you zip me into my costume?"

Stan did. "Did you know that when the first anteater specimens were brought

My Marriage, or A Cult Dedicated to a Perverse Fertility Goddess

from the New World, Europeans thought all anteaters were female because the males of the species hide their testicles inside their bodies?"

Midge sighed through her anteater snout. She hated when Stan relayed random animal facts. "Let's go save our marriage," she intoned nasally as she dragged him toward the car.

← ♥ →← ♥ →← ♥ →

Nearly a hundred other cars packed the church parking lot. "I think that's the mayor's Lincoln," said Stan, pointing as he scanned for a parking space. "And look! That's my old boss's Cobra!"

"Maybe he'll hire you back if I sleep with him," said Midge, her biting sarcasm muddled by the snout of her mask.

"Maybe so," said Stan, his sobering gaze obscured by the brim of his hat.

Doris Rhodes greeted them at the church doors. "Midge! You made it!" she slurred. "And your aardvark costume looks cheap, but passable."

"Anteater costume," Midge corrected. "And what's your costume, Doris? Are you supposed to be a baboon?"

"Howler monkey," Doris corrected back.

"Wrong habitat," Midge corrected back again.

"Howler monkeys are native to rainforests," Stan corrected back again further.

"Not all species of howler monkey," Doris corrected back again back. "Some are native to seasonal deciduous forests bordered by pockets of open savanna."

"Oh, you're right," Midge corrected herself back again back in reverse. "I do remember reading that."

"Quite right," Stan corrected himself back again back in reverse, too. "I remember reading that, too."

There was a silence as they each pondered whether there were any more corrections to be made regarding howler monkeys. "Maybe you should just come inside for the orgy," Doris said finally, swinging the doors wide.

Fifty-some women wearing savanna animal costumes and fifty-some men wearing safari outfits crowded inside the church sanctuary. In alphabetical order: antelopes, cheetahs, elephants, giraffes, kangaroos, leopards, lions, ostriches, and zebras mingled and cavorted with rifle-toting hunters among the rows of pews. Midge had to shout to be heard above all the mingling and cavorting: "Does anyone see Beverly?"

"What's she dressed as?" shouted Stan.

"A crocodile," shouted Doris.

"Wrong habitat," shouted Midge.

"Don't start that again," shouted Doris.

"Stop shouting," shouted a random woman dressed as an elephant.

Midge scanned the crowd. In the back row of pews, one of her high school teachers fluttered her ostrich-feathered arm as she stroked the inner thigh of Mr. Graceford, the school's head principal. In the center aisle, the receptionist at Schumacher and Sons Family Medicine nuzzled her zebra-striped face into Dr. Schumacher's bare chest.

The cult had erected a stage before the altar. At the foot of the stage, an entire

78

harem of women dressed as lionesses purred as they pawed at Mayor Whitman's back, neck, and shoulders. The dozens of other faceless women and their grinning men danced and gamboled and reveled and lolled, and above them all, a crocodile skin-clad Beverly Johnston, leathery and sharp toothed, stood tall behind the pulpit, sneering up at the agonized gaze of a plaster Christ hung upon the cross.

"I think that's her, making a weird face at Jesus," said Stan, pointing.

Midge gripped her husband's arm. "Don't try to sleep with anyone while I'm gone," she warned.

"I'll keep an eye on him," said Doris.

"You can't keep an eye on your own husband," Midge snapped back. She strode toward the foot of the stage.

"Midge?" Beverly called down. "Midge Garkowski? Is that you behind that aardvark snout?"

"Anteater snout," Midge corrected.

"Interesting choice. Did you know that when the first anteater specimens were brought from the New World, Europeans thought all anteaters were female because the males of the species hide their testicles inside their bodies?"

"I was just discussing that with my husband."

Beverly cocked her head. "You two must have a lot of interesting conversations."

"Not really." There was a silence as the two savanna-costumed women locked eyes. "Anyway," Midge continued, "what do I have to do to join this cult?"

High priestess Beverly flicked her tongue over her reptilian lips. "Simple," she said, her grin spreading impossibly wide. "Just harvest and consume Stan's organs in the Name of the Goddess."

←♥→←♥→←♥→

"I'm just not sure I'm comfortable removing and consuming my husband's organs," Midge whispered. Doris had called a huddle after it seemed like Midge might not go along with the whole ritual-human-sacrifice-and-cannibalization-of-her-husband thing.

Beverly reached out a scale-covered hand to stroke Midge's perm. "But think about it this way, Midge: you probably don't even like your husband."

Midge thought about it that way. "Well, when I think about it that way . . ." she said, still not quite sure what about the way she thought. "All I've ever wanted in life is a stable home," she mused. "I'm pretty sure I need a husband for that."

"But what if your husband is what makes the idea of 'home' an impossibility?" Beverly sneered beneath her crocodile mask. "What if our place is with each other, and being married to men is just a way to keep us apart?"

Doris nodded. "It's how they divide us," she slurred, taking a swig from the cough syrup she had hidden in the depths of her hairy, howler-monkey cleavage.

Stan placed his hand over Midge's anteater claw. "You do whatever you think is right, dear. I support your need for being allowed to make your own decisions."

Doris placed her monkey's paw over Stan's. It looked like the three of them were about to engage in an enthusiastic team activity. "Yes, do whatever *you* think is right," she emphasized.

"But what do I think is right?" Midge wondered. She looked at Doris, then at

My Marriage, or A Cult Dedicated to a Perverse Fertility Goddess

Beverly, high priestess of Shub-Niggurath. "Is this why I haven't seen your husbands around for a while? Were they sacrificed, too?"

Doris nodded. Beverly nodded.

Stan also nodded, but not because he had any prior knowledge of other ritual human sacrifices. "Don't forget, we need to pick up toilet paper before we go home today. We've got enough for one, maybe two more uses."

"It's time to choose, Midge." Beverly turned and made her way back up to the stage.

A hush settled over the savanna-themed congregation as Beverly raised her arms. "Shub-Niggurath, Dark Mother, Goddess of the Wood . . ." her voice reverberated around the church's ceiling. "We gather here, in this great house of patriarchal oppression, to shout and revel in Your Name."

The female members of the congregation burst into a chorus of whooping, shrieking, howling, snarling, and passive-aggressive nagging. Midge tried to catch Stan's eye amid the tumult. "What should we do?" she mouthed.

"I can't read lips," Stan mouthed back.

"I think they're going to make me kill you," Midge mouthed further.

"Did you hear what I said about the toilet paper?" Stan mouthed back.

Beverly stepped from behind the pulpit. In one hand, she raised a dagger, the ebony pommel carved into a goat. "Our men gather here with their rifles, which, besides being their primary tools of oppression, are phallic symbols."

A smattering of *boos* rang out in response.

"This ritual knife is also a phallic symbol," Beverly continued. She swept her gaze over the rows of pews. "Lots of things are shaped like phalluses!" She began listing examples, starting with small objects, like pens and pencils, then slowly building up to larger objects, like skyscrapers and presidential monuments.

While Beverly droned, Midge closed her eyes and considered her own mother. She thought about how difficult life had been once her mother had decided to leave her husband. The pressure, the never-ending responsibilities . . . Her mother had put on a brave face (made up with Elizabeth Arden makeup), but slowly the infinite number of responsibilities that came with being a single woman had taken their toll.

"Then again, my mother didn't have a cult that offered to help with living expenses," Midge thought, and then, for the first time since her wedding day, she began envisioning a life without Stan.

"And don't get me started on abstract concepts," Beverly roared as her sermon drew to a fiery close. "I mean, even abstractions are shaped like phalluses! You can't tell me that's a coincidence!"

The congregation murmured in agreement, and Beverly had to raise her arms again to silence them. "And now . . ." she continued, holding the sacrificial dagger high above her head. "Now our sister initiate, Midge Garkowski, will perform the sacrificial rite so that the rest of us can shout and revel in the Name of the Goddess."

Beverly turned to Midge, and the heads of a hundred-some horny, safari-themed cultists who were experiencing a sense of righteous indignation regarding the whole phallus thing turned in unison to follow her gaze.

Midge looked at her husband. Stan rubbed a scuff out of the brim of his safari hat, and, noticing everyone staring at him, draped his arm supportively over Midge's shoulder.

"Go ahead, honey," he whispered. "I know how important you think participating in feminist revolutions is."

Beverly moved to the front of the stage to loom over them. "Come," she beckoned, and she held the sacrificial dagger out for Midge to grasp.

← ♥ → ← ♥ → ← ♥ →

"This is a lot like the time I had to pull a dead tapeworm out of my cat's anus," Midge told her husband to lighten the mood as she drew out his intestines through the small incision in his abdomen. She knelt over Stan at the foot of the stage. Beverly and Doris flanked her, and below them, scattered among the rows of pews in the church sanctuary, the big-game hunters of the savanna-themed orgy-goers/cultists were watching with rapt anticipation.

"I didn't know you were a cat person," said Stan, wincing.

Midge always felt slightly uncomfortable being the center of attention, so she was happy her anteater mask kept her face hidden. She focused on coiling her husband's warm, squiggly bowels into the neatest possible pile. "I don't know if I'm doing the right thing," she said in a voice that betrayed the slightest hint of a quaver.

"It looks like you're making progress, at least," said Stan.

"I mean generally. Like, am I doing the right thing as a person?"

Stan screamed as a wave of agony racked his body, and for a moment, he lost consciousness. "I'm sure you're doing the best you can under the circumstances," he said once his faculties returned. "I know how important you think putting forth your best effort is."

"You're doing a great job, Midge!" chimed Doris.

"That monkey makeup isn't doing your face any favors," Midge wanted to snap back, but she held her tongue. Doris was her sister now—or she would be once the ritual sacrifice and cannibalization thing was over with. She turned instead to Beverly. "Do I have to eat *all* of his organs?"

"Just a few nibbles to show us you're serious about serving Shub-Niggurath."

"It's mostly a symbolic gesture," added Doris.

"I figured," said Midge.

There was an awkward moment as she finally reached the end of Stan's small intestine. It clung to her hand like a wet noodle, and she had to scrape it away with the phallus-shaped sacrificial dagger.

"I know this is difficult, but you're doing the right thing," said Doris. She flashed Midge what was meant to be a reassuring smile, which actually looked rather threatening due to the fake monkey fangs protruding between her lips.

Midge sighed as she took one last loving look into her husband's eyes. "Goodbye, Stan," she said, fighting to keep her voice steady as she reached back into his abdomen to feel around for his pancreas, large intestine, and spleen. "I'm sorry it came to this."

Stan wanted to reply, but as the blood and organs left his body, so too did his ability to provide emotional support for his wife.

Born anew, Midge turned to face the congregation with her former husband's pancreas in one hand and his spleen in the other. "I'm not going to eat his intestines," she told Beverly.

My Marriage, or A Cult Dedicated to a Perverse Fertility Goddess

Beverly shrugged. "I don't think the Goddess actually cares which organs you consume."

"It's less about which organs you eat than why you eat them," said Doris.

"It's just that Stan ate a lot of Thanksgiving leftovers. I tried a new stuffing recipe that calls for paprika."

"Oh, I've never tried that," said Beverly. "I always make mine with chopped apples."

"That sounds good," said Midge.

"I add sautéed mushrooms to mine," said Doris.

"That's disgusting, Doris, and everyone hates you," said Midge. "Anyway, we'll all have to get together and swap recipes for next year."

"But not the mushroom one," said Beverly.

"Right," said Midge.

Midge turned back toward the congregation. Shadows pooled in empty spots along the pews, and in their shifting darkness, Midge thought she could make out strange, horned shapes.

"Shub-Niggurath, Great Mother, Black Goat of the Woods with a Thousand Young . . ." she began in a voice that held new strength. "I partake of this flesh in Your Name, and in the name of my sisters." She bit into the pulpy, purple spleen, and the savanna-themed orgy erupted in a discord of triumphant, bestial shrieking.

The women pounced and raked the men's bodies, and the men surrendered their arms and abandoned themselves to their pleasure. There was a pulsing sound, and the smell of blood in the air. The shadows pooling in the pews coalesced into awful, fleshy masses riddled with boils, horns, and cloven hooves.

"At last!" Beverly shouted. "The Dark Mother blesses us with Her gift!"

The fleshy masses burst into sprays of milky slime that fell onto the congregation like diseased rain, and the congregation shuddered with heightened pleasure.

Beverly and Doris leaped from the stage. "Join us, sister!" they called, beckoning Midge into what was now a single, undulating mass of milk, flesh, church pews, and safari/savanna animal-themed costumes.

Midge hesitated. Had she finally found a place she could truly call home?

From somewhere beyond space and time, a darkly maternal voice called out to her: *Home isn't a place; it's a people.*

Oh, Midge thought back in response. *I guess that makes sense—in a cliché sort of way.*

Before she leaped, Midge swallowed the rest of her former husband's spleen whole.

←♥→←♥→←♥→

Joseph C. DiNallo is an Ohio native currently living in southern Louisiana. He writes fiction, poetry, and drama. His work has appeared previously in *Gyroscope Review, Amaranth Journal of Food Writing and Art, The Sow's Ear, Snowy Egret, Third Wednesday*, and *Miller's Pond literary magazines*, and the Skywatcher Press anthology*, The Dead Unleashed*.

Cyloptorus

David A. Kennedy

Those boys was dead when I found em, and no one ever said different. The questions they asked me, I tried my best to be honest. There was a lot, and sometimes I get confused. I ain't stupid, like they say, but I like to take my time thinkin things through. And they musta believed me, or they never woulda let me go.

Them bodies was in the woods behind the Hoover place. There's a trail runs right along the back fences of all those farms. Everyone uses it to get to the quarry, so don't ask how come I was there one time at dusk. It was summer, and I went for a swim. Yeah, by myself, what about it? Weekdays is pretty quiet, and the water's low this year, so you can't jump off the south cliff no more. Well, Johnny Deakins did, but he busted up his legs.

It was late when I skedaddled out of the swimmin hole, and I had to work that night. I'm a dough man. It's hard to make good pizza dough. An old woman showed me some tricks bout dough, and a few other things.

The dead boys was layin in the weeds in front of the oak trees. I seen this red thing, and I thought right away it was a shoe. Even though I knew it was a shoe, I was puzzled that it was pointin up. I stared at it for a while, then I looked around, cuz all of a sudden I got real scared. Goosebumps was comin up all over me, and I was shakin.

The shoe was a little ways from the trail, and when I walked over to it, the foxtails got all in my socks. The two dead boys was just layin there. They wasn't side by side. The one with the red shoe, he was layin on his back, and he was hurt grievous bad. Like his insides . . .

The second boy was taller, and he had his face in the dirt. His left arm was gone, and I couldn't see it nowhere. I got a little sick, I'm not too ashamed to say that. I wanted to run away and just forget all bout it, but I knew I couldn't. My poor dead mama always said to obey the laws, and I told her I would try. Besides, I get bad dreams if I try to run away from things. Very bad ones.

I walked hard on the trail until I fell and skinned my knee. I was cryin, not from my hurt leg, but cuz I kept thinkin bout those boys' mamas, and how they was gonna be so sorry their boys got killed. I was runnin and limpin at the same time when I got to the highway. By then it was dark, and I got scared all over again. There wasn't no cars on the road, so I had to go all the way to Ed's. He got a fillin station before you get into town, and he likes me. And Petey was there, and everyone likes Petey.

I come hustlin up to Ed's and I was yellin. When Ed came outside he saw me and his mouth got real wide. My clothes was dry when I left the swimmin hole, cuz everyone goes skinny-dippin—even Judy Wilder, and she's the prettiest girl in Gaddon. But my hair was wet, and cuz of all the cryin and stumblin in the dirt, I was a mess. Ed, he thinks I'm hurt real bad, and then he's yellin too.

The moon had come up, so you could see just fine. Ed ran up to me and asks *what's wrong, who hurt ya*, but I tell him, *no it's not me*. Now Ed is all confused, but Petey comes over and I start to feel a little better. He's the best dog I ever knew, and he likes me lots. And I say *hey Petey*, even though I'm still cryin, and all Petey wants to do is lick my skinned-up knee.

No one liked Sheriff Teeter, but I never knew how come. He didn't bother me much, so I was okay with him. But everyone is scared of the law, and when he drove up real fast in his car it was all lit up and the sirens was blarin, and it like to give me a heart attack.

I told em where those boys was, and yeah I was for sure they was dead. Sheriff Teeter seen I was bruised up a little, and he saw the fear on me. I thought he was gonna put his handcuffs on me, cuz he looked at my hands real close. Then he was yellin at his deputies to do stuff, and they was runnin around like chickens for a bit. Then he says to one of them, *stay here with the boy*, so that tall deputy named Jim stayed. Those two police cars left real quick right down the Harris Mill road to the quarry, but you can't walk that way cuz ol' man Harris is mean and he don't like folks crossin over on his fields.

Deputy Jim, he's real nice to me and looks at my knee. Even buys me a soda pop—*man* are those sweet! Ed's wife comes down from the house and asks me what happened, but Jim tells her she can't ask me stuff. Then she tells him she wants to clean me up some and he says okay, and all three of us go into the fillin station washroom. Maggie, that's Ed's wife's name, she washes my knee real careful and she don't even put the stingee stuff on me like my poor mama used to. She gets a big band-aid and puts it over my scrape, and it pulls on my skin when I walk now.

It weren't too much longer before the amb'lance shows up with his siren goin, too. It don't even stop at Ed's, and I was glad cuz I don't like hospitals, anyway it's just a skinned-up knee. The amb'lance scared up a big flock of crows when it turned on the mill road, and I got to thinkin of how those boys was just layin there, that maybe if I hadn't come along those crows would be over there right now. Even though crows was just birds, I thought they could do some awful things to a boy when he can't move or stop em.

Maggie asks if I'm hungry, and all of a sudden I am. She brings some peanut butter and jelly sandwiches, and she even gives Jim one. They get their milk from right next door, and it sure is good. Jim's got a radio that's always makin noises, but pretty soon I get a little sleepy. The next thing I know, Sheriff Teeter is lookin right

David A. Kennedy

at me, and I give out a little yelp. He says *it's okay, ya don't have to be scared*, but when the law tells you that, you gotta be careful, and even an idiot knows that.

That's when he asked all those questions, and I said I would tell the truth. Another deputy was there, too, but she was a woman. After Sheriff Teeter was through askin me bout the dead boys, he says Deputy Sherry would take me home. I say all right, and we go to her police car. She had a big gun on her hip, and she was real pretty. And I honestly don't know why, but when we started drivin I got this feelin bout her. Like she was thinkin bad thoughts or somethin.

I was sittin in the back seat, and I heard Deputy Sherry talkin to someone, cept it weren't me. I moved over just a little, and I saw she had one of those cell phones. Teeny little thing, and she held it tight to her face. I heard her say some bad words, and I looked out the window instead. All of a sudden, I had to pee real bad, so I just had to ask her can she please stop cuz I have to pee?

I thought she would be mad and prob'ly yell at me, but she looks in her little mirror where I can see her face, and she's smilin. Sure, she says, and right away she pulls over at the spider orchard. That's what everyone calls the old Wickman place. Those trees ain't bore fruit in nigh on a century, my poor mama used to always say, and those words stuck to me.

There was a ditch runnin along the highway, and I went down there to pee. But there was some water in there, and I membered that you wasn't supposed to pee in the water. Folks get sick that way, my mama told me. I could see the deputy talkin on her phone, so I crossed over and went into the old orchard, not far, cuz I had to go real bad. I was facin the moon when I unzipped my pants, and it sure was bright.

I wasn't finished when I heard the first noise, and I thought that sound came straight from the moon. The hair on my neck prickled up, and I tried to hurry but I couldn't. It was almost like thunder, cept there weren't no clouds. It was close and it scared me bad. Then I heard the car door open and the deputy callin out to me. And I was gonna answer, I swear it, but instead I just stood there. Cuz I just knew another noise was comin, and it came right away. This was more like a long, low rumble, but I thought it was closer too. Deputy Sherry says some swear words, and from behind a dead tree, I watched her get back in her police car.

I looked back at the moon, but the moon was gone. That's when I turned and ran. I heard a terrible hard sound, and I heard screamin. I knew it was Deputy Sherry, but I also knew I couldn't help her. There was a God-awful crunchin like her car bein torn apart, and may the dear Lord forgive me, but when her screamin ended I was grateful.

I was all cried out when I got to Camilla's porch, and I layed down on the glider-swing and slept hard. Sirens woke me up, and I was hopin it was all a dream, but my heart wouldn't let me. It was before sunup, but Camilla was in the kitchen makin tea. She came out and saw me, and she got a sour look on her as she pulled me inside the house.

Sheriff Teeter was mad, but I thought he also looked a little scared. *What the heck happened*, he keeps askin me, but he don't say *heck*, and when I tell him *I don't know* he gets red as the inside of a watermelon. I say *it's the truth, I had to pee, I can show ya where I did it. I didn't pee in the crik, that's a bad thing*. Told him *I was peein, and there was a*

Cyloptorus

loud noise. That's when I got scared, I tell him. *Deputy Sherry got out of her police car*, I say, *but then another scary sound comes, and she went back inside. When I saw that the moon was gone the screamin started, and I ran away.*

For some reason, Camilla was mad at Sheriff Teeter and they went outside, but I could hear the swear words plain as day. My ears hurt when I hear too much cussin, so I went into the kitchen. The oatmeal was fixin to boil over, and I turned off the burner quick. I sat at the table and waited for Camilla, and when she came back in, the door slammed and I jumped.

She's mad as a mongoose, that's what my mama would say. A mongoose is an animal that eats cobra snakes, and you gotta be mad to do that, I guess. When my mama passed, Camilla took me up, and she taught me a lot. Not just bout dough, but other stuff too. Like how to use my magination, cuz everyone has one of those, and if you knew how, you could do some pretty swell things with it. But if you got carried away, you could get into bad trouble.

Camilla asks how come I did it and I say *I didn't do nothin*, and I start to cry again. I thought all my tears was run out of me, but I guess I made more. She says *stop cryin like a baby, you's no baby no more.* I say *I can't help it, and I'm terrible sorry those folks got killed.* She says *ya should be*, and I start bawlin for real, and *how come it be my fault*, I ask, *when I'm just a boy and those folks was killed hard?*

Camilla is old, but she got clear eyes, black as night. She looks at me real close, and the only thing in this world I can't take is when she's mad at me. She says *go down to the cellar, and tell me what it is.* I say *I don't wanna do that*, and she asks *how come.*

Cuz they's scary, I say real loud. Camilla, she just crosses her arms and frowns down at me. And she says *if it's scary down there, well, mister ya made it that way.* And she asks *did ya see the moon last night?* I say *I don't wanna see the moon*, and she asks *don't ya member what I told ya?*

I look down and don't say nothin. Camilla gets her tea and goes in her sittin room. I was real hungry, so I put some oatmeal in a bowl. There's a little bear on the counter filled with honey. I love to squeeze a little honey from that bear, not too much mama said, or I might get sick. Camilla don't like cow's milk, maybe that's why it tasted so good over at Ed's last night.

After my oatmeal, I was sleepy again, so I ask Camilla real quiet *can I please go to bed for a spell?* She looks up from her tea. *All right*, she finally says, *but ya heard what I said, and don't ya wait till dark.* I say *okay, but I don't wanna think bout that right now.* I turned and ran up the stairs to my bed, and when I got under the covers, I closed my eyes extra hard.

I heard Camilla in the kitchen, bein loud to wake me up. She's always been real nice to me, even though sometimes I'm a snot. One time, I asked her how come she took me up, and how come she was nice to me, cuz we wasn't even kin. She said that everyone needs a little help when they's young. And when she was teener someone helped her, and you never forget when someone does that. Besides, she said, I had talents that no one else had, so she thought it was a fair exchange, but when I asked what that was, she just laughed.

It smelled real good downstairs, and I was handsome-hungry. That's what Uncle Bobby always said at Christmas, but he was dead now. I slipped into the kitchen and sat at the table, and Camilla says nothin. I love to watch her cook, and man you can bet it's always good. She had got a chicken stewin, and the counter was heaped up with greens. Greens is what makes boys strong, so I always eat mine. I start to get a little antsy-pantsy, but I don't say nothin. Then Camilla asks do I want a sandwich, and I tell her *yes'm I would.* She says *fine, soon as you're done.*

My mouth went upside down, and my eyes peeked over to the far door. I wanna say, *can I please eat my sandwich first? I'm hungry,* but I know the answer. And she says *ya better hurry up, mister, it's gettin late.* I could see the sun outside, but it was fallin low, I guess. I went to the door and opened it. It was dark in the cellar, but that's what cellars are for, Camilla once said to me. To keep things that must be kept in the dark, things that sometimes only magination can make.

The old stairs squeaked a lot when you used em. A string was hangin right inside the door, and I tugged on it. A little light came on below, and it weren't hardly enough to see yourself spit. I walked down those stairs to the cellar, which is filled with boxes. Some of em are paperboard, and others I think are made of steel. But the ones I like the most are those little cages people carry their dogs and cats around in. Cuz inside those ones, I keep some of my toys.

My toys are special, and Camilla helped me to learn how they was made. You see, for a boy like me, sometimes it's hard to find friends. Camilla taught me how to *make* friends, and I made a bunch of em. Cept they're not really friends, like you would have a friend be, anyway. See, these are monsters, cuz that's what I like to play with.

Maybe I am a little bit old to play with toys, but if ya had the swell ones I got, you would too. There's all kinds, cuz Camilla says I got a special-good magination, and some of em could scare you good. Cept they're all so small, smaller than Petey even, so's you could grab em up and put em away most anytime you wanted.

But it was Uncle Bobby who said there was somethin wrong with that'un, and by God with the moon too. Mama said to him to hush, when she was alive, and he was always mean to my mama. And Camilla, she didn't like him no how, and they used to say swear words to one and the other, but not after Uncle Bobby got himself killed at the slaughterhouse. Chester Langway thought that was just the funniest thing, didn't he? Gettin killed in a slaughterhouse. Then his daddy shot his mama, and after that, Chester didn't laugh no more bout nothin.

It was always spooky down there. My friends got woke up by the light, and inside them cages, things was movin. I tell em all to hush, I can't take em out tonight, don't they know the moon is full? Camilla says ya can't play with monsters when the moon is full. When I ask her how come that is, she says she don't know, that some things in this world just be. And I really don't mean to, but sometimes I forget stuff.

I looked into the big cage on the old desk, and inside is a Choolio. I made it, and I made up its name. Camilla says everything needs a name. This Choolio, he's bout one foot tall, and he got three legs. When I made him, I asked *can he have snake-scales, but fur too?* Camilla laughed and said sure, and she showed me how. It's really pretty easy if you know how, and I can't say what cuz it's a secret, but it's really just words. Words is pow'ful things. But if ya think maybe any ol' words might work, go on and try.

Cyloptorus

He don't say much on account a him gettin throttled one time when I wasn't watchin close. Sometimes, I take too many out, and monsters, well they like to cause trouble. This one I got is a real troublemaker, and I just call him the Hacker. He had aholt of that Choolio good, and he woulda choked him dead if I didn't hear the ruckus.

The Trisaurus was in his cage, and I was glad. I never told Camilla when he bit me. He don't mean it I know, cuz when you got three mouths and you are a baby dinosaur, stuff can happen by accident. Then I see the open door, and I got scared bad. Cuz I didn't member, that's what scared me. But I musta, cuz these cages, see, they got magic locks, and monsters can't open em.

I start lookin round, but I don't see it nowhere. The cellar ain't got no windows, and there's only one door. And I try not to cry, but how would ya feel if *your* Cyloptorus went missin?

I don't wanna tell Camilla, but them cages was really rattlin now, cuz monsters don't like to be teased. I go up to the kitchen and tell her what it was, and she ain't none too happy bout it. There's a sandwich on the table where I always sit, and I eat it up fast. Then I see a police car comin up the driveway, and another car behind it, but it don't look like no police car.

Sheriff Teeter says this here man is a tective, and he got some more questions for me. He's even taller than Deputy Jim, and his name is Mark. And Mark says *don't worry, son, we know ya ain't the one what hurt those folks. But you was there, and ya musta seen somethin.* I say *no sir, I didn't see nothin but the moon, and then it was gone too.*

Camilla, she don't like the law too much, but she don't take no lyin either. But when she says to me tell em what it was, I don't say nothin for a bit, cuz I thought we was secret bout it. Sheriff Teeter, he gets mad again, and asks *what does she mean*, and his voice is gettin loud. Mark says to him to calm down, and I didn't think anyone could tell that to a sheriff. Sheriff Teeter, he's mad as can be, but he closes his mouth for a while.

Real quiet, I tell em I don't know nothin but that I got a missin Cyloptorus. And Mark asks what is that? I look over to Camilla, and she just nods. I say *it's a monster, and I made it, but it ain't no more'n two foot tall, and it never hurt no one. The moon was full*, I tell em, *but I don't member lettin it out.*

They looked at Camilla, but she was starin out the front window. The sun was almost set, but it's still real hot. Then Camilla says to those men that when the moon is full, the wild things in this world are extra pow'ful. And if you conjured up one, you had to let it be when that moon was big, cuz you can control little monsters, but not big ones. And iffen a little monster got out under a full moon, then death is soon to follow. Cuz they can get big, too.

Well, that didn't sit too well with those laws, and they set to squawkin at Camilla somethin fierce. But she just stood there, and when they was done she says *ya best tell folks to stay inside tonight, else they might get killed.* After that, the moon ain't full no more, and we could catch the Cyloptorus. I thought Sheriff Teeter would get awful mad, but he just looks at the tective, and they both got these frowns on, makes em look like sad clowns they's so big. Like big kids what can't get their candy.

The sheriff asks if Camilla is tryin to be funny, and he don't preciate it one bit. She says *how dare you Stuart*, and it weren't even till later I thought that might be Sheriff Teeter's first name. She says *ya know goldurn well that was Peggy's boy got killed and we was close*. She don't say goldurn, but a cuss word I don't like to say. My poor ol' mama always said don't take the Lord's name in vain. Camilla don't believe in the Jesus-God, although she reckons he was an alright fella.

It was already dark when the laws finally went away. Camilla says, *well I warned em*, but she looked worry worn. I tell her I'm sorry, and I won't do it again, but I swear I didn't take him out. She says she don't believe me, and I start to cry again. She don't care, and goes to her sittin room. I ask *what are we gonna do tonight*, and she says *don't worry bout her, but you mister are goin to bed with no supper. And don't ya leave your room tonight*. I tell her how sorry I am those folks got killed, but can I please have a little supper cuz I'm so hungry? She don't even look at me, so I run upstairs and slam my door shut.

The moonlight didn't let me sleep, and my poor tummy wanted food. Over to the window I could see all the way to McHenry's, and I never seen a bigger moon. So bright you could see the highway, and that's when I knew I had to go.

The chimney goes all the way up from the livin room, made of rocks. When I was little, I learned how to get outside my window, so I could climb down that old chimney to hunt frogs at night. Then Camilla showed me how to make my toys, and I quit doin that. Now I got onto the roof, and I was real quiet. I shimmied down, and man I almost fell.

I had to go to the quarry, but I ain't for sure why. I never like to go there at night, and I needed some company. Ed used to let me take Petey for a walk. Yeah, I know I prob'ly shouldn't, but I was scared to go by myself.

Somehow, I was almost at Ed's, so I musta crossed the spider orchard but I swear I don't even member. Thinkin too hard makes my poor head hurt. But I could hear noises over at Ed's, so I stayed in the south pasture till I could see what it was.

Sheriff Teeter was there, and that tective, and a mess a other police, too. Everyone jumped when the boom came, specially me cuz I know that sound. They started scramblin around Ed's like they was ants that got themselves all riled up. And *whoosh* off they goes down the mill road in two, three, no *four* police cars, all of em with their sirens wailin. It hurts my ears bad, so I cover em up, but it don't help much. In a flash they was gone.

Now there's no one over at Ed's that I can see, so I go over for a look. Petey is layin right there like a good dog, and he's waggin his tail hard now that he sees me. He don't bark, that's what makes him so good. Ones that knows when to bark, that's what makes a good dog my mama said. So I say *hey Petey, do ya wanna go for a walk?* He don't answer, cuz he's just a dog, but I think he wants to go. I sure hope Ed won't mind, but it's awful scary outside when you got a big moon like this and a Cyloptorus, too.

Petey and me went down the mill road, since I wasn't worried bout ol' man Harris tonight. Weren't much after that when I heard the hollerin start. Petey got what are called hackles, and I got em too. I say *it's okay, Petey*, and he believes me. We come to the second field where there's a coyote trail. We turned onto that path, and that's when I heard shootin. Petey's cryin a little, so I hush him. I decide to run, and

Cyloptorus

I wanna run the other way, but I can't. The noise is wicked loud, like thunder comin out of the old quarry, and gosh those policemen can sure scream like little girls when they wanna.

A whole bunch of scraggly willows is what's around the quarry, and you don't see nothin till you's right there. But the road stops on top of the north rim where folks park their cars, and that's where the Cyloptorus was. Petey's barkin now, but no one hears him cuz it's a war zone right in front of my face. My mouth is wide open but ain't nothin comin out, cuz the monster is the biggest thing I ever seen. It was taller than the county building in Westfield, and that's five stories high.

The Cyloptorus got two big arms, and two littler ones. The big hands got a police car in em, with a policeman inside. He's gettin shook somethin terrible, and how I wished he could please stop screamin. Sheriff Teeter is hollerin as loud as them bullets those men is shootin, and when he sees me he yells *what the f-word are ya doin here?* I say *I'm sorry, and I never knew no Cyloptorus could grow this big, but I swear I didn't let it out.* He's so mad and red I think he might just have a stroke and die on his own, like my Aunt Martha.

The moon was up high over the quarry, and the ground shook cuz the monster slammed the police car down. Mark comes over, so I start to say *I'm sorry tective Mark,* but he's yellin at me too, and I thought he was nice. He got blood on him and he looks awful scared and he hollers *how can we kill it?*

I tell him *ya can't, not lessin ya got magic bullets.* I say *I had to make him strong, so as to last.* And that *Camilla told me if somethin gets made by magic, then only magic can kill it. I got this one monster. I call him the Hacker; he could do it, I bet, cept he's only yay high,* then I put my hand just over Petey's head. I tell him Camilla wouldn't let me take him out tonight anyway, cuz don't I know the moon is full. Tective Mark was gonna say somethin real hard to me, I think, but that Cyloptorus reached down and grabbed him up, and the look on his face gave me the willies for a long spell after.

It pulled him way up high, and on the top of its body there's a kind of stalk. It moves around like an elephant's trunk, but that's where the eye is at. That tective was wrigglin real hard, but he weren't goin nowhere. My growed-up toy roared as it brought him up to look real close. I never even heard a bed-sick baby squeal like him. Sheriff Teeter got a shotgun, but that don't work on a Cyloptorus, I just told em that.

I didn't give him but small teeth, but he got two mouths, and he put the tective inside one. It don't chew, so we had to listen to him screamin in there until he were swallowed.

Some more police cars come haulin tail into the quarry lot, and just in time, cuz these here was all tore up. One policeman tries to get behind the Cyloptorus, but it plucked him off the tar-sand and threw him real high in the sky, and oh my when he come down it made a horrible sound.

The new policemen got bigger guns, and they start blazin away. Cyloptorus don't care, and he ain't budgin. A roar comes out from down in the quarry. I think I peed a little in my pants. My poor mama always said I was a good boy and I believed her. And I don't know if a boy can be bad just cuz he don't member stuff too well. I only know I got a real bad feelin cuz I membered somethin I did, and it were a bad thing.

David A. Kennedy

See, this Cyloptorus, he don't get along with the other monsters. He got feelins, ya see, he ain't mean like the Hacker. Sure, he looks scary, he be a monster, ya know. Anyway, I got thinkin, he's just lonely. I used to get lonely somethin fierce, specially after my mama passed, but now I got my toys. Camilla always helps me, but I wanted to surprise her that I can do it all by myself this time.

Everyone knows ya can't keep two monsters in the same cage, even if they's nice ones. When you is ready to make a new monster, what you do is say your special words, but you gotta say em into the cage, cuz this magic takes a while to work. I was real careful to say the words right, but now I member that I did not set the lock, and I was late for work. I forgot, and I knew the moon was comin full so I let it be. And dear mama please forgive me, but I'm fearin my new Cyloptorus came alive, and got out cuz the cage weren't locked. And that durn one got the other one out, too.

Sheriff Teeter got hurt when a willow stump came flyin through the air, and when three other policemen rushed up, somethin comes up out of the old quarry. First, there was the eye, and ya never seen a bigger one. The stalk it's on kept comin up like a giant snake, then a huge dome and could that really be the body?

A second Cyloptorus rises up, and all of us just cower like puppies. This one's twice as big, and when it finally stood up on its fat feet and reached the parkin lot, even the moon disappeared. A horrible stench hung in the air, and some policemen was throwin up. Second Cyloptorus got an enormous boulder in each upper hand, and lets one fly. It whooshes ten feet over my head, and the wind like to knock me down. It hits two police cars, and they crumple up like soda cans, and there's screamin behind me, too. That giant monster took his other boulder and brought it straight down to the ground below it, where Sheriff Teeter and some others was. It was like a house fell on em, and the parkin lot jumped and pushed me five feet into the air.

Petey came loose, and *please no Petey, don't go over there*. Someone was yellin my name but it weren't no policeman. Petey's barkin hard as he can, but he's so tiny the monsters don't even notice him. I turn around, and it's Camilla, and was she mad as a mongoose! Then she looks up and sees the two beasts I made, and I never saw the fear fall on someone like that. I say *poor Petey is gonna get hurt*, but she just stares at me, and her eyes is blazin like the guns there ain't no more of. *What did ya do?* Camilla keeps askin me, *dear God in heaven, boy, what did ya do?* I wanna say to her, *ya don't believe in no God in heaven*, but I don't.

I was cryin hard, and so was Camilla. But I hear Petey yappin further away, and I look back for him. He's dashin off to the side, where folks can walk down to the quarry. I yell *stop Petey* but he don't, then he's around the corner below us all, still barkin, and I think it's okay, so long as Petey keeps barkin it's okay.

The policemen was all down. Some of em was still moanin, but I ain't no doctor, and I know it's awful selfish but we was still alive and those policemen wasn't gonna be much longer. Camilla got the shock on her real bad, so I took her arm, and we kinda scooted back around some willows near the quarry edge. Cuz there was somethin not right down there, and that really confused me, since we got two Cyloptorus up here, and I never made no more than that.

They got a little bench over there, where folks can look down. The smell was right gaggy, but it gets worse when we get to the cliff top. I looked back, but those monsters was just standin there, wasn't doin no more mischief. I still heard Petey, and could even see him, and my heart got better. He was barkin up a storm, and runnin back and forth, but there was somethin down there that made my eyes get wide as saucers.

Camilla lets out a little shriek, and I wanna say *don't holler Camilla, them Cyloptorus are way over there.* She acts like she don't care bout that now. She gets down on her knees, and starts prayin to herself, or to someone she didn't let folks in on. Then I ask *what is that?*

She whispers *it's* eggs*, boy, it's an egg sac and why, dear God, did ya do it?* And I say *he was lonely, he ain't got no friends, and I knows what that's like. I just wanted him to have a friend, that's all. And then I forgot I made it, and the lock weren't set, and I'm awful sorry, Camilla.*

She says she's sorry, too, but she ain't yellin now. She ain't even cryin, but the fear on her made my skin hop around like they's crickets all over it. I look down, and sure enough it do seem like eggs, kinda like the mounds of em that bullfrogs would make in the north pond. These is a lot bigger, and there's a whole mess of em. And if I looked real hard, I could see black things wigglin around inside em.

I'm so heavy tired now, and I see the moon is tired too. Pretty soon it be comin down, and I told that to Camilla. And won't things be just fine tomorrow? Cuz the moon would be wanin, that's what my mama called it when the moon gets smaller. And won't them Cyloptorus get small again, so's we can catch em, like ya said?

Camilla looked at me, and her eyes was empty. And my heart, well, it got empty too. She says, *no, son, things won't be fine. Never no more.* I'm cryin, *why, Camilla, why?* She says *these ones here, yeah they be gettin small come sunrise. But before dawn, yonder hatchlings be comin out,* and the chills got me good. Camilla tells me, *what gets made under a full moon, got the power of the moon inside it. For all time, not just when the moon is full. And there's thousands of em boy, do ya understand? Tens of thousands, even.*

Down below us, Petey was still barkin. I seen a dark shape pop out of the egg mass. Looked sorta like a pollywog, but it was already as big as a man. I turned and pulled Camilla up from her knees, but she's so frail I just picked her on up and started to carry her out of there. And even though I'm so awful tired and hungry, we gotta keep movin. We gotta find us someplace to go, and I don't like to tell folks what to do, and I'm terrible sorry, but ya might wanna stay inside tonight, or maybe start runnin like us . . .

When he's not tending to his rare plant collection, rock climbing, or spoiling his wife Debbie and cat L (probably not in that order), **David A. Kennedy** writes in a variety of genres but has always been drawn to the darker side of fiction. His thriller novel *Ricochet* (Acorn Publishing) was published in 2016.

Brandy

Alec Lownes

The bar stinks of spilled beer and old cooking oil. The voices inside are not loud enough to drown out the rain pounding on the shutters. Brandy polishes a glass after its fifth turn through the bar, the vessels used so many times that they resemble sea glass. None of the sailors seem to mind.

A raucous shout comes from a table at the far end of the bar. A thick-armed man motions Brandy over, and she puts the glass down. The men are drunk; this batch came in on the last trawler after a week out, and she can barely understand them shouting over each other for more whiskey. She returns to the bar to pour a shot for each of the laughing men.

"'Tis the big one, it is," an old sailor says, seated at a small table near the door, raising his voice over the downpour.

"You always say that, Marv." The middle-aged sailor wears a black slicker.

"I can feel it this time. Feel it in my bones."

"As far as I count, you've said it's the *big one* every year for the last twenty, and the sea hasn't swallowed us yet."

"My knees've never ached like this yet," Marv growls back and sips wine from his clay tankard.

"Damned be the day that I end up like you, Marv, stuck land-bound and complaining about my knees, prophesying doom every year on the dot," says the youngest of the three, leaning back in his chair against the kind of fluorescent-orange slicker only worn on the trawlers themselves.

"Ye don't know yer asshole from yer mouth, young scab," Marv shoots back.

"What'd you call me?"

"Settle down, Benny, he don't mean anything by it. Marv's as crusty as the rest of us, maybe even more so. Ain't none of us been on the sea as long as he."

"Aye, and ye've never felt her heart, never seen her depths."

"I've seen plenty of depths." Benny spits, stares at his empty shot glass and raises his hand.

93

Brandy

Brandy puts her glass down for the third time and crosses the bar to take his order.

When she's left, Benny says to the man in the black slicker, "D'ya see the tits on her? You know if she's taken?"

"That's Brandy, and she's taken."

"By who?" The young sailor shifts and glances around the bar for a target.

"Aye, she's taken all right," Marv nods. "By a man twice, no, three times the man you'll ever be."

"What'd you say—"

Brandy returns with a double-barrel and lays both shots before Benny. He doesn't waste the opportunity to look down her blouse.

"There's never been another," says the man in the black slicker.

"Not before, not after," Marv agrees. "Only the one for Brandy."

"Who was he?" Benny asks.

The man in the slicker sits back and strokes the long stubble on his chin. He raises his voice. "Brandy, what's yer feller's name?"

She calls a name out to the table, and the man nods at the rest of them, as if the sound they couldn't comprehend was an answer. Brandy smiles.

"Now that was a sailor," he says.

"What makes one man the better of another?" Benny whines. "We're all out on that sea, getting tossed and thrown and flung around."

"Something about him, young'un. There's just something about him. He came in one day, don't rightly recall what outfit he's on, but he told the strangest yarns," says Marv.

"Stories," Benny scoffs. "Tall tales."

"Nah, not stories. I couldn't say why, but I knew when he was saying 'em they was true as you and me sitting here."

"Then what made them so strange?"

"He talked of rogue waves," the man in the black slicker says. "Fifty, a hundred feet tall. Said the deck fell from under him and he chased it all the way down the well. Said the water closed up overhead like he'd been sunk deep, then the boat rose so fast and so quick, it slammed him to the planks. So fast the hull left the water at the peak, if you can believe it."

"That's a tale." Benny doesn't sound convinced.

"I don't think so."

"Something in that man," Marv says. "Something wild and salty. He was born on the sea as far as I'd bet."

"Born on the sea," Benny repeats, and laughs.

"With a cowl, more like. He said they hauled up a kraken."

"A kraken! Now that's a tale for sure!"

Marv shakes his head. "Not a tale. I seen one just once, and we were in deep, deep water. Night was dark, and the running lights were out. Everything's dark as an oil slick, when I hear someone scream down stern and *splash*. Sure, I called 'man overboard,' but afore the words left my mouth, I saw it. One thick, scabby tentacle wrapped around the poor feller's arm as he were dragged beneath the surface. We didn't find him."

"Your eyes were playing tricks on you, old man," Benny says, but when he glances at the younger sailor for agreement, he's met with a pale, drawn face.

"I saw one too," the sailor in black says. "Off the Maine coast. It skimmed the top of the water. No one else saw it, and I didn't tell anyone, but I saw those . . . things it has. The tentacles, as long as the boat. It was up on the surface, and I only saw it because of the twilight flare against the slick, but it rolled over and fixed me with one of its eyes. I thought I was a dead man, that we all were. But it just slipped down under the waves." He gulps beer. "None of the others knew how close we came."

"That's a load. You're talking about the giant squid? They've found dead ones, washed up. Squid can't capsize a boat. Hell, it can't even live on top of the water. Once it's up that far, it's dead."

"You young fellers with all your science and radar and satellites," Marv gesticulates toward the ceiling. "You think you know everything. Just 'cause you get it on a slide and cut it open, you think you can see its secrets. Nay, we ain't talking about the giant squid. Didn't you hear? We said *kraken*."

"It isn't a giant squid," the younger sailor backs Marv up. "It's . . . bigger than that. With fishhooks on its arms to snag you and pull you overboard."

"Then it's just some other kind of squid. Or there's no such thing."

"Bad luck to throw dirt," Marv says. "Not unless ye've got a story of yer own."

"I've never seen anything I can't explain."

Marv grunts like he's proven a point, and the younger sailor looks away. Benny aims a glance at Brandy, who's double-fisting six mugs as she crosses to another raucous table. A locket hangs around her neck, above those perfect, plump breasts. It's an oval, taller than it is wide, and looks like it's made of pure silver.

He'd like to see what she looks like wearing nothing else.

⟨ ♥ ⟩⟨ ♥ ⟩⟨ ♥ ⟩

An hour past closing time, Brandy has just finished cleaning the spilled beer from the last table. The floor can wait until tomorrow when the tackiness of being left overnight will help the sawdust stick. Sleep threatens to close her eyes, and she yawns against the back of her hand.

She's alone. Brandy is always alone at the end of the night in the empty bar, and she unclasps the braided chain from her neck. The smooth oval sits in her palm, surrounded by the coil of silver like so much fallen rope, and she digs her fingernail into the side seam to pop the locket.

The breath catches in Brandy's chest at the vermilion light that spills from the locket, and she snaps it shut before anyone can catch a glimmer through the closed shutters. She hadn't expected the light tonight, but she knows what it means. She realizes she hadn't prepared herself and she tries to think of what else needs doing before she leaves—is there anyone she should tell, is there anything she needs to retrieve—then decides that nothing really needs doing at all. Rain pounds at the windows from the storm outside like a rowdy customer trying to get in for a nightcap, but she leaves her coat behind.

She won't need it.

Brandy

Brandy exits through the front door and doesn't bother to lock it. She isn't alone anymore. A young sailor—one of the three sitting at the table closest to the door—waits for her in an orange slicker. He's taken shelter under the awning and looks half asleep. When she appears, he shakes himself awake and takes a step forward.

She doesn't step back.

"Hey," the sailor says, voice barely audible over the pounding rain, and she feels his eyes rake over her body even in the darkness. The drenching rain plasters Brandy's hair to her head and sticks her clothes to her skin, but she doesn't care.

"I thought you might like a chaperone."

Lightning flashes, illuminating the hungry look in his eyes. Normally she'd push him away, make some comment about the size of his manhood or the size of his catch, but she doesn't. The rain chills her and raises goosebumps on her arms, but she's filled with mixed excitement, elation, and terror.

"Sure." Brandy doesn't want to brave the walk alone, even if he isn't the company she would've picked. Brandy turns and the man catches up, giving her a sidelong glance that she knows psyches him up for the adventure he thinks is about to come.

It doesn't matter what he thinks.

They reach the end of the street before he speaks. "You've been here a long time," he nearly shouts over the driving rain.

"All my life." Brandy can't keep her gaze from darting into the night toward the town that should be there; the driving rain so thick it blots out even the streetlights. So many years, and she wonders if she should feel worse about what's to come.

"Seems like a small place to grow up in."

"It's big enough in the ways that count."

"The port, you mean?"

"Sure."

They walk with only the sound of the rain lashing the rooftops for a little while more.

"I heard you've got a man. Is he out at sea?"

"He is."

"Must be one hell of a man to keep a woman like you waiting."

"He is."

"You know, there are other men here, closer to home."

She almost laughs in his face at the thought that he thinks he's anything like her man. "When he came, I knew he was different, just from the first time I saw him." She feels the sailor's mood sour beside her. She'd be afraid of the coiled violence in his body, of the kinds of thoughts being alone and womanless for a month or longer can put in a younger man's head, if they weren't walking through air as thick as water.

"What was so special about him?"

"It was the way he talked. When he talked, your whole world was his words. He could sweep everything else away until you were there with him, and he'd show you the most amazing things."

"What kinds of things would an old sailor have to show a young woman like yourself?"

Alec Lownes

She laughs, but there are no echoes in the downpour. "What if I showed you a shark swimming down this street? What if octopuses sat at your dining table, and your hair waved like seaweed as eels feasted on your brains?"

He recoils. "Is that what he told you?"

"That, and so much more."

"Those don't seem like the kinds of things to tell a lady."

The street's been sloping down steadily the whole way, and the black ocean tosses past the edge of the dock.

"You wouldn't know what to tell a lady. Not like me."

"I could tell you some pretty sweet things." He grabs her arm but seems surprised at the sounds of waves crashing against the pilings.

"Do you live near the docks? Is your place close?"

"It's close enough." Brandy reaches up to her locket. "Do you even remember his name?"

The young man screws up his face and tries to recall, but can't.

Brandy knows he can't; she's teasing him. She barely feels the pressure from his grip against the pelting rain. "You can't even fathom his name. Here, let me show you."

She slides her fingernail along the seam in the locket, and it pops. Crimson light spills across her throat.

He sees alien glyphs the color of blood against the shining silver.

Reflected in his eyes, she remembers the first time her lover revealed his name. The understanding of what he is, of his long past and his terrible future. His name is his essence, and to know it is to know him completely.

The young man in orange drops to the slick cobblestones in terror. In the pummeling rain, she hears something slide out of the water at the piling. The man scrambles backward, then flees. Brandy turns to see who she's been waiting for all these years.

He hasn't changed. The same stubbled jaw and wrinkled brow, but that face is a disguise. She knows him, knows his name, and she can see through that to his true form. He reaches out, and she folds against his wet body.

"It's time." He's looking toward the town. Toward the land that rises so proud over its mother sea. The sharks will swim in the streets, and the eels will feast on her customers.

"I know." She breathes in his deep, briny musk.

He steps back, and she falls with him into the sea.

The ground shakes. The young sailor stumbles as he runs back into town.

←♥→←♥→←♥→

Alec Lownes is a former software engineer turned writer who lives with his wife, son, cat, and fish in Western Pennsylvania. He has work published in *The Colored Lens Speculative Fiction Magazine* and *After the Storm*. He can be found online at aleclownes.com.

I Lost You to the Summer Wind

John Opalenik

Everybody's got that one special someone. And I don't mean the person you spend the rest of your life with. Not everybody gets a happily ever after. Hell, not everybody gets a "rest of their life." Anybody who watched even the news that summer knows that lots of people on the Cape didn't. I mean that special someone that breaks in your heart, teaches it what it can take, and teaches you to be more careful. I met that special someone three summers ago when I was spending the summer working at my uncle's bookshop.

Harbor Books was nestled in Mattapoisett, Massachusetts, a small town people drive through on their way up Cape Cod. Uncle Everett opened the shop hoping that it would become a cultural centerpiece of the area, with poetry readings, open mic nights, and author signings. Instead, it was mostly a place where people on their way to Cape Cod grab a book to read on the beach, and sometimes sell it back to the used section for a couple of dollars on their way home.

I needed a change of scenery that summer. When I went home for winter break between college semesters, I realized that my old hometown friends and I didn't have much in common anymore, now that we weren't stuck together in the same high school. When my uncle asked if I could take over the store for the summer between my freshman and sophomore years of college, it seemed like just what I needed.

Then she walked in.

Dark hair framed her olive-skin-toned face. She wore an old T-shirt that read, "Mermaids smoke seaweed" with a military-style green jacket over it. Her eyes were so dark they nearly looked black, and for the brief moment our eyes met, she looked through me as if she could see truths that I didn't even know about myself.

I stared at the young woman in the doorway, dumbfounded. I waited for her to speak first, and then I regained enough composure to remember the social script. "Welcome to Harbor Books. Is there anything special you are looking for?"

"Nothing just yet." She tilted her head as if studying me. "Are you new here? I thought someone older ran the shop."

"That's my uncle. He owns the shop, but I'm running it for the summer while he's away."

We kept up the small talk while she started browsing. Unlike a lot of the customers I'd seen those first few days, she steered clear of the popular beach reads and instead spent most of her time in science fiction and books on astrology and star charts. "Sci-fi and astrology. You must really like the stars."

"I guess you could say that." She glanced up as if a starry sky waited just above her. "I just think it's interesting to think about our place in the universe at special times in our lives and how it all syncs up. Like you and I meeting today. What are the odds that this is the summer that you are taking over your uncle's shop, and it's the summer that I'm spending in Mattapoisett?"

"When you look at it that way, you could even wonder what the odds are that my uncle would decide to open up the shop here instead of the many other little beach towns in Massachusetts."

Her eyes lit up as if the universe aligned right before her eyes. "Exactly! The more you zoom out, the tinier we feel in the grand scheme of things, but on the other hand, think about all the things that had to line up perfectly for us to be here, for books to exist, for life to have evolved on this planet. It's what I live for."

"What is?"

"Those moments when the stars are right, and something special happens." She blushed and looked down at the book cradled in her arms like something precious. "Sorry. I'm rambling. I don't even know you, and I'm standing here talking about . . . well, things like this."

"No. It's fine." I wanted to come out from behind the counter, but I didn't want to seem too eager. "Honestly, this is the most interesting conversation I've had all day." I had never told her my name, and the longer I waited, the more awkward it would be when it finally came up. "I'm Jonah. It's been really nice talking with you."

"Jade." She shifted the books to her left arm and shook my hand. "Thanks for putting up with my rambling, Jonah."

"My pleasure."

She went back to browsing, but when she saw the doorway leading to the back room, one of the books slipped, causing the rest to cascade to the floor. I rushed out from behind the counter to help her pick them up. We squatted down at the same time and bumped heads, her forehead into my lip, not hard enough to hurt, but just enough to make us both stop and acknowledge the awkwardness.

"I'm so sorry." She rubbed her forehead, more in embarrassment than in pain. "Are you okay?" When I assured her that I was fine, she continued. "I was just distracted by that dark room in the back. What's in there?"

I scooped up the rest of her books and handed them to her. "That's the used book section. The lights are off because they're on a motion sensor, and nobody's been there all day."

She hefted the books in her arms. "Is there anything interesting back there?"

"Most of it's just the same stuff as out here. Lots of people buy beach reads and then return them on their way home." I shrugged my shoulders. "Every once in a while we get a bunch of stuff from local estate sales if you're interested in old leather-bound books."

"That sounds cool, kind of like a treasure hunt." She bought her books and then asked. "Will you still be here if I come back tomorrow to look through the used stuff?"

"Yep. It's just me until August twenty-eighth."

"Cool. See you then."

"Looking forward to it."

It may make me sound like a dork with a crush, but if I'm being honest, I was . . . I spent the next morning at the shop glancing at the door every few moments between sips of coffee and ringing up customers. When I unwrapped the second half of the foot-long sub I started for lunch the day before, the little bell over the door rang, and there she stood. "I was hoping I'd catch you at lunchtime. Is there any chance you can hang up a *Be Back Soon* sign and let me buy you lunch as a thank-you for letting me talk your ear off yesterday, and as an apology for headbutting you?"

I pretended to consider my options and then replied. "It's been slow today. I guess it couldn't hurt."

Jade took me to an unassuming taco stand embedded in a strip mall between a liquor store and a local realtor's office. When I saw that the taco stand was BYOB, I joked that they must have some sort of deal worked out with the package store.

"What do you mean, package store? It's not like there's a UPS nearby."

"You know." I gestured. "A liquor store."

"Who calls it that?" she asked with a doubtful tilt of her head.

"Doesn't everyone?" I pulled out my phone, googled it, and quickly found out the truth. "Oh. I guess it's a pretty Connecticut-specific thing. That's strange."

"It sure is. Where in Connecticut are you from?"

"New Haven."

"You grew up right by Yale? They've got a beautiful library."

"Sort of." I didn't want to contradict her, but I couldn't lie to her either. "There's a lot more to New Haven than just Yale, and not all of it looks like Hogwarts. My mom used to take us for walks around there, and at first, it felt like I was a knight at a castle, but as I got older, it became obvious that we were the tourists, there more so than the families from around the world visiting before dropping their adult children off."

"Fair enough. For better or worse, lots of cities are like that."

We sat down with a platter of tacos and a tray of hot sauce samples arranged in order of spiciness ranging from playful to dangerous. We worked our way up the selection until we each found our limits. I settled on a poblano-based sauce with a hint of cherry, and she kept going until she hit a pineapple habanero sauce.

"So, are you from around here?" I asked, unable to notice any linguistic hint of her personal history.

"My family moved around a lot. We spent time on the shoreline in the Pacific Northwest, in New Orleans and Nova Scotia. But we're from the area around the Paphos Forest in Cypress."

"Your family seems to have a pattern of living in places where water meets forest."

John Opalenik

"I guess we inherit more than just possessions from our ancestors. Maybe places that feel like home, too." Jade glanced out the window and then down at her empty plate. "I'm stuffed! Do you want to go for a walk on the boardwalk?"

I planned to leave the shop unattended for an hour or two tops, but it turned into an entire afternoon. When we got back, Jade apologized for keeping me away so long and I told her there wasn't another way I'd have rather spent the day. Just the same, she offered to help me add new books to the used section to help me catch up on what I could have been doing during the day.

Jade opened a cardboard box full of books. "How is the used section organized?"

"Alphabetical by the author's last name," I hesitated. "Well . . . mostly. If it seems like popular stuff people will want for their vacation, it goes up here. If they're classics or old stuff from estate sales, it goes wherever it fits on the shelves in that little nook in the back."

She looked at the dimly lit cutaway in the room that someone might miss at first glance. "Looks creepy. Why do you keep it there?"

"The dim light keeps the old books in better condition," I replied. "And something to do with the level of humidity back there. I don't know. Uncle Everett explained it to me, but I don't remember the details."

Jade offered to go through the boxes and put away the older books in the back while I dealt with the popular paperbacks in the front, and we did it that way for a while until I realized it was getting late. "Jade. Technically the store closed an hour ago." I paused. I didn't want to sound like a creep and chase her off, but I figured she didn't mind being alone with me. "Do you want me to give you a ride back to your place?"

She turned around, almost surprised that I had gotten close to her. "No thanks. It's not far. I can walk."

I thought about what my mom taught me about making sure a girl gets home safe after a date, and while Mattapoisett isn't exactly downtown New Haven, it still felt wrong. "Are you sure? It's the middle of the night."

She gave a look as if she were searching for the right words, and then said, "It's not that I don't appreciate it. It's just . . . I'm here with my family. I know. I'm twenty-two. It's not like I'm a middle-aged woman still in my parents' basement, but it feels strange to bring a guy home. Besides, you'd probably think they're weird."

"I'm sure they're fine." I promised myself I wouldn't persist after one last counter. "Everybody thinks their parents are weird. I grew up with an overprotective single mom who was a germaphobe. If I brought you to her apartment, she'd make you wash your hands before you made it to the couch."

"They're . . . religious in a way that some people might find weird." She flinched, almost interrupting herself. "I don't mean 'religious' as a code word for racist or homophobic. They're just, spiritual, kind of New Age." Then a thought occurred to her she probably guessed would shut me up, and she guessed right. "Maybe I could just stay with you tonight."

101

I Lost You to the Summer Wind

When I woke up, Jade wasn't in bed, but the bathroom door was closed, so I guessed she was in there. I drove to a bagel shop nearby. I remembered her saying she liked smoked salmon, so I thought I would get a nice surprise in the form of bagels with lox. The strange thing was, when I pulled my car out of the parking lot, I noticed someone walking toward the state beach wearing jeans and the oversized, green military-style jacket that Jade always seemed to wear, either over her shoulders or tied around her waist, as if the nineties never ended.

I was more self-centered back then and immediately asked myself what I'd done wrong. Had I pressured her to spend the night? I hoped not. I wondered if maybe I should have offered to call her an Uber. Then my mind leaped to sex, and I thought about who initiated what the night before. She had taken the lead in every way. She'd told me what to do, and how she wanted me to do it. It wasn't until I thought about it at the stop sign I realized how much she'd taken charge. It was almost as if the idea of questioning it didn't even occur to me.

The car behind me honked, jolting me back to reality. I turned back toward town, realizing how creepy it would be to follow her. Sticking one bagel in the refrigerator in my uncle's apartment above the bookshop, I sadly gnawed at the other one as I minded the store. I thought about texting my mom but decided against it. She would ask how things were going and I wouldn't be able to avoid mentioning Jade, and then she'd have lots of questions that I couldn't answer.

"Jonah. Are you here?" Jade's unidentifiable accent issued from the doorway. She wore a cardigan the same shade of green as her jacket, but with a black tank top tucked into dark jeans leading down to even darker Doc Martens. She looked like a cross between Mr. Rogers and a soldier, in a way that really worked.

"Jade . . . when you weren't there when I got up in the morning, I thought that . . ." my voice trailed off.

"I know. I'm sorry." Her head dipped down to her shoulders. "I had to go to a thing with my family. They're pretty serious about that sort of stuff. I felt weird waking you up before dawn to tell you about it, so I just left. Sorry." She held up a bottle of golden liquid. "I was hoping I could make it up to you tonight. Dinner and drinks on me?"

"What's that?" I smiled and looked at the unlabeled bottle.

"It's my secret family recipe for mead, basically honey wine. If you want, I can come over, make dinner, and we can split the bottle."

I thought about what the little one-bedroom apartment looked like, and while it was good enough for an impromptu one-night stand, it seemed way too messy for the date night she was proposing. "Can we make it a very late dinner? I just need an hour or so after I close up shop to clean up and make sure all the pots and pans are clean."

"I can watch the store for a bit if you need to get things done," she offered.

I expected to be cleaning the apartment above the shop for at least an hour, but after five minutes, I realized I'd left my phone behind the counter. When I ran back down to get it, Jade was standing in the back room holding a book bound in worn, black leather with an image of a golden tree on the cover with roots stretching down in a deep shade of red. Gold lettering spelled out the title in a language I didn't understand. When Jade saw me, she looked at me as if I'd walked in on her doing something wrong. I waited, assuming she would explain herself.

"I was just sorting things out. This one's so pretty." She drew her fingertips across the cover the way one would something precious.

"Can you read it?" I stood closer. The cover image seemed to glisten despite the limited light. "You were looking at it like you understood. Is it in Greek?" I paused, recognizing my faux pas. "I'm sorry. You said your family was from Cyprus. I assumed."

She waved her hand as if my remark were smoke and she could fan it away. "It's not Greek." She hesitated, considering whether to tell me. I guess the only reason she told me was that she knew I'd eventually find a way to look it up. "It's written in Enochian." When she saw my blank stare, she explained. "According to legend, it's the language of angels. They taught it to John Dee, Queen Elizabeth's astrologer back in the 1500s."

"And you can read it? Is that part of your family's belief system?" I almost didn't ask since any mention of her family sent her running for the hills, but I had to know.

"Sort of. I don't know if they believe in angels, at least not the way other people do, but my mom knows a lot of languages. She's trying to teach me, but it's a lot."

"Can you read the title?" Again, she must have figured that I'd eventually be able to look it up, so she told me. "The Mother of a Thousand Young."

The title made me shudder, and not just because it gave me a flashback to Jade insisting she was on birth control and throwing away the condom the night before, but because it felt bloody and ancient as a stone dagger. "What is that supposed to mean?"

She shrugged. "I can barely read the title. I was just looking at it because the cover was pretty, and you don't see Enochian every day."

I let it go. Two families on their way to Provincetown came in looking for something to read on the back patio of their rental. Jade excused herself, saying she'd be back in time to make dinner. I was utterly charmed, by Jade in general, but also at the idea of a cozy night in. It felt so grown-up compared to either bringing a girl back to my mom's apartment or to my dorm room. I passed the afternoon imagining what it would be like if nights like the one I was waiting for became my new normal.

←♥→←♥→←♥→

My uncle hadn't used his wine glasses in ages, so I had to wash the dust out of them before Jade poured my first cup of mead. It tasted like the rich honey she'd promised, but with a bite that reminded me of whiskey. It had an earthy aftertaste that served as a constant reminder that Jade's family made this, not a factory.

"Do you smoke?" Jade held up a joint that looked out of place in the age of vape pens.

"I get sleepy, especially if I've had a drink or two." I held up the glass of mead. "I don't mind sitting on the back deck with you if you want to, though."

I Lost You to the Summer Wind

We sat out back while she smoked and looked out at the dying light turning the sky orange, and a peaceful quiet fell over Mattapoisett where the people visiting for day trips had gone home, and the people waiting for night to fall and the bars to open hadn't truly come alive yet. The only constant was the distant sound of waves crashing.

"What are we making?" I set down my glass and looked at the cast-iron frying pan.

"A bunch of veggies with garlic and olive oil. The purple you're seeing there is the stem of a beet." Jade explained. "It's all vegan. Actually, can you get some water boiling? I like to serve it over noodles."

We put on music, kept cooking, and drank our way through half the bottle. The intoxication came on quickly and felt more like a high than being drunk. I convinced myself that it was the combination of my infatuation and the contact high from when she smoked earlier. Eating would even me out a little, but after dinner, I asked her if we could sit on the couch, more because I felt lightheaded than for any other reason.

She seemed to have picked up a different signal because she started kissing me and unbuttoning my shirt. I thought about stopping her, saying that I wasn't feeling well, but it just felt so easy to melt into her arms and go wherever she led me. I'm surprised I noticed, but I heard a sound downstairs in the shop, as if some books had fallen from a shelf.

"What was that?" I picked my head up, suddenly more alert.

"I didn't hear anything." She let the cardigan that hung loosely from her shoulders drop. "Come on, Jonah. Forget it. Let's go to bed."

Floorboards creaked.

"Hold on. I should really check." I pulled my unbuttoned shirt over my shoulders before approaching the stairs. "Wait here. If it looks like someone broke in, I'll call the c—"

Something heavy hit the back of my head, and I tumbled to the bottom of the stairs. My body stopped abruptly at the bottom, but my vision kept swaying back and forth as I stared at the light fixture at the bottom of the stairs that connected the bookstore to the apartment. The blurred vision of a woman stood looking down at me. At first, I thought it was Jade, but then I saw the gray hair and more severe features. Perhaps it was her mother, maybe even grandmother. It was hard to tell with my vision blurred from the concussion and whatever was in that mead.

"We have the book, daughter. Finish him and meet us by the road. We have much to accomplish tonight," she ordered before she left, followed by another half dozen figures, all wearing black and green.

Soon, only Jade stood over me. "I'm really sorry it worked out this way, Jonah." She tilted her head sadly. "You could have ignored the sound, taken me to bed, and woken up in the morning with me and a single book missing." She looked toward her departing family and back to me. "For what it's worth, I really did like you." She thrust a combat boot at my already throbbing head, and everything started to fade out.

I don't know how much time passed before I was aware of what was happening to me. She could have been just outside the door, or long gone.

John Opalenik

I struggled to think about anything other than the throbbing pain in my head, but I was able to remember that morning. She was walking toward the beach where there were campgrounds. If her family were here trying to do something bad, they might stay there to avoid a paper trail. She described her family as being crunchy and new age, so camping felt more right than a motel.

When I got to my car, someone had slashed the tires. It must have been Jade, because as far as her family knew, she had finished me off. I don't know why I felt like I had to catch up to her. She stole a book that I would have sold them, but maybe they needed it right then or they wanted to erase any sort of record that they had it or that we ever did. Truthfully, it didn't matter why. I just needed her to look me in the eye and explain.

I tried to run toward the campground, but between having banged my ankle falling down the stairs and the pain in my head, I had to slow to a hurried walk. When I got close to the campground, a thunderstorm started, but it felt like so much more than that. Electricity buzzed in the air, and I felt pulled forward toward the raging campfire as if I were caught in a riptide, but on land. All that wind started blowing in a wide circle once I got closer to Jade and her family. Her mother stood in front of the fire, silhouetted against the blaze. The rest of her family circled her, chanting in a language I couldn't understand.

Outside of their circle stood a ring of skinny trees that blew in the wind, bending but never breaking. I don't know if it was the storm, or whatever she gave me to drink, but reality started bending above the flames. At first, it was small, like the distortion in the air on a hot day, but soon the clouds became viscous, like boiling jelly reaching out with arms and hooves and long tongues. When the otherworldly cloud touched the willows, they stopped moving with the wind and started moving on their own, dislodging themselves from the earth and tearing their way through the campsites I passed on my way to her.

Wispy branches became whips heavy and fast enough to cut someone in half, while the thicker branches hit campers hard enough to turn them into a gory mist. Gnarled knots of wood turned into toothy mouths devouring the campers' remains.

I stood frozen between the horror behind me and the summoning circle ahead of me that had conjured it. One of the swaying shadows broke the circle and ran toward me frantically.

"Jonah. You can't be here!" Jade shouted. "You aren't one of us, and the Dark Young are hungry after their centuries-long slumber. Nobody else is safe."

I held up my arms. My mouth couldn't decide whether to ask what, how, or why, so I stood there with my jaw hanging open. Jade looked at the carnage, back at her family, and finally at me. She took a black Sharpie out of her pocket. "Hold still." She grabbed me by my chin and scrawled something on my forehead. She pulled a pocketknife out of her back pocket, drew the blade across her palm, and rubbed the blood into whatever she had drawn. "Hopefully, this will keep you safe long enough to get away." She looked back at the massacred campsites. "Now get out of here!"

The wind and the waves intensified, blurring the line between the ocean and the campground. The trees-turned-into-monsters finished their meal and turned toward me. They rushed forward and surrounded me, but never got close enough to

I Lost You to the Summer Wind

touch. I didn't know whether to scream, run, or call out to Jade, but soon, a massive wall of water engulfing the campground took away whatever choice I had.

They found me the next morning, the only survivor of a historic storm that turned the campground into a ruinous monument to nature's fury.

I tried to tell people what I saw, but between the concussion and the sheer amount of alcohol and hallucinogens in my system, they didn't think that any of what I claimed to see had actually been there. When the police investigated, it looked like nothing more than a campground party that got way out of hand and then also got hit by a severe storm nobody predicted. I thought about pressing the matter, but I realized nobody wanted to hear it. They had a sane explanation for what happened, and they weren't looking for another version of events that could open doorways to madness.

It's been five years, and I haven't seen Jade since. Part of me is glad because I don't know whether I'd demand answers or ask to join her family. Of course, there's that dark corner of my heart that aches to see her again, monsters and mass destruction be damned.

John Opalenik is a horror writer and educator from Connecticut. He is the author of The Primeval series, *The Blue Beneath the Mountain*, and the short story collection *Among the Willows & Other Strange Tales*. He has been a teacher for more than ten years and his books have been featured at indie bookstores, online, and at horror events. He currently serves as the secretary of the Connecticut chapter of the Horror Writers Association. He lives in central Connecticut with his wife, son, and dog.

Keep up to date on future releases and events by visiting johnopalenik.com, and following @JohnOpalenik on Instagram and Threads, or @john.opalenik.7 on Facebook.

106

Shub-Niggurath's Shindig

Nora B. Peevy

Shelly and her twins, Lechuza and Camazotz, were arranging black coconut shavings on the goat lying on the violet-strewn grass cake when the phone rang. Greg warmed himself next to the great hearth of the fireplace dividing the kitchen from their family room. He drank Scotch, the amber drink reflected by the firelight. The diamond in his pinky ring flashed like a tiny, white quasar.

"Baphomet's residence, Shelly speaking." Pause. "What?" Pause. "Surely, you're joking. That can't be." Pause. "The ceremony is less than twenty-four hours from now. Oh, how deliciously funny and naughty. Someone is going to be praised to high Shub." Shelly ran her fingers through her cropped, red hair. "Of course, they didn't do it this time. My girls would never think to put themselves in the running for 'Best Prank of the Year.'" She turned. "Lechie and Camie. Did you two steal Shub's goats?"

"No." The twins shook their heads in unison.

"Patty, they said 'no.'" Shelly glared out the window over the kitchen sink. "Well, I don't know what to tell you. If my girls said they didn't do it, they didn't do it." She checked her black nail polish. "Why don't you try asking your two boys? They're always pulling pranks. Just last week, Greg caught them spray-painting the church." Pause. "Yes, it was hysterical that they wrote, 'Jesus can suck my balls.'" Pause. "No, I'm not *saying* your boys did something with the goats. I'm saying they *possibly* did something with the goats. They're certainly funnier than my girls. Toodles." Shelly hung up.

"Patty Carver's boys . . . Shub just loves them." Greg finished his scotch, tears in his eyes. "It's just a shame we couldn't buy the kids the ponies they asked for as a reward for pulling the best prank." He shook his head. "A darn shame."

Shelly *tsked-tsked* her daughters. "I'm very disappointed it wasn't the two of you this time. Stealing Shub's ceremonial goats would surely have won you that award."

Shub-Niggurath's Shindig

←♥→←♥→←♥→

Pan sat in his naked, firm glory, drinking a light-bodied grenache with a subtle white-pepper flavor in the middle of a dark forest. The trees still held their leaves. Pan couldn't see the stars through the old growth.

Busty goat-legged women, servants of Shub-Niggurath, surrounded him. Tiny goat horns pierced their nipples. They wore tiaras fashioned from copper and wool hair wraps, with miniature bunches of grapes, goat heads, Baphomets, small sigils of Shub-Niggurath, or tiny pentacles. The goat-legged women played cat's cradle with black wool. One adorned Pan's phallus with bunches of grapes as he set down his wine and picked up his pipe. A group of the women smoked from a green hookah fashioned to look like a grapevine.

Pan's music sped up. The goat-legged women whirled in time to the Ruska Roma melody with exaggerated hand movements and giant grins, their hair spinning around them like wheels of fire.

Sitting on fallen tree limbs covered in lichens and mushrooms, a group of Shub-Niggurath's older servants wrapped themselves in cloaks the colors of the night forest, huddling near their crackling fire, warming their bodies as their blood pumped through their horns, circulating to their entire system. One knit a tiny, black wool sweater, fingers holding knitting needles and moving faster than the dancer's feet, while the one beside her held the skein.

←♥→←♥→←♥→

Somewhere in the dark tapestry beyond our unimportant galaxy, Shub-Niggurath floated, a giant evil cloud. The Mother Goddess drove a chariot through the starless cosmos pulled by two valiant lions. She drank elderberry wine. Sadly, nobody could hear Her divine unholy *burp!* as She rode, unaware of all the humans, her sleeping sacrifices below in the universe.

←♥→←♥→←♥→

The Carver boys couldn't sleep. They hid under their Cthulhu sheets with their flashlights, reading Lovecraft comics and singing what all children sang around the time of Mabon and the ritual at The Temple of the Black Goat with a Thousand Young, dedicated to Shub-Niggurath.

The Goat Song
A little tiny goat
Hanging from a tree,
Coloring all the leaves,
And dripping blood on me.
Yellow leaves turn red.
Brown leaves turn red.
All falling down on
My waiting head.
The trees will soon be dead,
The ground painted red.
And all of Baphomet's children
Will soon go to bed!

108

Nora B. Peevy

In the gleaming copper temple in the dark wood, giant creatures with black tentacles, goat's legs, and dripping fangs played tag around the sacrificial tree in the center of the room, smacking each other's mouths. They would have delighted in wearing purple and black ribbons on their tentacles in honor of tomorrow's ritual, but the priests and servants of The Temple of the Black Goat with a Thousand Young forbade any nonsense denigrating The Mother Goddess.

The Young began to yawn. It was past their bedtime, so they were herded into a glass nursery with the symbol of their mother on each wall, three goat heads attached at their necks, with their horns pointed outward to form a circle. A sea of giant cryptids now floated together, frightened of the forest beyond. One of the young suckled on its tentacle, careful not to bite it with its dripping fangs. Another uttered, "Mama," in the cloak of darkness. Like the sound of a falling log in the woods, no one heard the monster speak, but oh, the precious beast sounded darling. If only Shub-Niggurath was there to record it in its baby book. It was a pity because they grew up so fast.

←♥→←♥→←♥→

The day of Mabon was overcast, with a slight chance of rain, but the Weather Channel was about as reliable as Shelly's children growing horns, though a mother could dream. *I'd be the talk of the PTA if that happened.* Shelly sighed as she drank her coffee and gazed out the window, wondering where the goats were. She set her coffee mug on the granite counter. It read: *Excuse me, sir. Do you have a moment to talk about our lord and savior, Cthulhu?*

The ritual at The Temple of the Black Goat with a Thousand Young was upon them. Shelly began to cry. She couldn't bear to think about being parted eternally from her beloved Greg, although it was such an honor to be chosen. She wiped her eyes. "Lechic! Camic! Are you ready? We're going to the salon to get our hair done for tonight's ritual. Greg, honey, are you coming with us?"

Greg ate his scrambled eggs and bacon at the breakfast bar. "No. I think I'll go over to the clubhouse. Hang out with the boys and reflect on my good fortune and the beauty of the season and all that." He dabbed egg from his beard with his white, linen napkin embroidered with a cute pygmy goat baaing, *I ♥ Shub-Niggurath!* When she went upstairs, he pulled a family photo from his wallet and smiled. He was the luckiest husband and father. Now he would be one of the *gof'nn* among The Blessed at The Temple of the Black Goat with a Thousand Young.

Shelly wrangled the twins, who were headbutting each other like young goats. "Come on, girls. Let's go. We have a million and one things to do before tonight's festivities. And Grandma and Grandpa are coming for dinner with the rest of your dad's family. I need to pick up the dinner rolls from the bakery, the goat-shaped butters I ordered, and the hot ham from the deli. And make that Jell-O goat mold your grandpa wants every time he comes to dinner." She sniffled, trying not to think about the last night sleeping beside Greg.

Shub-Niggurath's Shindig

←♥→←♥→←♥→

"What's the special occasion?" The hairdresser snapped her gum as she washed Shelly's hair.

"Not The Ritual of a Thousand Goats but summoning the Scarlet Circle."

"Oh. The Ritual of a Thousand Oaks. I've read about that. That's Hindu or Buddhist or something like that, isn't it?"

"No. I said The Ritual of a Thousand Goats."

The hairdresser began rinsing Shelly's hair. "Oh, you mean the yoga place on Fifteenth and National? I love that place. Where you do the goat yoga? It's so relaxing—or are you talking about the jewelry store? I got a bracelet there for my niece. It's so cute."

Shelly sat up in her chair, her hair dripping wet.

"Ma'am, you're not supposed to leave your chair, yet."

Shelly clomped away from the hair-washing station in her Louis Vuitton heels, one twin's wrist in each hand.

"Ma'am, you still have conditioner in your hair."

Shelly glared at her.

"Did I say something wrong?"

"How dare you disrespect The Temple of the Black Goat with a Thousand Young. How *dare* you!" The little bell jangled above the door.

"Well, bless her heart. I didn't know the women around here took their goat yoga so seriously. You'd think she started a new religion, or I said I heard Jesus fart on the crucifix when I was in church, the way she stomped out of here." The hairdresser laughed. "Adelia, did you see her lips purse up like she was taking a dick up her poop chute, but didn't want her hubby to know she enjoyed it?" The two hairdressers guffawed.

"Come on, babies. We're going to run our errands. Lechie, give Mama your hat. I'll just do my hair at home."

"What about my hair?" Camie tapped her foot.

"Yeah, what about our hair?" Lechie tapped her foot, too.

"I'll do your hair too." Shelly blew a raspberry at the salon as she got into her minivan with the *I brake for Shub-Niggurath!* bumper sticker.

←♥→←♥→←♥→

The Blessed stood outside before The Temple of the Black Goat with a Thousand Young, flabbergasted. A bunch of goat-legged women and goblin-like creatures mingled, the priests and servants of Shub-Niggurath.

"What in the Goddess's dark tapestry is this?"

"I believe, my dear priests, you are looking at what is called a 'yarn bombing.'"

Heads swiveled and focused on Pan, who leaned against a copper pillar. Pan and his goat-legged women had wrapped all four pillars multiple times in what looked like a never-ending scarf. Pan held a wineglass, his hooves crossed, stroking his erection.

"Oh, put that thing away. The ceremony hasn't even started." One priest glared.

"Take that down," another of The Blessed ordered Pan, pointing at the yarn bomb.

"No." Pan pulled his pipes from his butt and farted. "Excuse me. Oooh, that is rather ripe." He traded his wine glass for his pipes and played a rousing tune. From the forest pranced a dozen pygmy goats wearing black woolen sweaters and wreaths of oak leaves with candles on their heads between their horns. All had shaggy black wool and stood two feet tall at their withers. They had red eyes and slightly upward-curving horns, with wiry beards hanging from their cute little chins.

"Oh. My. God. You. Didn't," one of The Blessed said.

"Oh. Yes. I. Did." Pan gestured to one of the topless, buxom goat-legged women with twenty bells in her hair and bells on her hooves.

She jingled as she romped toward him. "Your horniness." She bowed her own horns. Pan hung a bunch of grapes on each horn and lifted her chin, kissing each cheek. She blushed and fluttered her eyelids.

"Oh, this is disgusting." One of the The Blessed muttered to himself.

"No more disgusting than watching Shug enjoy a delicate pink human tartar." Pan gestured to his wineglass. Another goat-legged woman appeared with a pitcher of wine and another glass. "Join me, my lovely."

"Your horniness." The goat-legged woman with the grapes on her horns curtsied, and all her bells jingled.

"The Temple of the Black Goat with a Thousand Young is not your playground."

"Oh, but I believe it is." Pan danced a happy jig, clicking his hooves together. "I believe it is, my friend."

"We are not your friends. Take the sweaters off the goats before Shub-Niggurath's summoning. There will be trouble." The Blessed ground their teeth as one.

"Oooh. I'm so scared." Pan skipped circles around The Blessed. "But they're so fuzzy-wuzzy cute, and the nights are getting cooler. Don't you think The Mother Goddess wants to know Her children are warm and cozy?" He scratched one goat behind his ears. The goat bleated with pleasure. "As for the yarn bombing, I can't control what my women get up to while I'm busy rutting. You know how randy I get this season." Pan grabbed one of his consorts and simulated taking her from behind. All the goat-legged women laughed.

"Disgusting. Remove the yarn aplomb from the temple." This Blessed one was a little touched in the head.

"Bomb."

"Aplomb."

"I said 'bomb.'"

"Bomb? Where? Where's the bomb?"

"You idiot," one of the goblin-like *gof'nn* rolled its eyes. "He meant the yarn bomb."

"There's a bomb in the yarn? Why would anyone put one there?"

"Never mind."

"Pan, remove the yarn bomb," the closest Blessed ordered.

"Why is there a bomb in the yarn?"

"Shut up," all The Blessed said to the addlebrained one.

"Oh, all right. I've had my fun." Pan snapped his fingers, and the yarn bomb disappeared. "You are all party poopers. Poopy pants. Party poopers. Poopy party poopers with poop in their pants. That's what you are. I'm going to go poop in the woods. Excuse me." Pan capered off into the dark forest.

At that moment, the guests arrived. Everyone saw the goats in sweaters cavorting and butting heads, romping so hard they sent their oak-leaf wreaths and candles sailing in the air.

Greg caught one wreath and placed it on Shelly's head. "My love." He kissed her sweetly. "You will always be my teddy bear."

"And you will always be my fuzzy-wuzzy bee." She kissed him on the lips.

"And you will always make me want to throw up," Pan said. "Wine for the sacrifice? I've heard Shub-Niggurath prefers a light red this time of year with a hint of white pepper. The grenache is quite good and doesn't overpower the meat." He eyed Greg's biceps, licking his lips.

"Don't mind if I do."

"Oh, Greg! Look at the goats! They're adorable. Who made those sweaters? I'd like to purchase a dozen for my goats at home. Are they in style this season? Could I get them in blood red or bruised purple? Perhaps a softer black like cashmere?" Shelly ran over to pet one goat and pulled oats out of her pocket. "Who's the designer?"

"I am." Pan pointed to himself.

"You did a smashing job, old buddy." Greg clapped Pan on the back. "And here we thought the Carver twins had stolen Shub-Niggurath's goats. Girls, you're still in the running! Think of something creative. Something like tiny booties with bells or Elizabethan collars. Those would make any goat look regal. They worked for Queen Elizabeth. She was *not* as cute as the goats." Greg elbowed Pan.

Shelly choked back her tears and watched her children tapping the glass cage with Shub's babies in it. "Lechie and Camie, don't tease the poor things! They can't get out." One baby pressed its tentacles against the side of the glass, sliding down mournfully.

The Blessed entered the temple and formed the Scarlet Circle. The Gate would soon be open, and Shub-Niggurath would ride in on Her grand chariot drawn by two lions from the dark tapestry of the unknown and incomprehensible cosmos to give Her gift to Her lucky initiate.

"Oh, Greg. I'm so proud of my fuzzy-wuzzy bee." Shelly put her arm around her husband for the last time, her eyes damp.

Greg kissed the top of both his twins' heads. "You two be good and promise to help your mother with the dishes. And do your homework." Greg stepped into the center of the circle next to the sacred tree. A goat hung, hogtied, its throat slit, its blood filling the symbols carved on the floor as The Blessed each sacrificed a bit of power.

Moments later, Shub-Niggurath arrived in all Her glory and swallowed Greg. Shelly and the rest of the guests turned their gaze not to look upon the cosmic glory of Her, but that didn't stop their ears from enjoying the bone-crunching symphony accompanying The Blessed's wide, black eyes. Pan drank a glass to another sacrifice gone well while Greg's relatives ate cheese puffs and pigs in a blanket.

Nora B. Peevy

The twins sang "The Goat Song."

"Darlings, come here," Shub-Niggurath summoned Her trio of goats. "Who made these marvelous sweaters for you? You look divine." She gestured for someone to get Her a glass of wine, and Pan hopped to Her side. "Honeybunch," she purred. "It's been too long. Shall we?" And together, they left Her future offal to go walking in the dark forest green while Greg's family laughed and ate the appetizers Shelly had prepared for this blessed occasion.

And that is how Shelly threw a shindig for Shub.

Nora B. Peevy is a cat trapped in a human's body. Please send help or tuna. She toils away for JournalStone and Trepidatio Publishing as a submission reader, is a cofounder/editor for Alien Sun Press, a reviewer for *Hellnotes*, editor in chief, artist, and writer for *Weird Fiction Quarterly*, and has been published in *A Walk in a City of Shadows: Tales of Urban Legendry* (Alien Sun Press), *The Wicked Library Podcast*, and other places. She has a  bachelor of arts in English with a concentration in creative writing from Cardinal Stritch University and is also a contributor for Getty Images. Usually, you can find her on Facebook asking for help to escape her human body or to get tuna. Tuna is nice. Cats like tuna. She also likes cat naps in Milwaukee, Wisconsin.

Emissary of Love

Rob Smales

It wasn't my fault.

The other members of the group blame me, but they're all jealous. Even Jill and Cathy Dansbury, who seem to be perfectly in love from the outside, and Scott Woodman, who claims—loudly, and to all who will listen—to, and I quote, "catch more ass than a toilet seat." They all wish they were in my Tevas, and every one of them would have acted the same way had her eye fallen upon *them* with favor. But it didn't. It fell upon *me*. And what with it being the only eye she *has*, well . . .

But I'm getting ahead of myself.

We at the Inquisition for Deities Ineffable Offering Transcendence (which makes a poor acronym, but no one noticed until it was pointed out at the Secret Societies and Personhood's Convention, down in DC, and by then we were stuck with it) had seen where other groups such as ours had gone wrong—especially those morons at Roanoke. We didn't set our sights too high—or too low, as the case may be. We didn't try to wake Cthulhu, or go knocking on Amon-Gorloth's door asking to borrow a cosmic cup of celestial sugar. Despite all of Bradley Ligit's demanding, we didn't roll up on Inspeca to request surfing tips—I swear, the only reason we even let that man *speak* at our gatherings was that he owned the space in which we met. We put it to a vote and set our sights more *realistically*. Practically down to earth.

After all, he was awake and frequented this earthly plane, so who better—who *closer*—to ask for other-, extra-, or interworldly knowledge than Nyarlathotep? Besides, the rituals looked easier, and it would take less time overall, which worked out well for many of our members: Dillon is totally swamped with his new business, the Dansburys had childcare issues, and a couple of others work nights. So we did our homework, put The Mighty Messenger in our crosshairs, and began to prepare.

Bradley's warehouse—which isn't near a ley line, but *is* right beside those high-tension wires coming in from the highway—was set about with all manner of sigils and signs, symbols of power we'd cribbed from the oldest books we could find: *The Necronomikin*, *The Ebook of Eibon*, and *The Book of Azathoth's Cousin Irving*. Not exactly the great grimoires of power, but not bad for a cult whose Lord High Inquisitor spent his days managing a car wash. We drew our patterns, set our wards, and carved a summoning circle into the floor. Bradley bitched holy hell about that last one, it being his floor and all, but the Dansburys had seen one just like it on *The Dresden Files* so he shut up about it. Mostly.

Finally, the night came: some celestial thingamajiggers had moved into place, and the Grand Conjunction was at hand. The Lord High Inquisitor said a bunch of stuff about signs and portents when he showed us the copy of the *Times* he'd found in some customer's car, but his horoscope *did* say "Your stars are in alignment." Funny: I'd never figured the LHI for a Taurus. He'd always struck me as a classic Virgo. But there it was, right in the *Times*! We'd found out about it kind of last-minute, so the whole Inquisition hopped to it, bustling about like ants from a kicked-over anthill—if, that is, ants wore robes of midnight black embroidered with silver thread, and the head ant shouted a lot and wore a big, tall pope hat with the Inquisitor's All-Seeing Eye emblazoned on the front, *and* if, instead of stolen picnic grub and sugar cubes, ants carried around pots of incense and things intended as sacrifices. But other than all that, we were *just* like ants.

Finally, the moment came. Cheryl Bernham, our meeting timekeeper, set a countdown on her iPhone, so we knew it was accurate. The chanting began, low and sonorous, but over the course of an hour, it swelled in volume and rose in tempo until it reached a final crescendo. I couldn't tell you *exactly* how the chant went, or what it meant, as I'd never actually *learned* it. I'd brought a cheat sheet, copied out of *Azathoth's Cousin*, and I wasn't the only one: Kim Lake kept pulling a piece of paper from her sleeve, and it looked like Tim Greene had written it on the backs of both hands.

I hadn't even learned the entire ceremony, to be honest with you, just what I needed to in order to get my job done. I watched Dillon Ryan—he of the startup home gerbil massage business—and when Dillon rang his bell, I'd give a two count and then light my incense pot. It was one of the pots sitting on the floor touching the very edge of the summoning circle, which the LHI had said was *very* important. I'd been practicing diligently so as not to screw up. *Bong*, one, two, light: that equation formed my contribution to the summoning of an elder power; not *the* elder power—that's where those Roanoke yobbos screwed the pooch—but *an* elder power, one with ties to multiple *the* elder powers, so it seemed like a good place to start.

Now, the fact that I'd practiced so much didn't mean I wasn't nervous when the actual time came. In point of fact, I was pants-shittingly terrified. Oh, not of Nyarlathotep, though, of course, there was a healthy dose of respect there. I was a hair away from pooping my eldritch robe over the fact that if I screwed this up, the whole Inquisition would be furious with me, and the Inquisition has a reach both long and affluent. Between Ken McSweeny, the mechanic, and Barb whatshername, the meter maid, I'd be afraid to go anywhere in my car, or get it repaired, and while Lenny Barber had gotten me a great deal on both a phone and a wireless plan, as my local Verizon tech he could pull my SIM card out of network in about a second. My life would become *very* difficult if I messed this up—thus the flop sweats. And thus . . .

I'd been keeping track of Dillon's bell from the corner of my eye, so I saw right when he picked it up. The bell rang. I counted under my breath, throwing a hippo in between to avoid giving a nervous fast count.

Bong!

One hippopotamus. I lifted my match.

Two hippopotamus. I struck my match.

Three! A runner of sweat dropped into the corner of my eye just as I reached forward with my lit match, and it stung like a mad bastard. I flinched, nearly knocking the incense pot over, but I managed to catch its very rim just before it clanged to the floor. The incense cone was still stuck in place, so I thrust the flame against its tip as I set the pot back *precisely* where it was supposed to be.

Disaster averted.

Well . . . almost.

Remember when I said I'd diligently practiced lighting the incense? Well, what I *hadn't* been diligent about was cleaning the pot after practice. Incense burns down to ash, you see, and after burning a lot of incense, there was a lot of ash in there. Enough that, when jogged sharply enough—say by nearly tipping the thing over and then snatching it back—a good-sized foop of ash fell to the floor in a fine and dusty spray. A spray that not only cut right across the circle I was supposed to be reinforcing with sweet-smelling smoke, but filled up and obscured more than half of one of the somewhat ancient symbols giving the circle its power.

Now, the LHI had been *seriously* intense when he forbade anyone to either break the circle or mess up those symbols, and here I'd gone and done both in one swell foop. Visions of massive parking tickets and shitty cell service filled my head as I glanced around, panic-stricken. It didn't look like anyone had noticed, though, and I breathed a sigh of relief. I turned the sigh into a quick puff, trying to blow some of the ash away, but I'd have had to bend right down to it to have any real effect, and I wasn't doing anything *that* obvious. The floor was gray, the ash was gray, and we were doing all this by torches and candlelight. If I was lucky, no one would notice, and I'd have a chance to scrub it away with my foot when it was all over.

Determined to ignore the ash for now, I looked up.

And gasped.

In the center of the circle, a column of smoke rose, not from our incense pots, because all those produced was regular looking—if sweetly smelly—gray smoke. But this wasn't gray, and it wasn't regular looking. It swirled up from the floor in a tiny tornado, a tornado of many colors—but more than the colors, it was the *un-*colors that struck me. There was blue and the opposite of blue, red and the opposite of red. All the colors of the spectrum were there, and all their opposites as well. And if you think the opposite of blue is yellow, or pink, or anything else you'd find in ROYGBIV, you are sorely mistaken. The opposite of blue is the color of the heat that bakes off a tarmac parking lot frying in the summer sun. The opposite of green won't be found in any rainbow you'll ever see, but is the exact shade of fingernails screeching down a chalkboard. Every wavelength of every color you can imagine has an opposite, a negative, and they all shimmered in that expanding column. And if you think that *sounds* confusing, you should have *seen* it. All about me, black-robed figures clutched their stomachs at the mere sight of all that color and un-, whirling and swirling, lit up by its own glow and unglow. Many vomited, turning aside so as not to spew on their own incense pots or some mystic symbol or other. Many wept at the suddenness of the sickness, at its violent strength, but all I could do was stare, because it was the most beautiful thing I've ever seen.

For about eight seconds.

That's how long it took the expanding psychedelic twister to completely fill the confines of the circle. I caught a whiff of the smoke when it flattened out as if contained by an invisible wall sitting atop the ring of sigils in the floor, the disgusting miasma of a spoiled corpse wearing a soiled diaper, the whole thing soaked in gasoline and set afire, plus the opposite of that odor, which somehow turned out to be just as rank. It pulsed, the roiling, spinning everycolor *flexing* against its imprisoning circumvallation, once, twice, thrice—

And then the contained cyclone collapsed inward, all those colored (and uncolored) particles rushing together with the force of a thunderclap. The sound smashed out of the circle, washing over the gathered society at the speed of . . . well, sound. All about the great chamber, members were knocked back a step—some lost their footing, slipping in their recently upchucked dinners to land in those putrid puddles of their own shame—all but me. My robes rippled as if caught in a high wind, and that smell washed over me again, putrid and repugnant—but alluring just the same. More than alluring: I realized I was sporting the boner of all boners, the kind so hard it hurt a little. I'd have looked down to see whether I'd managed to actually pop a tent in my robe right through the jeans I wore beneath, but my gaze was riveted to the center of the circle, to the spot where all those particles of many colors had come together.

To where *she* stood.

She was tall, and I'm not really sure what *statuesque* means, but I think I was looking at it. She was extremely curvy, and in all the right places—and I could *see* all those places because she was gloriously naked. Her breasts were like   well, *breasts*. I hadn't seen a great many in person, not without those stupid disco-ball strobes they use at every strip club I've ever been to, but they even had every boob I'd ever seen on PornHub beat, hands down. There were little mouths where her nipples should have been, but that was barely a distraction. Her skin was smooth and pale gray, and—smooth, without wrinkle or crease or hair to be seen, like an extremely soft-looking mannequin. I raised my gaze to meet her eyes and immediately understood the why of her mouth placement: her single eye was six or seven inches across, taking up so much of her face there was no room for any other feature. I'd no idea where her nose wound up, but it sure as hell wasn't under that eye.

That eye was round. That eye was liquid. That eye was *soulful*. And its color . . .

Its color was that of the swirling maelstrom she had been before she had been her, flashing through all the colors and the un- in a rippling, swirling, *mesmerizing* pattern, all faster than my eyes could follow, but I couldn't tear my gaze away. I was falling into that limpid lake of luscious luminosity—literally falling forward, about to go flat out, chest and chin on the floor, damn the circle, damn the symbols, damn the parking tickets and poor coverage—when those mouths spoke. One had a voice flutingly beautiful, the other buzzingly strident, the pair of which stiffened my spine just as that smell had tightened my tallywhacker, locking my knees and halting my topple before I missed a word.

"We are The Emissary."

The LHI had made it perfectly clear, on pain of having your Inquisition dues tripled, that *absolutely no one* was to speak to the summoned being but him. He'd told me, specifically, what with my reputation as a bit of a talker, several times. I was well aware of what the LHI wanted.

"Of course you are," I said.

"Oh, great Nyarlathotep," said a cracked and rasping voice from the other side of the circle. I looked past one smooth, gray shoulder to see the Lord High Inquisitor himself, staggering a bit but at least keeping to his feet. All about the chamber, Inquisition members were swooning, gabbling darkly to themselves, or gargling and choking on the last of their regurgitated pot roast; apparently, being the day manager at the Sir Suds-a-Lot Drive-Thru Car Wash (undercarriage cleanup at *no* additional charge) required the man to be made of sterner stuff.

He raised a hand that trembled so violently he may have been playing an invisible maraca. "We, the Inquisition for Deities Ineffable—"

"We are not Nyarlathotep," said the sweet-speaking left breast.

"Do you not listen?" asked the terrible-toned right.

"We are The Emissary," they thundered in unison. Her head whipped around 180 degrees, or maybe the eye simply zipped over to the back side of her head; it was hard to see in the flickering candle- and torchlight.

With a squawk like a man doing a shitty parrot impression, the Lord High Inquisitor fell, his body bending back as far as it would go. Then farther. I'd never seen a man shaped in quite that manner, not even on YouTube. Oh, how he screamed! Then, with one last jerk and *crack*, his heels touched the back of his skull, the screaming stopped, and he lay still.

That eye, so beautiful and wondrous, circled back around to face me.

Now, after seeing the effect of her gaze on the LHI, you'd think I might have been terrified to have that beautiful orb fixed upon me; after all, I'd been in danger of soiling myself at the mere thought of the Inquisition's anger, and all they could do was *mess* with my life. This being could apparently *take* it, swiftly, and with what had sounded like a lot of pain. I'll be straight-up honest here: I'm not known for my bravery—see above, regarding parking tickets and cell service. I *should* have been terrified. I *should* have been dry-mouthed and tongue-tied, unable to say anything even as eloquent as the LHI's shitty parrot squawk.

Instead, my hands rose to throw back my ebon cowl. Rather than carefully lifting the hood from my head, as I usually did, the casual gesture swiped the satin hood liner across my pate, and I felt the static it generated lifting the back of my hair into a ridiculous plumage, like a baby bird with pillow-head.

I didn't care.

"How *you* doin'?" I said, in my best Joey Tribbiani.

The big, beautiful eye blinked. The smooth, gray lid was the size of a dinner plate. *"What?"*

"I said," I said, but was suddenly shoved aside.

Rob Smales

Roger Tupper was standing behind my incense pot. The Assistant Lord High Inquisitor's left hand was twisted into some kind of mystic finger-sign. His right hand clutched a fistful of his robe a little beside and behind; it pulled the grand garment out of shape, but at least kept the fresh puke stain out of sight. The Lord Not-So-High Inquisitor had decided to step up and make the most of the recent vacancy in the LHI position.

"Oh great and powerful Emissary," he intoned—and I had to give him this: the dude could intone like a motherfucker. "Please forgive our confusion. We, the Inquisition for Deities Ineffable Offering Transcendence, performed the rites to summon Azathoth's Messenger. To find—"

"We are The Emissary of The Faceless God," said the left breast.

"The Black Pharaoh is otherwise occupied," rasped the right, "with things beyond your mortal ken."

"*We have answered your summons in his stead,*" they said together.

"I . . . What?" said Roger, forgetting to intone in his confusion.

"*We have answered your summons in his stead,*" they said again.

"I . . . What?" Roger squeaked.

I tapped Roger's trembling shoulder. "I think they're the PA."

The not-so-LHI whirled. Out in the center of the circle, the dinner plate did its slow blink again. Three voices spoke: one fluting, one rasping, and one definitely *not* intoning.

"*What?*"

"The PA," I repeated. "The receptionist. The 'I'm sorry, Mr. Nyarlathotep isn't in right now. If you leave your name and a brief message, the Floating Horror will get back to you as soon as he damn well pleases.'"

No longer facing the double-mouthed, single-eyed beauty standing—rather fetchingly, I thought—in the protective circle, Roger rediscovered both spine and voice. He straightened from what had become a confused and fearful crouch, and his words bellowed out somewhat louder and deeper than they had before; he was showing off for The Emissary. "Now *look*, you! You were told, numerous times, *not* to speak during the ceremony, and I will *not*—"

"Silence," rasped the right breast, and all sound in the great chamber died. I hadn't really been paying attention—it wasn't like I'd known the chant anyway—but once it was gone, I realized the whole Inquisition had shifted from droning in unison to a quiet montage of babble, everyone not unconscious or dead muttering distractedly to themselves, like some kind of great big bag-lady convention.

"We wish to hear the plumed one speak," sang the left.

Cringing, Roger turned back to the circle. "But—"

"*You are not the plumed one!*"

Roger suddenly—Well, he . . . I'm not sure how to . . . You know how you can reach all the way into a sock and grab the inside of the toe and yank the whole thing inside out? Something reached up inside of Roger and, well . . . Look, I had no idea there was that much stuff inside a human body, but what came out the bottom of his robe that day should *not* have fit into a Roger-size package. The mess was thick and spread wide, and I half expected Bradley to start bitching about it—it being his floor and all—but that order for silence still held sway; I didn't hear a *pin* drop, but I detected bits of ex-Roger dripping from the walls. And ceiling. And people.

Except for me. I'd somehow been spared the literal bloodbath, which I was more than okay with; those robes are dry clean only, and try explaining *that* to the counter guy down at Martinizing. A light breeze tickled the three-finger spray of hairs my sliding hood had raised atop my head, and I thought about what that sweet-sounding tit had said. I took a breath, and then a chance, and tapped the front of my strangely clean robe with a finger.

"Am *I* the plumed one?"

"*Of course you are*," those breast mouths said in unison, parroting my own words, and in exactly my voice.

I found myself grinning. "Hey! That's pretty good!"

"Hey!" mimicked the left.

"That's pretty good," said the right, both still in perfect reproduction.

My forehead crinkled with confusion. "What are you doing?"

The Emissary gave an extra-slow blink (wink? Hell, who knew?), and with an eyelid that size, it took a while. Then, the left mouth said, "Why did you say that?"

"What? It *was* good! I love those impressionist clips on YouTube, and that—"

"Not that," said the right, in a voice that would have looked the *exact* opposite of the color green.

"Before," the left fluted. "When you said, 'Of course you are'?"

I sucked air through puckered lips, buying a second to think. Why the hell *had* I said that? "Well, you are, aren't you?"

"Yes." The right sounded angry and suspicious. It had just the voice for it. "And we just said as much. It needed no verification."

"So," added the left, oddly sweet for a being connected to so much blood, pain, and madness, and all that within just the past ten minutes. "Why did you?"

The bullshit machine in my head whirred away, roared in fact, but it was like some asshat had jacked the drive wheels off the ground in a practical joke TikTok: the engine was screaming but accomplishing bupkes. I opened my mouth, praying for some line to pop out of it—perhaps swiped from a movie or TV show filed away in my subconscious—and was horrified to hear the *truth* slipping out. "Because I usually get all tongue-tied around beautiful women, but that popped into my head, and it just seemed like the thing to say at the time."

I felt heat creep into my face at the openness of the admission—and then, with a terrible prickle of fear at the back of my neck, recognized the strange ache I was feeling as a reminder that I was still sporting a blued-steel erection. I'd never checked the front of my robe and locked every muscle in my face and neck to keep from doing so now and possibly calling attention to my state. I merely stood there, idiot grin frozen on my blushing face, and thought *no tent no tent notentnotentnotentnotent* for the duration of another of those epoch-spanning blinky-winks. I had plenty of time for it to occur to me that I'd just spoken rather forwardly to this being, and for that thought to trigger memories of all the times I'd been slapped in the face for being forward with a woman—read: *every* time—and for some perverse section of my brain to cross-index all that with what I'd just seen happen to the LHI and his loud-mouthed understudy—and all *they* did was speak to her—and come to the conclusions that (a) I should probably kiss my ass goodbye and (b) all the twisty, splattery evidence in the room said I'd likely be able to do just that, soon, one way or another.

As that smooth, round lid rolled slowly upward, allowing the ginormous orb beneath to once again pin me with its stare, I was almost overcome with the urge to close *my* eyes in the childish insistence that if *I* couldn't see *her*, then *The Emissary* couldn't see *me*.

But that was the problem: I wouldn't be able to see The Emissary, and my brain, my heart, and my pecker all agreed that *that* would be intolerable. It was my heart's desire (an organ that had never *ever* spoken up before in my dealings with the opposite sex) that if these were my last moments on Earth, I'd spend them gazing upon The Emissary, and that the last thing I'd see as she jammed my head up my own ass would be that great, round, gorgeous eye, the most wonderful window into the most wonderful soul of the most wonderful—

"Do you really find us beautiful?"

The poetry dancing through my heart tripped on my tongue and fell on its face. "I . . . You . . . Uh . . . Beg pardon?"

"Do you really find us beautiful?"

The poetry struggled to rise, but my regular old tongue kicked its feet out from under it again.

"Does a bear shit in the woods?"

The lid fluttered in confusion, clapping out the drum solo from "Wipe Out" and fanning up a breeze that tickled my hair.

"Are you asking us if the large, hairy mammals of the family Ursidae perform solid elimination in a rural, tree-filled setting?"

"Uh . . . Yes?"

"Yes."

"Then, yes."

The great lid tapped out a Buddy Rich solo as the God of the Bloody Tongue's Girl Friday puzzled through all the affirmatives. "So . . . you do?"

Poetry had regained its feet by then, but common sense rose up behind it to kick it squarely in the nuts. "Yup."

When she wasn't speaking or blinky-winking, The Emissary had been quite still. She was still now, motionless not in the way of people, or even trees, but with the immobility of stone. A stone resting upon another stone sitting upon a stone shelf in a still shot. She *radiated* stillness, the silence of the void between stars, the absolute zero of the timeless nowhere between worlds. Her surface—I wasn't sure she had *skin*—darkened, the gray deepening toward black.

I took in the color change and finally felt that blued steel melting away as my nuts shrank to the size of sesame seeds. Small ones. I'd seen The Emissary do *terrible* things to people, but she'd never actually *looked* angry. She'd destroyed the LHI and his understudy as casually as you or I would flick away an ant we'd found crawling on the toe of our shoe. But me and my big mouth, we'd actually gone so far The Emissary was darkening with anger. I mentally told my asshole to be ready—it was already puckered, trust me—because when the *kissing it goodbye* chance came, it wouldn't be a long one, and I had no idea what direction I'd be coming from. Or even if it'd be from the outside.

If I'm really lucky, I thought, *I'll just explode. Too fast for pain, and the last thing I'd see would be The Emiss—Wait-a-hold-it now! What's this?*

The darkening color was changing. It was no longer strictly gray, not from where I was standing. Some red was flowing into the picture—its opposite, too, but I won't go into the visible shade of a smell right now—spreading out from her eye and mipples (nouths?). But it wasn't a deep, volcanic tint, nor the bright scarlet of blood from a freshly inside-outed Roger; no, this was paler somehow, and lighter, and not really *red*, I thought, but . . . pink?

I gasped. *Oh my God*—and not the god *usually* referred to in this chamber—*is this being from Beyond, from Between, from Elsewhere . . . is this summoned creature who can kill with the mere concept of a thought . . . is this representative of an Elder Power . . . blushing?*

She was! That great eye was downcast, its sail of an eyelid lowered to half-mast, and those odd mouths of hers hung slightly open, as if they searched for something to say, but that damned TikTok joker had been at it again, and her wheels were just spinning. Even as I watched, one smooth leg slid into motion, knee bending so the big toe—she didn't actually have toes, I now saw, but the movement of that spatulate appendage was the same—could grind little circles into the poured concrete floor.

"Do you really think so?" said the sweet left mouth.

"*Do* I!"

"That's what we asked," said the sour right. Apparently, they don't have sarcasm or rhetoric in the outer dark.

Before I could answer, a passing blood-covered hag started shrieking, a shrill, gurgling yodel of pain and insanity far beyond that cat-lady babble I'd noticed before. It was Cheryl, the timekeeper, though she looked quite different with the living eyes scooped from her head, dangling from her hooked fingers by the long extraocular muscles like disgusting yo-yos. Without warning, she detonated, the wet splash of a bursting water balloon coinciding with her innards becoming her outards and spreading themselves over several square yards of the scenery. The smell was truly horrendous; apparently, Cheryl hadn't had time to use the facilities before the ceremony'd begun, and that was mixed into the blood froth now painting the room.

The smell only assaulted me for a heartbeat before it was propelled away in the wind created by The Emissary *batting her eyelid at me*.

"She was rude to interrupt," shouted the right mouth.

"You were saying?" purred the left.

"I, uh . . ." I was a little disconcerted. I'd known Cheryl for a long time, even borrowed money for lunch from her a week ago. Her face—just the skin, I think— had come to rest on the floor off to my right, and I could see it in my peripheral vision, and it didn't look like she'd undergone the quick, painless transition into oblivion I'd envisioned back when I'd been hoping to explode myself. Those eyeless holes opened and closed, and the mouthless lips writhed in what looked like agony, and I *knew* I should have been devastated by what had just happened to my friend. The devastation seemed tempered though—a *lot*—by the thought that I wasn't going to have to pay that money back. Besides, poetry finally stood, clutching its bruised plums but ready to continue the fight, demanding its turn to be heard.

"Every sunrise and sunset, every full moon cresting the horizon, even Salma Hayek in *From Dusk 'till Dawn*, back when she was young and wore a lot less clothes, you add all those together, and they *still* don't equal how beautiful you are."

Well. Okay. Maybe not poetry, but at least it was better than that "bear shitting in the woods" thing. But now comes the slap. Or transition into a sludge pile capable of feeling nothing but pain until she lets me die. Or whatever.

The blush deepened. That toeless flipper-foot-thing scored the floor, cracking the concrete in a random back-and-forth pattern. All around us, the entire Inquisition—all those not currently absorbed in a new career as either an experimental geometric design or a Jackson Pollock monochrome—raised its collective voice in song. I can't be sure it wasn't the same chant—I'd lost my cheat sheet—but it didn't sound the same. Maybe it was the opposite of the chant I'd failed to learn, or maybe it was just that all the chanters were weeping as they sang, but it definitely sounded . . . darker.

"You say the sweetest things."

Both voices spoke in unison again, almost as if the two parts of her (she did refer to herself as *us*, didn't she?) were in agreement that I *did* say the sweetest things. That gave me a little shot of confidence. I took a breath and sifted through my mental files for a line, a Joey Tribiani *How you doin'?* or maybe the old *What's a nice girl like you doing in a place like this*; tried-and-true words women respond to because they're not associated with schlubs like me.

But it *had* been me, hadn't it, who'd said the words that had made her blush deepen, that had apparently won both those voices over? The poetry from my own heart, applebag swelled up like a mason jar but still getting the job done.

"You, uh—You ever been to Kelly's?"

"Where?"

"Kelly's Roast Beef, over in Revere."

The Emissary thought it over. *"No."*

I took a breath, then took the plunge. "You want to get out of here and head over there? Maybe get a bite? Or something?"

"With you?"

I gulped. "Yes?"

There went that lid again: slow down, slow up.

"We would like that very much."

I grinned. "Well, all right, then! Shall we?" I turned toward the exit and stuck out an elbow, offering to escort her arm in arm. I'd never done that before—it had always seemed kind of dweeby—but there was something here, perhaps the involvement of my long-silent heart, urging me. Being a proper gentleman was probably beyond me, but I'd at least try not to be a *total* dick.

The Emissary left the exact center of the protective circle for the first time. My mind flashed on that smoke of many colors and un-, flattening out against the perceived perimeter of the Inquisitor's work just before collapsing inward to form the being I was now hoping to take on a date.

Emissary of Love

What if the damned circle is working? I worried. *What if she can't get out?*

I had a quick thought of running to Kelly's for takeout and coming back to heave one of the bags into my love's prison. It'd be like an indoor picnic, wouldn't it? That's romantic, right? But as she approached, her form wavered and flattened as she shifted back into smoke. Her misty shape slid sideways across the circle, slipping through the air just above that foop of ash I'd completely forgotten about. She rippled into solidity once more and hooked a hand through the crook of my elbow. I shuddered with pleasure at her touch, though my skin still crawled at the cool, soft, marble feel of her, strangely weighty though so smooth and frictionless I barely felt it.

We slid through the shadowy crowd that was left of the Inquisition, all of them babbling and singsonging and weeping like brokenhearted children, and slipped, arm in arm, into the night.

That was a week ago, and none of the Inquisition members will return my calls, though I've left countless voicemails on dozens of phones. They're all angry, I can tell, because The Emissary and I have become what my mom would have called *an item.* We went to Kelly's that night—watching her eat a roast beef sandwich and a double cheeseburger at the same time was quite a treat—and closed the place. The next night, we closed Mooncusser. The next, the Sail Loft. Seven restaurants in seven nights. Mainly because when I've tried to bring her back—she really did enjoy Kelly's—it seems the places we've closed have *stayed* closed. All of them. I've always asked why, but only gotten an answer from the woman who answered the phone at James Hook. She was snuffling and crying so hard I could barely understand her, but what I *think* she said was the whole staff had gone mad.

I asked Em about it, and she suggested it might have been all those people seeing her as she really is driving them over the edge.

"But babe," I said. "Don't *I* see you as you are?"

"*Yes,*" she said. "*Where would you like to go tonight?*"

I think there has to be more to it than that. I mean, *I* see her all the time, and I'm just as sane as sane can be. Besides, that whole *spreading madness wherever we go* thing, that doesn't sound like my Em. That's more the purview of her boss, Nyarlathotep, the God of a Thousand Forms, and I . . . I . . .

Hey! Wait a minute!

When asked what he does, **Rob Smales** tends to answer, "I write words." When feeling particularly full of himself, he may go so far as "I write the words that occur to me at the time." Groupings of these words, referred to as stories, have appeared in nearly four dozen publications and anthologies, been nominated for three Pushcart Prizes, won a couple of readers' choice awards, and appeared three times in Ellen Datlow's honorable mentions list regarding her Best Horror Of the Year anthologies.

His most recent stories have appeared in *Wicked Sick: An Anthology of the New England Horror Writers* and *Strangely Funny X* (Mystery and Horror, LLC), plus a pair of novellas in 2023, *LaundryLegs* (Weird House Press) and *Spearfinger*. He hails from Salem, Massachusetts, where he works, writes, and, occasionally, sleeps.

Mother's Blessings

Ngo Binh Anh Khoa

I.

My nerves can't possibly be further strained
As I clutch my belovèd's limb when he,
As promised, takes me to his home to see
His Mother, whom he worships, and obtain
Her blessings for our union. How I dread
This meeting; my mind's filled with what-ifs and
Scenarios where I shame myself. My hand
Grows sweatier as fear festers in my head
While I'm led through a forest out of town,
Where gnarly trees cast shifting shadows on
The treacherous ground, and each footfall upon
The crackling dead leaves echoes all around
Amid the sounds of hidden beasts. My heart
Speeds up as my composure falls apart.

II.

We walk for thirty more minutes until
We reach his Mother's place, a massive cave,
Whose entrance is a maw, abyssal, grave,
The sight of which makes me grow tense and ill.
"You'll be fine," says my belovèd as he
Holds my hand tightly as we onward go;
His steadfast grip assures me. I don't know
How this will play out, but I know that we
Will be in this together till the end;
Thus, with a calming breath, I forward tread
Through this maze where the shade looms overhead,

125

Mother's Blessings

Whose yawning pathways stretch and twist and bend,
But my belovèd never once slows down,
And for the cave's heart we are steadily bound.

III.

I stare, wide-eyed, unable to believe
What my own eyes are feeding my stunned brain;
It's like I've entered a new, eldritch plane
Not meant for outsiders to thus perceive.
Most foreign and bewildering is the view:
This space beneath the Earth is vast, where Time
Appears to stop, and each part's drenched in slime
That reeks and glows with a harsh, alien hue.
Though large, there's no free spot within this place,
For there are younglings running everywhere,
Whose shrill and disconcerting cries would blare
Incessantly in this chaotic space.
And there she stands, from whom all lives are sprung:
Shub-Niggurath, Mother of a Thousand Young.

IV.

I've heard of her from my belovèd's tales
So many times before, but now that I
Behold her with my bulging eyes, a cry
Bursts through my gaping mouth as my skin pales.
Her figure towers over everything,
And her relentless tentacles wrangle any
Unruly child that disobeys her. Many
Have tried, including my belovèd's kin,
Who were all punished with a long timeout
Inside her stomach. Most of them grew tamed
And changed their ways whereas the rest were maimed
Into oblivion by her acid. Out
Of terror, my whole being then goes numb
The moment she sees us and nearer comes.

V.

Her countless mouths, in concert, open wide,
From which a singular scream tears through the place.
Reality glitches in the silenced space;
Her will is law and must not be defied.
The younglings, therefore, dare not make a sound,
And neither do I when her myriad eyes
Are trained on me and my belovèd's sights;
In unseen chains and shackles, I stand bound.

126

Ngo Binh Anh Khoa

She stares, unblinking, at our limbs entwined;
My webbed hand in his tentacle shivers, pale.
Her breaths sweep over me, each one a gale
That makes me shudder as fear drowns my mind.
But, Dagon's scales, it's too late to retreat!
I raise my head; her glacial glare I meet.

VI.

I do not know how long the quietude lasts.
I'm but a fish upon the chopping block,
Watched by the thousand eyes around me, locked
In place, awaiting judgment to be passed.
Then, suddenly, the goddess turns to my
Belovèd. Both of them begin to speak
In their own tongue, with growls and grunts and shrieks
And weird, impossible sounds both low and high.
I've tried to learn the language, but due to
The differences in physiology
Between my race and my belovèd's, we
Have learned the words I can conceive are few.
As such, I listen, understanding naught
As they converse. A fierce war's being fought!

VII.

Half of the Mother's eyes are fixed upon
Her prodigal son, the other half on me,
Which note my every movement carefully,
And then, they squint. I swear my strength is gone
In that one instant. What does that act mean?
Is she unsatisfied, or angry, or
Disgusted with my presence? Many more
Internal questions haunt me in between,
But they're still talking; louder are their voices
Which soar and ricochet around the cave.
Lord Dagon, grant me power to stay brave!
I pray amid the harsh, conflicting noises.
Then, swiftly as it came, the battle ends
When all sounds die and fragile stillness reigns.

VIII.

I hold my tongue, but only barely so;
The torturous itch to know what has been said
Makes my scales rise, and in my ringing head,
Doubt wars with hope; both in time stronger grow.
I wait till my belovèd turns his gaze

127

Toward me, his tentacles gently tightening
Around my wrist, a subtle sign that brings
Me out of doubt's cruel clutch. Upon my face,
A small smile blossoms when he stands by me
And pulls me close against his body. How
I've yearned for this, his soothing heat, and now
That I have got it, I melt blissfully.
His Mother's watching us still with her eyes
That gleam like patches of dusk-painted skies.

IX.

"She says you are a delicacy," my
Belovèd whispers in my ear as we
Sit down for dinner with him next to me;
His solemn Mother, meanwhile, looms nearby.
"And that's a high praise coming from our kind,"
He speaks, and on my quivering lips, a kiss
Is placed, one from each mouth. Great is the bliss
I feel as his soft words make me unwind.
Then, something heavy suddenly falls onto
The table, which groans under that new weight.
I, shocked and speechless, view what's on my plate
And find a youngling served up, drenched in goo!
I sit there, body frozen, my brain numb
Till instincts move me, and I yell, "Oh yum!"

X.

To say that dinner is a horror show
Is one gross understatement of all time.
Though I've seen my fair share of gruesome crimes
Across the centuries that I've lived through, no
Sight's ever filled me with such awe and fear
As this one where a family feasts upon
Their kin's fresh corpses, all cooked and served on
Plates soaked with pungent cosmic slime. How drear!
Wan is my face reflected in the eyes
Of my belovèd when he offers me
An eyeball from his plate, on which I see
His Mother pour her breast milk. Foul scents rise
And stab my nose, but I try to stay calm
And squeeze the tentacle in my trembling palm.

XI.

I swallow each bite agonizingly,
For she is watching every move I make,

Ngo Binh Anh Khoa

A test to see if I have what it takes
To integrate into her family.
I power through the smells, the taste, the sight
Of my half-finished plate. I smile and eat
And compliment her skills at cooking meat,
Which my belovèd translates with delight.
His Mother makes sounds like a bleating goat's,
Apparently satisfied with my display,
And slaps the table as her tentacles sway
And flail. "She's happy!" my belovèd notes.
I take the final bite and force it down,
And claps and laughter thunder all around.

XII.

Shub-Niggurath and her children chant and cheer
For me as my belovèd holds me close;
His calming, musky scent then fills my nose
As I suppress my bile. His voice I hear,
"Well done, my dear!" His words soar through the screams,
And pride unbridled blossoms in my heart;
Long is our hug, and when we come apart,
I still feel like I'm floating in a dream.
A heavy tentacle nudges me, and I
Look up to meet his Mother's steady gaze,
Within whose pinkish orbs I see my face
Wear one huge smile. With much relief, I sigh
While listening to her speech, a fluttering song.
"Welcome, my child!" her voice rings, clear and strong.

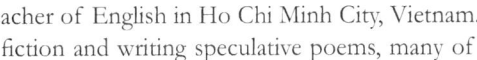

Ngo Binh Anh Khoa is a teacher of English in Ho Chi Minh City, Vietnam. In his free time, he enjoys reading fiction and writing speculative poems, many of which have appeared in *Star*Line*, *Weirdbook*, *Spectral Realms*, *Penumbric Speculative Fiction Mag*, and other venues and anthologies. He also writes haiku, some of which have received awards and honorable mentions in different contests in the US, Japan, Canada, and elsewhere.

The Gift of the Calamari

Robert Dawson

One dollar and eighty-seven cents. That was all. And sixty cents of it was in pennies.
—O. Henry, "The Gift of the Magi"

Della looked at her little hoard once more. Sixty pennies. Nine silver dimes, six nickels, and . . . what? She picked out the offending disc, tarnished and strangely heavy, for a closer examination. *Seven* cents?

She turned it over. Whose head was *that*? Not Liberty, or even President Taft, not with all those writhing snake-things and that horrible smile. Della quickly shifted her attention to the tiny letters around the edge. Whatever they said, it wasn't English or Italian. French, perhaps? Some jerk must have given her a Canadian nickel in her change. And how, for crying out loud, how was she meant to buy a Christmas present for her Jim with *that*?

There was nothing to say but "Aw, nuts!" So Della said it. Twice. And a third time, to show that she really meant it.

The air in front of her shuddered like jelly, and a Thing materialized. It was clearly unaccustomed to small New York apartments: its head brushed the ceiling, leaving slimy spots on the cracked plaster. Was this the figure on the coin? It was just as ugly, and equally well equipped with tentacles, like one of those calamari things Nonna used to fry. It slouched against the mantelpiece, dripping onto the rug, and gave off a faint aroma of spoiled fish.

"You have summoned the immortal Aunutz, puny mortal," said the Thing, in a squelching, bubbling voice like stepping in wet seaweed.

"Well, I didn't mean to. Skedaddle, ya creep!"

"From my sunken palace beneath the polar ice, you have summoned me."

"Oh, is that why you're dripping on my rug?" She softened her voice. "Well, mister, I'm sorry your palace sank, but you can't stay here. This here's a respectable apartment building, and the superintendent won't even let us have a cat."

"You have summoned me, mortal. You may have one wish—if you dare to ask for it."

Yes sir! A wish! That was more like it! Della gave an excited little squeal and tried to explain, all in one breath, about Jim, and the hoarded coins, and the necessity of finding a suitably magnificent Christmas present, and the complete impossibility of doing it for so little.

The Calamari-Thing listened. As Della finished, it gave a twitch that could have been a nod. It extended a tentacle and traced a complex figure in the air, trailing a sickly pale light.

When the eldritch sigil was complete, the Thing shimmered and disappeared. Della blinked. Had she been dreaming? The puddle on the carpet, and a lingering smell of seaweed and old sardines, suggested that she hadn't.

For a minute she stood silent, her pounding heart almost drowning out the faint clatter of horseshoes on the cobbles four stories below. Eventually, like timid petals unfolding, her fingers opened. She peeped at the coins, but they had not multiplied. In fact—oh, *hell*! The strange coin had vanished! *One dollar and eighty cents* . . . Muttering under her breath, Della opened a window, then settled down to chopping the onions for the corned-beef hash, vowing to dig up Nonna's recipe and cook calamari the next time she saw some at the fishmonger's.

Six o'clock passed, and Jim hadn't returned from his bookkeeping job. At first, Della assumed he had stopped at Kelly's Tavern to celebrate some friend's birthday. She covered the hash to keep it warm and spent a satisfying five minutes rehearsing the mild scolding he would get for not letting her know ahead of time; but as the hour hand crept further and further around the clock face, she realized it was nothing so simple.

Just before midnight, she ate a very small half of the hash, and went to sleep alone, her mind full of fears.

At daybreak, she walked eleven blocks to the police station in the rain. A desk sergeant with a kindly face and a soft Irish voice took notes, while the matron plied her with fresh handkerchiefs. But it did no good.

After a week they dragged the river; but no trace of Jim was ever found. Della's Christmas shopping problem was solved.

Everywhere, they are the wisest. The wisest—and the most cruel.

They are the Elder Gods.

Robert Dawson teaches mathematics at a Nova Scotian university. His work, including both science fiction and fantasy, has appeared in the *Nature* Futures column, *The Year's Best Military and Adventure SF* (Baen), and numerous other periodicals and anthologies. He is an alumnus of the Sage Hill and Viable Paradise writing workshops.

In his spare time, he volunteers with a Scout troop. He believes the world needs more bicycles.

The Birthday Party with a Thousand Young

Andrew Leon Hudson

After rolling past what must have been the visiting vehicles of every family in the entire suburb, the Jamisons pulled up outside just the biggest house imaginable.

"On a teacher's salary," said Mike, "are you kidding?" He shook his head in disbelief. Mansion barely covered it. Ziggurat might. "Who'd they have to sacrifice to land that pile?"

"I hear they need the space," said Faye. "And it's two teachers, honey."

"Sure, and I'll bet those dollars really add up." He squinted along the endless rows of cars without optimism. "Are we gonna know anyone?"

"Well, *I* don't, not yet, but when the school year starts I expect I'll know everybody. And who knows who has kids at the company, you tell me."

"Our department chief might. He said they'll be here, anyway, so . . ." Mike sighed. "Why don't you guys go ahead while I find somewhere to park? Maybe I'll be able to join you before the beer is all gone."

Faye kissed his cheek. "I'll hold on to the last one for you. And since you're such a lightweight, I'll even drive us home."

"Thanks, babe." He cast a happy glance at his wife's fine rear as she got out and opened the back door. He twisted in his seat to give Mike Junior a big thumbs up. "Now, you go have fun, kiddo. And woo haf vun, too," he told Janey, tickling her belly with wavering fingers.

"Thanks, Dad," Mikey lisped through his giant top-row gap, scooting onto the sidewalk. Janey gurgled as Faye prized her from the booster seat, instinctively groping for a boob.

Faye bumped the door shut with her butt and leaned down to the passenger-side window to give Mike a view of her goods, and an arched eyebrow. "Don't take too long. Just in case—"

"—they're all freaks," he finished. "I know. Don't worry."

He watched Faye start up the artfully crooked path that wound its way across a flawless sea of millimeter-precise grass, Mikey at her side, Janey propped against her hip. Beyond, the house rose like some mystical, angular island, spreading across the landscape, the neighboring plots fading to insignificance, his family dwarfed before it.

What kind of square footage does that *monster have?* he wondered as he pulled away.

←♥→←♥→←♥→

The door—one of those towering affairs that always seemed to Faye at least six feet taller than was strictly necessary—swung open to reveal a veritable domestic goddess: brilliant smile, perfect hair, comfortable heels, and a dress right out of the fifties.

And that bosom—Faye was simultaneously glad Mike wasn't there to swallow his tongue and fraught at the thought of whether Mikey's eyes might be bugging out of his skull. She didn't dare check.

"You must be Faye," the vision said, "it's wonderful to meet you, do come in!"

Faye blinked, her mind suddenly blank. "Thank you . . ." *God, what's their name again?*

The nameless hostess turned her attention to Mikey. "And who's this handsome youth?"

"Michael, ma'am," he said on politeness autopilot, and Faye relaxed a fraction.

"Well, it's a pleasure to meet you, Michael. Why don't you run through to the garden where the kids your age are playing? We girls can go meet the other crowd." She waved them inside, and Mikey charged toward a spectacular kitchen.

Faye hitched Janey up and entered, admiring the glorious hallway. Its ceilings were so high the corners seemed eager to meet in the middle.

"I'm afraid I don't—" *remember your name*, she began to say, then courage failed her. "You have a beautiful home," she finished lamely, feeling a little dizzy.

The lady of the house twinkled. "Oh, you're sweet—but not as sweet as *this* one!" She popped Janey on the nose with an elegant finger. The baby goggled. "Can I get you a drink? G&T, perhaps? My man's quite the connoisseur, we've got all the brands."

Faye shook her head ruefully. "I'd love to say yes, but I'm still serving drinks for Janey here."

"I know how you feel. Maybe just a virgin, then. He swears by Miska Tonic." She opened a door and led the way through.

"You'll think I'm awful," Faye started again, bracing herself to accept the uncomfortable duty of asking her hostess's name, "but I've completely forgotten—"

She stopped, frozen in the doorway.

Wall-to-wall babies, all of them staring back at her in silence.

"Oh, my God."

"Don't panic, they aren't *all* mine!" The hostess smiled wistfully. "Well, maybe I think of them that way, but I'm just looking after them while everyone takes a break." She scooped up the nearest, a darling little boy in blue shorts with some kind of cartoon squid smiling on his T-shirt, held him up and nuzzled his belly. "I just love kids to pieces."

"I simply don't know how you cope," Faye said, pulling Janey a little closer.

"Comes with the teaching territory, or it does for me at least. Yes, some of the

The Birthday Party with a Thousand Young

Old Ones act as if kids are an inconvenience to fight with or ignore, but that's never going to happen to me!" The baby boy rumbled, and she cocked a knowing eyebrow. "Uh-oh, someone's hungry. Up you come." She hefted him into the crook of her arm and, without warning, unleashed a full breast from the plunge of her blouse and directed the teat into his gaping mouth.

"You don't mind, do you?" she asked as the little boy went to work.

"Er, no," Faye answered, "no, not at all," though she felt vaguely flustered by the unexpected move.

"Some people, you know? And it's perfectly natural. *Super*-natural, even. I've always got more in the tank than they can manage in one sitting."

Faye could believe it: the suckling baby was almost spread-eagled on the mighty boob, like a tiny lizard basking on a sea-smoothed boulder. She caught herself staring and glanced away.

All the other babies gazed at her. Quiet and still, in the warm, warm room.

She turned back to the feeding, bouncing Janey, feeling lightheaded.

"Don't be shy," the hostess chuckled, "we're all mothers together."

Faye was suddenly reassured, relaxed, even a little sleepy in the muggy atmosphere. This time, when the woman disengaged the boy from one side of her mighty chest and swung him to the other, Faye didn't look away and was rewarded with a big, blue-eyed stare.

"Pfuh," he said. "Nuglooie."

"What's that, sweetie?" asked Faye with an uncertain beam. "What's that, then?"

"Muglewuh narfuh." His chubby little fingers clutched the giant, spongy breast.

Faye chucked him under the chin, and he drooled milkily on her fingers. "He's a chatty one, isn't he?" She desperately wiped her fingers against her jeans, then blushed at her rudeness.

The hostess waved a dismissive hand. "Don't worry, when you've got this many or more to deal with, you get used to a bit of cleaning up, believe me. As for *chatty*, that's nothing; just wait until he gets started. He's always going on about his big brother, Cuthbert the birthday boy."

"That's such an unusual name these days." Faye frowned to herself like a drunk who lost the keys to her apartment.

"We try to keep the old traditions alive."

"Cuth oolhoo!" blurted the baby.

"See what I mean? There'll be no stopping him now."

"Cuth oolhoo, rurl yeh," said the baby. "Wagar nagle."

"*Wagar nagle*," repeated Janey, emphatically, and Faye stared at her daughter in dreamy surprise as the boy turned his attention back to the breast.

How about that? said the hostess's expression. "First words, do you think?" she asked—then Janey shifted in her diaper and made a sound that could only be rendered as *fhtagn*. Faye blushed brighter, but the woman laughed like a hyena.

"I'd better change her." Faye wondered where Mike was with the baby bag.

"*I* could change her for you," said her hostess. "I could change her completely." *That would make things so much easier.* ". . . would that be okay?"

134

"Of course." The hostess gave her a rosy smile. "I could feed her, in fact."

Faye frowned again, not sure if she'd heard right. ". . . what?"

"Feed her!" She laughed. "This little guy's almost done. More than enough to go around."

". . . yeah, I noticed." *Was that rude?*

If it was, the woman didn't seem offended. "Let me take her off your hands."

". . . okay." Faye watched herself handing Janey over almost as though in a trance. The hostess deftly accepted her one-handed, held her up to the unoccupied nipple, and Janey latched onto it with a ready enthusiasm, nestling in.

". . . thanks," Faye mumbled.

"It's my pleasure." The little boy had fallen asleep, and the hostess unplugged him from her breast and laid him down on the thick rug without disturbing Janey in the slightest. "And *hey*," she said as she straightened, "since little Janey is taken care of, *you* could have a drink after all!"

". . . yeah, I guess so," said Faye.

The abandoned breast jutted invitingly forward.

When he got back from parking the car, Mike wandered into the enormous yard from the side of the house, keeping a low profile as he took the opportunity to check out how these Joneses were doing for themselves.

Was it the Joneses? he wondered. Faye would know. Three months in this new neighborhood and he still couldn't keep all the names straight.

Up close, the house was impressive as hell, but God only knows how a realtor would describe it. Having "personality" wasn't the word, unless prefixed by "overbearing." Had the look of a home-improvement job to Mike's eye—not that it wasn't flawless work, but there was an odd shape to it he couldn't put his finger on. How could so many straight lines feel so . . . bendy?

He checked out the yard instead. A nice slice of land: good-sized pool and trees down at the boundary, waving gently in a breeze that didn't seem to reach the decking here at the house. And in between, acres of grass for the kids—and right now they were playing follow-the-leader or something like it, a long snake of little bodies each mimicking the one in front, a procession of jittery, lurching steps that would put John Cleese to shame.

Mikey danced and stomped at the back of the conga, fitting in like a champ. Just how many kids were there? He lost count as they wove around. *Almost looks tribal,* he thought, before his guilt resurfaced to absorb a dose of the white middle-class, and he internally reprimanded himself.

"Well now," said a rich, friendly voice, "if it isn't Mike Jamison. Fancy seeing you here."

Mike's new boss, Robert Roanoke, stood with a tall, thin figure beside a smoking barbeque and a dew-beaded cooler, an icy-green bottle of beer in one hand. Mike approached, cursing the awkwardness of uncertain social strata. "Afternoon, er, Robert."

"Robert, hell, it's Bob. Let me introduce you to our host."

The garden chef raised his tongs in greeting, a wide smile on his face.

The Birthday Party with a Thousand Young

Mike held out a hand to shake while he waited for that introduction, but big affable Bob seemed to falter. "Oh hey, you look like you need a beer!" Bob fairly lunged at the cooler, leaving the job half-done.

"Pleasure to have you here, Mike," said the chef. "Make yourself at home."

"Good of you to have us over."

"Not at all! My wife would have my hide if she thought she'd let someone's kids slip through the net!"

"Here you go, Mike." Bob handed him a beer, and the three men tapped bottles.

Mike swigged his beer and gazed over the garden. The kids had moved on to a stone-cold classic, *Statues*. Mikey was "it," standing by the wall of the house with his face in his hands, back to the slowly approaching crowd.

The kids had their hands up like chubby talons, the tykes. "Turn around once in a while, Mikey," he called, "don't make it too easy for 'em!" but Mikey just shook his head. *Ah well, gotta learn sometime.*

"So," he said to the menfolk, "which of those little monsters is the birthday boy?"

"None of that pack," the chef said with a grin. "Check the pool."

It didn't look like anyone was using it, but Mike wandered closer. He was just about to say as much when he spotted the form lying motionless at the bottom of the pool.

"Jesus—" Mike set down his bottle, hurriedly treading off his shoes.

The chef's smile never faltered. "Nothing to worry about," he called. "He does that all the time. Can't get him out of there. I'm serious."

Mike hesitated, but the kid's dad seemed just as chipper as can be, with enough teeth on display to make a dentist nervous. "You sure he's okay?"

"Positive. The boy couldn't be happier." He sucked on his beer, smiling still, and somehow didn't spill a drop. "He likes to give us a scare, pretend he's 'sleeping beneath the waves' as he puts it."

Mike peered doubtfully through the ripples. "He's been down there a while."

The chef smirked. "He'll rise when his time comes, don't you worry about that."

"And speak of the devil," announced Bob, "er, so to speak."

They turned to the house, where a chorus of *oohs* and *aahs* heralded the appearance of—Mike assumed—their hostess. She stepped onto the deck by the kitchen, smiling radiantly, with a wide serving tray held up before (he was distractedly glad Faye wasn't there to scowl at him for noticing) an utterly phenomenal pair of tits. A mountainous cake balanced on top (*of the tray*, though either could have borne the burden), an impossible concoction of angles and peaks, and chocolate on top of chocolate, so dark the eye fell into it.

The adults, standing scattered around the garden, applauded as childish voices started to sing the inevitable song.

And, behind them, he whose day it was finally emerged, wet and glistening, from the depths.

←♥→←♥→←♥→

At the end of the evening, the partygoers went their separate ways, promising their hosts they'd all return the next year to do it again. The Jamisons headed back to their

Andrew Leon Hudson

car alongside Bob and his wife, Cindy, the gals chatting away while the guys brought up the rear.

"Don't get me wrong," said Bob, more quietly as the ladies drew ahead, "it just struck me as a little weird they'd invite childless couples to their kid's birthday."

Mike shrugged. "I guess it says a lot for the sense of community. And, kids or not, you've got to admit they threw quite a party."

"You said it," said Bob. "Good thing I don't have to get behind the wheel, that's for sure."

Mike faked a drunken veer, and they both chuckled. "Never let it be claimed that a wife is worthless."

"As long as she has a driving license—" Bob gave Mike a cheeky look "—or a figure like Faye's. You lucky dog. Swinging party next time, you feel me?"

"Watch it, boss!" Mike said, feeling both cocky and flattered.

Bob slapped him on the shoulder. "Had to be worth a try." They walked on in companionable silence, but after a moment he grunted reflectively. "It's a different life, right?"

Mike tore his gaze from Faye's seductive sway. "What's that?"

"Being in a family way, you know. Never really gave it much thought, myself, but you see the way those folks are, with that big crazy brood of theirs . . ."

Mike gave a little laugh. "Make you think about starting your own?"

Bob looked puzzled but pleased at the thought. "I dunno. Maybe."

They reached the Roanokes' ride first, went their separate ways with handshakes and hugs and a promise to get together for a regular drink sometime, and then the Jamisons strolled on, hands gradually a-wandering as the darkness drew in and they found themselves in the quiet, sparsely lit area where he'd managed to find a parking space.

When they arrived at the car, theirs was the only one still parked. Mike pushed Faye against the trunk for a breathy kiss, beeped the remote blindly, and then yanked the door to the back seat open. "Get in there, you," he snarled, and she complied with a giggle.

"Ouch!" she yelped as he crawled in on top, and Mike reached past their heads to pull a bulky obstruction out of the way. As he tossed it on the sidewalk, it caught in the streetlight glow—*one of those baby seats?* He shook his head. Faye must have put it there as a joke. Weird way to drop the hint, but . . .

"Great minds think alike," he said, as she fumbled for his zipper. "Let's make us a little Mike Junior, honey."

"Or maybe a Jane," Faye breathed in his ear. "I've always liked that name."

Andrew Leon Hudson is a technical writer by day, and is technically a writer by night as well. He lives in Barcelona, Spain, which he recommends as an ideal place to wait for the world to end. His short fiction has appeared in zines including *Metaphorosis Magazine*, *Cossmass Infinities*, *Little Blue Marble*, and *Dark Matter Magazine*, as well as anthologies such as Parsec Ink's *Triangulation: Dark Skies* and *Dark Matter Presents Monster Lairs: A Dark Fantasy*

The Birthday Party with a Thousand Young

Horror Anthology (Dark Matter Ink).

He is coauthor of *Archipelago*, an alternate history naval adventure serial now available in book form, but his first solo novel sank without a trace so now he's very slowly working on another. He is also the editor of *Mythaxis Magazine*, a free-to-read genre zine that lives at mythaxis.co.uk. His presence on social media brings to mind the concept of negative space, since it is more often the space around his posts that is interesting or artistically relevant. He owns books, plus a gorgeous painting of a robot in love, and he loves it back. Anything else you've heard about him is speculation at best.

Hearts Synchronize

M. Stern

Studies continue to show that when people fall in love—love in the most spontaneous, instantaneous, intangible, inexplicable sense—their hearts physically synchronize when in close proximity, giving biometric confirmation to what had been previously presumed metaphorical. Greg Beaman saw these findings as representing the closest thing to applied metaphysics humanity had discovered thus far. Written right there into the script of the universe was *love*. Not other states often mistaken for love or treated as its synonyms. Not a safe harbor from the abyss of isolation. Not the practical decision to cohabitate and split rent. Not the excitement of a wedding, or the subsequent thrill of being gifted a lifetime's worth of kitchen accessories. Not even the well-satiated reproductive impulse. No, those things are all great, but they won't sync up two hearts. Because beneath your ribs sits a Rosetta Stone to decode the mysterious language of matching souls, a poetic thread woven as firmly into humankind's infrastructure as pi is to architecture.

"Hearts!" Greg said, charging into the house through the front door. "Hearts synchronize!"

He sprinted through the living room, around the corner, and down the stairs. In the living room, his roommate Dean Binski sat on the couch while Camilla Edmonds sat in the bucket chair. The downstairs bathroom door slammed.

"What was that all about?" Camilla asked.

"He's got a thing for the girl from Caffeinerati," said Greg's second roommate, Adam Witz, emerging from the kitchen. "It's inspired this new spiel about hearts. Every Taco Tuesday, he drinks a bunch of two-dollar Miller Lites and runs around yelling about it."

"Which girl?"

"The one with the haircut," Adam said.

Camilla thought. "Wait, *that* girl?"

Water ran through the pipes, shoes stomped back up the stairs.

"Where you going, Beaman?" Adam said. "We made a gravity bong in the sink!"

Hearts Synchronize

"Can't," Greg said, spiraling back out the front door. "I'm going to Caffeinerati. I'm on a mission."

←♥→←♥→←♥→

A half hour later, the three sat around a pizza, eating with a certain blurred focus.

"Where's Greg?" said Camilla.

"He went to see the chick with the haircut, remember?"

"Oh yeah."

After a long pause, Camilla said, "I don't think that's good—"

←♥→←♥→←♥→

Greg walked into the glistening spring night, off to see Carla.

He first saw Carla at Caffeinerati while sending resumes to temp agencies from his half-broken laptop. She looked like Simone Simon. Try as he might, he could not stop catching her eye and looking away. He got self-conscious about seeming fixated and relocated to a seat facing the wall, only to find that it was impossible to avoid seeing her in the wall's decorative mirrors. Seeing her reflection stocking some napkins, he thought she noticed him again. He glanced down quickly.

Looking in the mirror once more, he saw her approaching. He turned and began apologizing.

"You left your bag over there," she said. "I didn't want it to get stolen."

"Thanks, yes, that'd be bad." Greg stood to collect his laptop bag. Bag safely in hand, he said, "Has anyone ever told you that you look like Simone Simon?"

"Sure," she said. "Well, no, actually, who's that?"

"An actress. She was in *Cat People*."

"I haven't seen that one," she said. "But I have two cats!"

"Cosmic," Greg said softly.

"That's what my fish is named!"

"I'll be," Greg said. "What about your cats?"

"Their names are Marla and Darla. And I'm Carla."

"Nice to meet you, Carla. That's like something from a Haruki Murakami novel, those names, those cats."

"I've never read him."

"He's a cat person," Greg said.

"Was he in the movie?"

They locked eyes, smiling on exactly the same dreamy frequency. Carla walked backward, stumbled, spun and scanned the floor for whatever invisible thing had tripped her, saw a customer waiting impatiently and dashed behind the counter.

Over the following weeks, Greg visited the shop more frequently, standing there chatting with her. Carla started giving him the employee discount.

Discount notwithstanding, Greg had a rule about falling for women in the service sector. It was their job to be friendly, so developing romantic inclinations based on interaction at their workplace was a category error. Only if she was friendly elsewhere, say at a party, could he possibly have a shot.

It happened the weekend before he started at a new temp job.

Greg went to a party with a few acquaintances from the bar at last call. After an hour of drunken small talk with strangers, he realized those guys were gone, and he knew no one else. He was studying the bookshelf when he heard a commotion in the backyard.

"She's in a tree!" someone yelled.

"Anybody know her?"

Greg walked out to investigate.

From the back porch, he saw a cluster of tall trees. Carla was in one, about fifteen feet off the ground, crawling between branches with impressive dexterity.

"Come down!" yelled a woman in a small group near the tree. "They're calling the cops!"

"You're jealous!" Carla yelled. "Y'all don't have my climbing skills!"

"Yo—seriously, who knows this girl?" someone yelled from the porch. "Get her out of here!"

"I'm moving into this tree!" Carla yelled. "Cowards!"

Greg walked under her. He cupped his hands and shouted, "Hey Carla, it's Greg! I'm really impressed by your—"

"Hi, cat person!" She looked down and waved enthusiastically before she lost her grip and plummeted.

"Oh no," Greg said. His arms were out. Her weight dropped into them. He stumbled and thudded gently to the ground with her on top.

There was applause and whistling. Carla rolled off him and stared up at the tree, then at him, and said, "Don't feel good."

He pulled her over to a distant bush and looked away as she vomited loudly. He realized at some point that he was holding her hand.

"Y'okay?" he said after a while, hearing only teary sniffles and spitting.

"Uh-huh, barfed."

"I know. Do you know anyone at this party?"

She turned to him and nodded.

"Who?"

She pointed at him.

"Anyone else?"

She nodded.

"Who?"

She thought for a moment, glanced over his shoulder at the house, then back at him. She shook her head.

"We've gotta get you home," he said.

She shook her head again.

"No?" he said.

"Can't."

"Why not?"

"Keys."

"You lost your keys?"

She nodded.

Greg sighed.

"Do you have anywhere you can stay?"

She nodded.

Hearts Synchronize

"Where?"

She shook her head.

"Want to stay at my place? That guy over there is gonna make us leave soon."

She nodded.

Soberer of the two but nowhere near sober, he led her hand in hand down the silent street. They got to his place and he showed her the bathroom, went into his bedroom across from it, left his door open, and tried to read words in a book on which he could not focus. She eventually left the bathroom and came into his room.

He said, "There's a couch upstairs, I can—"

Carla turned her back and casually began undressing.

"Here," he said. "Put that on the floor but keep that one on."

She ended up in her T-shirt, using a pair of his boxers as pajama bottoms. Before he could say much about it, she got into bed next to him.

Greg wrapped his arms around her and she was entangled with him. Outside of a single autonomic reflex he was powerless to prevent but too exhausted to utilize, it felt beautifully, atypically chaste. A pleasant pulsation filled him like he was being directly administered a vitamin he was deficient in. He dissolved into sleep.

Carla was gone when he woke up.

A few days later, while playing on the internet on a break from doing data entry, he stumbled onto the relevant literature about hearts.

The temp job kept him from encountering her much since the party. He knew she worked Tuesday nights. After a number of Taco Tuesdays ramping up to this, he decided he had to let Carla know. What, exactly, he was not sure. He knew only that, on that night, their hearts had synchronized. Were there a cardiac monitor in his room, it would have revealed this. The data was on his side.

He walked into Caffeinerati. Inside, there were a few straggler customers finishing sandwiches and a kid mopping the floor.

He saw her.

Back near the bathrooms stood Carla. Greg's face lit up. From alcohol or from excitement, the room swirled. She was half turned away from him. He waved and walked toward her.

←♥→←♥→←♥→

"—I think she lives with her boyfriend," Camilla said to Dean and Adam. "The bassist in that band, The Muckies. *Eric Keys*."

←♥→←♥→←♥→

Greg reached Carla just as a guy came out of the bathroom, took both of her hands as he began speaking, then leaned down to kiss her. Carla turned and saw Greg and froze.

There was a second-long, pregnant silence.

Vomit exploded from Greg's mouth onto the couple in front of him.

The rest unfolded like a piece of dissonant music in a frantic time signature. A shriek from Carla, swearing from her boyfriend, a pleading *bro* from the guy mopping the floor, scraping chairs from the remaining customers, and a manager storming from the back room, his diatribe while dragging Greg to the front of the store ending with, "never come back in here *again*!"

Greg never did.

M. Stern

Running. That was how Greg had spent his days over the three-or-so months since moving into his parents' basement. Back in the suburb where he grew up, Meisner Falls, far removed geographically and culturally from the college town he left. Daily, he ran miles out into the nearby farm country. It balanced out, he figured, the copious nightly drinking. This yin and yang felt consistent with living life in limbo.

Jogging up the stairs from the guest room where he slept, run getting underway, something in the kitchen stopped him.

Before they left for Florida earlier that day, his parents had collected a comical number of empty beer, wine, and liquor bottles from his room and arranged them on the table, counter, and surrounding chairs. Reaching for a sticky note stuck in a difficult-to-reach spot, he sent bottles clattering to the floor. He read the note:

Find a job before we're back or move out.

"Can't even have a nervous breakdown in peace," Greg muttered.

The gray September sky and cool wind returned him to his comfortable sense of stasis. He was five miles into the middle of nowhere on his run, feeling energetic, and turned up a road he rarely traversed, not realizing the road was an after-work traffic thoroughfare.

The sun was setting, and Greg ran against a stream of flipped-on headlights heading toward and zipping past him.

The darker it got, the closer cars seemed to veer toward him. Growing nervous, he considered stepping down the large hill to his left into the ditch and waiting for traffic to abate. The choice was made for him at the next curve.

Two headlights jittered in his direction. A horn sounded. The lights jerked straight, but not before Greg screamed and tumbled three feet into the ditch.

Moisture soaked the back of his hooded sweatshirt. He lay there, feeling the world throb.

Scooting around in the bramble, he turned toward the farm the ditch abutted. Far off was a dilapidated barn. Leaning back, his left hand squished against something.

He looked, yowled, and scampered back.

The thing he had touched was the size of a fish one would expect to see held by a proudly grinning fisherman. Its body resembled a maggot, but the greasy white gave way to a black tentacled head. It was slightly curled in apparent death.

Without a phone to photograph it, Greg paced in the ditch, wondering what to do. He was preparing to flag down a car when he looked back at the thing.

A slit opened in the night air and sucked the creature in.

Greg got on his knees. He could not find a trace of it.

Walking back home in the dark, he tried to forget what he had—or had not—just seen.

The big bookstore in Meisner Falls had a coffee shop, and Greg sat there the following Monday afternoon, clicking through job search websites, committed to sending out one application before leaving. After two unproductive hours, he needed more coffee.

Hearts Synchronize

Looking up to assess the line, he saw, two tables away, the familiar face of Lyra Andrews—once the object of an earthmoving crush, albeit so far back he could not recall how it felt. He knew only the fact of it, that it had seemed as real as anything and at some point, dissipated.

Might as well.

He walked to her table. "Lyra?"

After a second, recognition flitted to her eyes. "Is it—Greg?"

"Yeah! We had sixth-grade science together."

"*Right.* Here, sit!"

"You still live in town, I take it?" Greg sat.

"Moved back in March," Lyra said. "Stayed here for three years after high school. Then I made some changes. Moved to California. Just earned my master's in composition, actually."

"Musical composition? What instrument do you play?"

"I build my own. It's *experimental* composition. It's hard to explain."

Greg tilted his head thoughtfully. "Like Stockhausen? John Cage? Fluxus? That kind of thing?"

Lyra's mouthed an empty syllable before smiling. "You know about it!"

Surreal. He remembered Lyra as first a cheerleader, later a bit hippieish. The type of girl tied to the suburban soil of Meisner Falls, who married a conventional guy with a conventional career. That she was now a sound artist made him think that people could always surprise you.

"Oh yeah," Greg said. "I love that whole aesthetic project, you could say. Appreciating the process as much as the output. Seeking more challenging, less obvious kinds of beauty. Rethinking what performance even *is*."

"I *never* have anyone to talk with about this."

"Cosmic," Greg said.

"That's what my new piece is called!"

"Yeah? What's the concept?"

"So, there are these cycles in nature. Complex statistical fluctuations. Ways that things—"

"Synchronize?"

"Exactly. In all sorts of ways. Raindrops falling in a field. Trees crackling in the forest. For the piece, I identify them, collect audio and video data of them, and analyze it using AI to find trends. Then, I generate tones based on the live analysis of the data, creating two separate drones from a speaker in either corner of the room. Between them sits an instrument I invented called a Resonator. It takes in the two separate sounds and finds where *they* match up and generates its own tone in response to the resonant frequencies."

"Sounds like Iannis Xenakis on steroids."

Lyra's face brightened, but before she could speak, a guy sat down. Greg recognized Kent Clay, doughier than decades earlier, sweeping in on a cloud of aftershave. Greg felt like someone had aerosolized his most Freudian nightmare and gassed him with it.

Kent said, "All good for the moment."

"Kent, this is Greg," Lyra said. "From middle school."

"High school, too," Greg said.

"Oh, right!" Kent said. "Always nice to see an old classmate! Good to see you again, buddy!"

A glad-handing slickness had replaced the doofy aggression Greg remembered, as if the stereotypical jock was the larval form of the stereotypical used car salesman.

Kent scooted closer to Lyra.

"What's on the agenda today?" Lyra asked Kent, suddenly tense.

Kent casually slung his arm around her. "Found a cement vendor I'm meeting with—there's the guy!" Kent stood, gave Lyra a long look, patted her on the shoulder, and darted off.

"How long have you two been together?" Greg said.

"We're not. I mean, we were a long time ago. We got married right after high school. We're divorced."

"Wow," Greg said. "You're still really affectionate?"

"Meh. Our families are old friends. He's around, whether I like it or not. So, are you in town visiting?"

"No, I'm back for a while. I'm—uh—between things. Looking for work."

"What sort of job do you want?"

"Ideally, I'd like a job discussing experimental composition."

"Now hiring," Lyra said, smiling.

He felt a flutter in his chest.

←♥→←♥→←♥→

It was dark when Greg arrived at Lyra's house, out in the woods, a few days later. She answered the door, and Greg found that whatever it is women do to make themselves smell like vanilla, Lyra was doing it. He noticed it when he caught her surprisingly long-lasting hug.

"Where's this instrument I'm supposed to see?"

"Dinner, then music." She floated from the hug and led him by the hand.

Greg nearly stumbled at the dining room's ambiance, at its dim lighting, candles, and multiple other features fancier than his presence had ever merited.

"Did you mistake me for someone important?" Greg sat down as Lyra went to the kitchen.

Lyra returned with a bottle of wine into which she was screwing a corkscrew. "You're from Meisner Falls. How often do you think I find someone who wants to discuss Xenakis? This is a special occasion."

The cork came out with a *pop*.

"I doubt I'm moving soon. We can discuss New Music any time," Greg said.

"Then we'll have more special occasions." She filled his glass.

←♥→←♥→←♥→

Everything seemed fun. Greg was enveloped in a kind of easy enjoyment and starry drunkenness he had forgotten existed.

Lyra opened the third bottle of red, pouring with no apparent intent to stop. "More? More?"

"Glass ain't getting any bigger!" Greg said, funnily exasperated.

Hearts Synchronize

She honked a laugh, pulling back the bottle just as the glass filled to the absolute top. "Watch." She lowered her head and slurped at the surface tension. "That trick takes a great deal of skill."

"Color me impressed."

"*Color*," Lyra said, affecting gravity. "Wait, do I have wine teeth?" She bent toward him and made an exaggerated grimace.

"Fine so far," Greg said.

"Let me check you," she said. "Here, scoot it out."

Greg slid his chair back. She crouched near his face, again grimacing and vocalizing an *ah* through clenched teeth. Greg mirrored her expression and sound.

She moved her face and her index finger closer and scrutinized. "Nice enamel."

"*Thnnk nyh*," he responded.

"You might be developing a clinical case of wine teeth tonight, though. Right—there." She ran the tip of her index finger down the front of his tooth.

Greg's heart was thundering.

"This is a serious condition. Don't move. We're going to have to operate." She lowered her face to his, stuck out her tongue, and gently licked the tooth. Then she drew her head back.

"How'd the op—" Greg managed before her mouth returned to his, tongue pressed far into his mouth, her body orchestrated like an *r* that she seamlessly transposed into an *L*, sliding into his lap.

They continued in a slow, hungry exploration, tugging at and working around obstructive clothing but too caught in the moment to pause, move, and remove it.

Something slapped against the window. Greg pulled his hand back as if chastised. Lyra reached for that hand and placed it over one breast.

"Wait," Greg said. "What was that?" He shuffled her off and approached the window.

"Probably just a bat," she said.

"Do bats leave slime on windows?" Greg observed a viscous, black blotch.

The distant darkness was impenetrable, but closer to the house, the porch light illuminated the ground from an angle. Greg looked down. Panic seized him.

There lay one of those squid-maggot things, tentacles damaged. He reached for Lyra. "Those *things*. I've seen one before."

"What?" Lyra asked.

"Down there! It's some sort of—bug, or mollusk. See?"

Lyra craned to see where he had been looking. "I don't see anything."

He looked down again, face pressed to the window. "It's—it's gone," he whispered. Greg stepped back. "I'm sorry. I'm afraid I'm going crazy."

"Come on," she said. "Moving home is stressful. Stress does weird things to people."

She put her hand to his face and said, conciliatory, with feigned shyness, "Would it make you feel better if we went upstairs? I'll show you my Resonator."

←♥→←♥→←♥→

Greg awoke in Lyra's bed feeling great, unconcerned that he never got a musical performance. He got up and encountered a handwritten note.

Had to run out for the day, text you later!

There was a heart doodled beneath the message, next to a cartoon approximation of the portion of him with which she had newly become acquainted. He got dressed, grinning, and pocketed the note.

His smile fell as he looked out the window. He was looking at the dilapidated barn he saw the other night, only from the opposite side.

Something told him to investigate.

Outside, he located a crack in the barn's facade, got on his tiptoes, and peered through it.

He saw eight of the squid-maggots, squirming in piles of goo and shattered, black shells. And in the center, Kent, butt naked.

Greg fell backward, stifling a scream, scrambled to his car, and sped off.

←♥→←♥→←♥→

When he got Lyra's text the next afternoon, he was vacillating between questioning his own sanity and Kent's, and needed time to think. After texting a few flirtatious pleasantries back and forth, he texted:

I'm going out of town to visit my grandmother for two weeks.

The deception proved stressful, distracting him almost entirely from his job search. Greg felt compelled to text Lyra casually throughout his fake vacation, concocting stories to flesh it out. He kept introducing new plot twists to make it feel more realistic, forcing him to keep a list to be consistent. Moreover, he was terrified of running into her somewhere, and so confined himself to his parents' house, ordering food for delivery and neither jogging nor running errands.

At the two-week mark, he was feeling a taxing social starvation. He wanted to be surrounded by people. The moment he had that thought, the television informed him that the Thanksgiving Pilgrim Parade was the following day.

It promised a quaint scene he normally hated, but offered plenty of people— and one last day distracted from more pressing matters.

←♥→←♥→←♥→

The next afternoon, traffic was backed up behind an overturned cement truck near the parade's entrance, but Greg still reached the event quickly. He parked and walked down the town's main drag, passing parking lots decorated with seasonal signage and inflatable turkeys. Couples and kids milled around wearing paper pilgrim hats, eating themed snacks.

He reached a parking lot where a news van was setting up near some bleachers. Two authoritative, if bored-looking, police officers stood nearby.

Greg gasped. He saw, in the distance, a squid-maggot wiggle across the concrete blindingly fast and disappear into a bush.

"Did you see that?" Greg asked two cameramen, mid-discussion, near the van. They did not acknowledge him.

He said, louder, "Did you see that—uh—animal by the bleachers?"

"Excuse me?" said one cameraman.

A ruddy-faced man in a beige sport coat Greg recognized as local news personality Tim Penske arrived, drawing the men's attention. "We're going to get rollin' here, soon as Sandy—" he began, then turned to Greg and said, "Can I help you?"

Hearts Synchronize

"I'm just—" At that moment, in the distance, Greg saw another squid-maggot zip by. "Oh God, I think there's something strange happening here."

"Uh-*huh*," said the newscaster.

One cameraman, meanwhile, had left and now returned with a police officer. "Seems to be the problem?" asked the officer.

"I'm glad you're here," Greg said. "There are these—animals. I've been seeing them lately. They're really fast, and when they die, they disappear. I just saw two."

"Son, what've you been taking this afternoon?" said the officer. He gestured to his partner a few feet away.

"*Taking?* You don't understand—"

"Let's discuss this by my car, so these gentlemen can—" The cop got a strange look on his face. "*Gggrk—Gggrk.*" He reached for his back and spun around.

"What in God's name," whispered Penske.

A squid-maggot hung from the officer's back, tentacles hungrily gouging his flesh. Blood soaked his shirt. He screamed.

The curious attention the scene was attracting quickly turned to panic. The other officer charged over, wild eyed. "Jeffries!" she cried, pulling her gun.

Greg backed up and felt Penske jerk him by the arm.

"What's going on here, you little punk?" Penske shouted, bourbon on his breath.

Behind the newscaster, a squid-maggot slithered, bounced into the air and landed, body pointing straight up, tentacled maw down, engulfing Penske's head.

"*Glllrgbbrrrl!*" cried the flailing newscaster.

Greg ran. The path to his car was screaming pandemonium. Squid-maggots snaked around, bounding onto victim after victim. Bodies and paper pilgrim hats littered the streets.

A parked tractor with *Carl's Corn Hut Gives Thanks* painted on the side had hitched to it a wheeled cart filled with hay and ears of corn. A man stood in the hay, pitching corn at MLB speeds at the creatures encircling him. He nailed one midjump, sending it flying. As it soared, one of its tentacles somehow snagged the air. A portion of the empty sky tore like a piece of fabric, revealing starry purple behind it.

"This is a real problem," Greg remarked.

As Greg reached his car, a squid-maggot slithered toward him. He dodged as it jumped. The thing slammed into his car door, denting it.

Greg grabbed the creature and took a roll of duct tape from his car.

"You're not disappearing on me, you slimy little shit-banana," Greg said.

He duct-taped around the creature's tentacles, left one long piece of tape hanging, got into his car, and slammed the tape's free end in his glove box. With the creature riding shotgun, he peeled out, fleeing the chaos.

Greg texted Lyra: *I'm back! On my way over. We have to talk.*

←♥→←♥→←♥→

Greg pulled into the dirt driveway, where Lyra was already waiting for him. He parked, nearly jumped from his car and said: "Nice haircut."

Something registered and Greg narrowed his eyes suspiciously, like he was concerned he might be the object of a prank. Lyra's haircut was precisely the same exercise in angularity that Carla from Caffeinerati had made her calling card. He shook off the strangeness. Before Lyra could hug him hello, he said, "Come clean on the squid-maggots."

"I have no notion of what you mean!"

Greg twitched his nose and blinked. He charged back to his car, wrestled the duct-taped beast out, slammed it on the hood, and extended one arm, presenting the creature for Lyra's appraisal.

"Look familiar now? They're at the parade, eating people and ripping holes in the fabric of reality. Full confession, I wasn't really at my grandma's house. I was cagey about hanging out because I saw Kent naked in the barn with a bunch of squid-maggots the other morning."

"You *snooped in my barn* and then *lied* to me?"

"Yes, but you still don't have the moral high ground here."

"Okay, I haven't been entirely forthcoming."

"Do tell."

"Those animals." Lyra pointed to the squid-maggot. "Kent gives birth to them."

"Dear God," Greg sat on the stairs. "They're your ex-husband's—rectal offspring?"

"No, no, it's nothing like that. I mean, it's sort of like that, actually. He projectile vomits black stuff with eggs in it, and those things hatch from them."

"Then why butt naked?"

"It's an attachment thing, I think."

Greg sighed heavily.

"Every May, Kent's family and mine go on vacation together," Lyra said. "When I moved back, divorce notwithstanding, I still had to go. It was less awkward than you'd think, honestly. It had been years, and I never *hated* him in the first place. We just grew apart. Those two weeks, he had this whole shtick about learning to be friends with the *new me*."

"Sounds reasonable," Greg said.

"When I moved into this house, which belonged to my great-grandparents, the barn seemed like the obvious spot to do music stuff. I figured I'd invite Kent to watch the first rehearsal of Cosmic. In retrospect, I think he read some symbolism into it."

"How's that?"

"Well, that barn—high school—we first got to know each other there."

"He thought the invitation signaled you were getting back together."

"On some level, I think so," she said. "Anyway, I did the performance. Everything sounded incredible. Midsong, I saw Kent was kneeling, frozen. I tried to help him, but I couldn't move either. Then through the speakers came, in a drone with a timbre I can only describe as *darkness*, the word *Yog-Sothoth*. Kent's mouth opened. A creature materialized made of, like, crystal balls, but the reflections on them were—wrong. The creature sprayed a stream of bubbles into Kent's mouth."

"Heck of a show," Greg said.

Hearts Synchronize

"Then the music cut. Power outage. The creature was gone. Kent was in the fetal position. We avoided the topic until I found him in there days later, naked and barfing up eggs. Since then, we've just been trying to figure out how to manage it. The plan was to fill the barn with cement."

"Cement?"

"Kent said he only got the urge to barf while in the barn. We figured that meant the barn was the gateway."

"I don't think that cement's coming." Greg scratched his head. "And given how the parade was looking, I don't think the barn has anything to do with it, anyway."

"This is all so confusing," Lyra said, sadly. "Stuff's moving too fast, and I can't figure out what to do."

Greg pulled her close and they hugged tightly.

"I know," Greg said softly. "It's stressful."

"See this haircut?" she said, stepping back, sniffling, and pointing to her head.

"Yeah, it's really—idiosyncratic."

"The other day, I woke up like this."

"Really? It looks sort of hard to maintain."

"No, I mean, I didn't receive this haircut at a salon. I've been working on a new arrangement on the Resonator. The morning after I rehearsed Cosmic II in my bedroom, I suddenly had this haircut."

"Woah," Greg said. "So you used it again? Even though the debut performance opened an extra-dimensional portal?"

"I had to," Lyra said. "I've found a new aesthetic realm! I'm giving voice to the universe's songs! How could I stop?"

Greg sighed and rubbed his temples. "I dig it. So, how is Cosmic II different? Since you're not barfing eggs, I'd assume you've tweaked something."

"I'll show you."

←♥→←♥→←♥→

Ascending the stairs to Lyra's bedroom, Greg felt something brush his leg and looked down and saw a cat.

"You have a cat?" he said.

"Strangest thing," Lyra said. "I had this incredible urge to buy two of them."

"Their names?" Greg said.

"Kyra and Myra."

"Uh-*huh*."

In the bedroom, Greg noticed speakers in two corners. Lyra grabbed from her closet patch cords, laptops and a Kleenex-box-sized conglomeration of circuitry—the Resonator.

"Sooo, I forgot to mention something else," Lyra said.

"Yeah?"

"Remember how I left before you woke up the other day?"

Greg nodded.

"That morning, I ran to the bookstore to work on Cosmic II. I didn't want to lose the flow."

"Dare I ask what was so inspiring?"

150

"While you were sleeping, I recorded our heartbeats," she said. "I read some studies about how people's hearts sometimes *synchronize* when they're—near each other."

"You don't say," Greg said. "So, you used our heartbeats in Cosmic II. I think that might explain some stuff."

"It's perfect. Cosmic II sounds completely different from Cosmic, too. You'll like it."

"Wait, you're going to actually perform it now?"

"Uh, that's what I said?"

"Yes, but I thought we were going to just have sex like last time."

"*That's* how much you care about my work? You, Kent, *half* the guys in grad school, is there just no interest in appreciating music anymore?"

Greg paced the room. "I care! It just seems—dangerous? Whenever you use this *Resonator* something incredibly weird happens. Extradimensional portals, extrabeauticianary haircuts—"

Greg nervously pulled up the window shades. "Ah nah," he said.

The view outside the window was terrifying.

Rifts were tearing into the early evening sky, as if the world were a two-dimensional painting and someone gouged it at random, revealing patches of another, differently orchestrated painting beneath it. Through the rents was visible a moonlike landscape with a purple sky, its *up* oriented as Greg's *down*. The geometrical confusion provoked a vertiginous nausea. Greg and Lyra collapsed and huddled together.

"At this point, what could it hurt." Greg reached up and closed the shade.

←♥→←♥→←♥→

Data read out on laptop monitors, mixing board diodes flickered, speakers droned, and the *Resonator* radiated sound responsively. A sonic pulse took shape. A polyphonic overtone emerged. Then another, which braided itself with a third. Greg held Lyra's hand.

A sonic *mise en abyme*, an endlessly building, incalculably complex swelling of sounds wove together, auditory fractals tessellating along heretofore inconceivable lines.

The sound dropped Greg in the middle of a mash-up of forgotten memories. Lyra in middle school turning and smiling at him. Carla almost twenty years later doing the same. Both aspects of a single gesture. Love, a characteristic of unfolding time. It's not so insane to see significance in symmetry. Coincidences are connections, and love is a fundamental physical property expressed through individuals. Time is threaded together with the synchronized song of heartbeats.

The music ended.

←♥→←♥→←♥→

They came out of it, gasping. Greg felt different.

"*Gah!*" Greg said. Lyra echoed the sentiment. They were shirtless, and tubes of clear organo-plastic, through which deep-red fluid flowed, connected their chests to one another.

They stood and walked apart backward, tugging on the tubes. They were as firmly connected as fingers. While such a metamorphosis made suddenly, unexpectedly, without regards for the conventions of the human form, might seem

Hearts Synchronize

panic-inducing, the opposite was true. It felt to Greg like it addressed all humanity's physical inadequacies.

Lyra did some quick scissor work to make their shirts fit, and they dressed and left the bedroom. At the bottom of the staircase, they stood enjoying the shared autonomic synchronization, the pleasant omnipresent tickle, the blissful second-by-second spasm of the doubly-embodied heartbeat, eight chambers ideally aligned, pumping the fluid blood that transmitted the substance love.

"I've gotta—" Greg said, motioning toward the bathroom.

Happily, the tubes stretched painlessly and surprisingly far, not precluding the closing of the door.

Utilizing the facilities, Greg thought about cycles. While the world was very likely ending outside, he had at least glimpsed confirmation that cycles were there, that the way things in life matched up and mirrored others was often no accident.

Greg washed his hands and left the bathroom. When he rejoined Lyra, he held her hands in his, tubes hanging between them.

"Hearts synchronize," he said, softly, leaning down to kiss her.

They both turned to see that someone had arrived.

Kent, butt naked, looking insane, stood before the open front door. Outside, the world had fallen away, leaving a purple sky and a desolate, white landscape, with hundreds of squid-maggots slithering busily across the ground.

There was a second-long, pregnant silence.

"I suppose I had this coming," Greg said.

← ♥ →← ♥ →← ♥ →

M. Stern is an author of weird horror, sword and sorcery, and science fiction whose stories have appeared in more than a dozen magazines and anthologies, including *Weirdbook*, *Startling Stories*, and the *From Beyond the Threshold* anthology from Eerie River Publishing. For news on the latest M. Stern stories to synchronize your heart, your eyes, and your pineal gland with, visit msternauthor.com or follow on Facebook @msternauthor.

You Can Still Have a Life

D. A. Salvatore

We're standing at our property line, staring at the massive tentacle-shaped spire that fills the space where Russ and Jan Wright's pool had been. Russ, slack jawed and wide eyed, tells me he thinks a big change is coming. I give him an *oh really* look and gesture toward the protrusion. He says nothing and walks off toward it, Jan following.

My wife, I notice, also has that same vacant stare. I give her a nudge.

"Maybe we should, you know, check it out," she says.

"I *do* know that we *definitely* should *not* check it out." I try to lead her away. "Look what it did to my raspberry bushes."

"We need to keep an open mind," she goes on, undeterred by the roots of the monstrosity snaking their way into our yard, displacing soil and vegetation indiscriminately. "It'll only be harder for us if we don't try to adjust."

I'm glad one of us is taking all this in stride, but I can no better adjust to this than to the temperature of the ocean while getting keelhauled. I say as much, but being overly dramatic can be a conversation ender. In this case, it is. Anyway, there is nothing to discuss. She has decided, but I won't find out until too late.

The tentacle is an eyesore, towering above Russ and Jan's two-story house, looming like a biopsy result. It drips with blackish-green iridescent pus and stinks like rot.

The first one shot up a few weeks earlier in Szarvas, Hungary. *Where?* Exactly. No one knows what happens there on any given day, so why couldn't *anything* happen there? Wild speculation began. Was it man-made, an elaborate hoax? Was it part of some ancient creature thawing out? Well, whatever it was, it was far away in a place folks like me had never heard of.

Life went on for a while until reports emerged of the good people of Szarvas going missing. People went *into* the Szarvas spire and didn't return, and if they did, they were "changed somehow."

Then a similar spire went up in Bonners Ferry, Idaho. And the same thing

153

started happening to the people there. I'd hoped that was it. One for Europe, and one—just one—for the USA. Two is plenty! No such luck. Just over 400 miles southwest, we got another.

I find a note on the kitchen table the morning after our argument. I know it's my wife's writing, even though it's composed of strange symbols. Part of me can almost decipher it, and I get the impression that she'll be back later.

I have little to do. Spires going up everywhere have unpredictable impacts. I have no job anymore, and no means of contacting anyone outside of walking distance, because anything that uses electricity gives up and dies. Honestly, going over to the Wrights' place and, well, just "checking out" the spire seems compelling. Another part of me screams at that idea. I shake it off. I decide to check my raspberries.

They look surprisingly okay after being partially uprooted. I'll pick as many as I can, even if they aren't ripe. If the bushes die, I'll have none. From the toolshed, I grab a basket we'd bought from a yard sale. At the time, I thought we'd overpaid— eight bucks, come on!—but the concept of money seems pointless now. We have no need for currency. We have no needs or wants, and we will be cleansed of—

—I snap back to conscious thought after what must have been hours. Time doesn't work the same anymore, or at least it doesn't feel like it works the same. The sky is always a dull, aching red. My basket is overflowing. I take my harvest into the house, hoping my wife would be back.

She is. And she looks happy to see me with my bounty. Aside from the smile, she looks different, glowing somehow. Ah, yes. She is literally glowing, covered with the same iridescence that shimmers on the spire. She points at the basket, smiling supernaturally wide, almost like she wants to show off her new mouth, radiating with purulence. I do a silly little wave in response. (I still feel silly about it.)

But she is still pointing at the basket. So I look. Oh. Okay. I had spent an unknown amount of time harvesting, but not raspberries. My basket is full of bloody little red eyes.

She drips across the floor and holds me tight in a slimy embrace. We say nothing, but nothing needs to be said. I can feel it. An undulating presence within her. Something from beyond the knowable universe called her. My wife of ten years answered.

←♥→←♥→←♥→

In the days following, I discover my sole purpose on this new Earth, the only logical and available pursuit, the only thing that makes sense in this chaos—gardening.

Aside from my prized raspberry eyeball bushes, I have a modest produce garden. I don't know what season it is, but they thrive in the sky's red luster. My climbing beans struggle against their own vines, their outer casings turned to maggot flesh. When I lean close, they scream at me. My hot pepper varieties pulsate with each heartbeat. My potatoes claw out of the ground and try to drag themselves away. But they're slow, and I can track them by following the trail of blood they leave behind. My lush garden has adapted to this climate and fits in nicely. Everything but the kale—still inexplicably green and leafy.

It's not traditional gardening, but I lose myself in it. The plants need no water; they need no fertilizer. They regrow their fruit nearly as quickly as I pluck it. I bring these offerings to my wife in the overpriced basket each day.

After I deliver the basket of "veg," my wife dumps them in the organic cauldron-like orifice that has grown out of the kitchen floor. The insides are constantly boiling, and she stirs the contents rhythmically while whispering incantations. When she's done, we eat. Or rather, she eats, and I choke back the slop as best as I can. I don't want to hurt her feelings. (I've asked her to make me kale on the side, or at least include it for my sake since it doesn't have innards like everything else, but she can't stand the stuff.)

Despite this, I immediately vomit. Violently. There doesn't seem to be any way around it. I don't know if minimal digestion keeps me tethered to the life I once had, but vomiting after eating anything these days is a foregone conclusion. Maybe I'm just stubborn.

I'm wringing out my shirt over a waste orifice when my wife tells me we're going to the Wrights' tonight. "Tell" might not be the right word anymore. She has lost the ability or the capacity or maybe the will to use human languages—I don't know. Her body is changing so fast, it's hard for me to keep up, but I'm trying to be ready for anything.

She's making *cookies*. How she's making them, I don't know, but anything that's not stew or stew-like is a breath of fresh air. Some of the cookies have my raspberry eyeballs, and I suspect they can see, but I don't know who or what's looking in from the other side.

I'd rather not go, and besides, why can't they come over here? The reason for the visit is ostensibly ritualistic—something I am afraid to disrupt—but inside, some of us are still social creatures. (For example, my wife didn't have to make cookies. We could have just brought eyes from the eye bush, and everyone could have just had plain eyes, but I got the sense that she wanted it to be fun.)

Oh, and it *used to be* Russ and Jan's house but I don't think they're using names at all anymore. And it's not so much their house as it is, well, it's Russ. Russ kind of *is* the house? Or has been absorbed by it? (Right! That's why they don't come over to our place.) It's more of a temple now, anyway. Lots of people, or things . . . beings? Let's just say folks—lots of folks come by. It's a twenty-four-hour Russ of worship these days.

And every time we've gone over, it's been a progressive overload of insanity. In the time before the spire, it was just Russ and Jan boring me to death over dinner.

Then it's, "Oh, hey! We live in a big, wiggly tentacle. We're so trendy and hip, and we shall be spared in the Great Cleansing and Ascension!" (The use of "shall" is directly proportional in proximity to the Great Cleansing and Ascension—my running theory.) "Come look inside our tentacle house, the Tabernacle of Twilight. (Incomprehensible consonants!)"

Now? Regrettably, and I suppose inevitably, there are some other elements.

My wife and I walk—some of us walk, others crabwalk, and I'll leave it to you to infer whom; just don't comment or stare—over together. It's harder for her to go bipedal, so I'm carrying the eyeball cookies on a slab and some of them are crying.

We enter through Russ's flaps, which open to face our yard. The inside of the Russpire is a space like a big tent. There's no ceiling, even though I can see where the spire ends from the outside. Above us is a void that goes on forever. Kinda neat! And lots of folks are here tonight. That's good!—easier for me to avoid participation in a bigger crowd. I set the cookies down on the big, menacing table (the only furniture). I wait.

Usually, one or two things happen. We all stand around, someone leads us in a chant, then we leave. That's one of the newer elements. Sometimes there are refreshments. The other more regrettable but probably predictably inevitable thing that happens is we walk in and there's someone strapped to the menacing table. That person is probably screaming and struggling. *Then* there's some chanting, and *then* that person gets stabbed to death, and only then can we leave.

I guess the one good thing about get-togethers now is that there's no more small talk. No weather to talk about, for instance.

Looks like everyone who's going to be here is here. We form up.

Jan's in charge and she surges forward, holding a robe at me. Oh, a third thing? I tell her thanks but no thanks. Black's not really my color, and I prefer active wear. No one likes this. I look at my wife. Oh, no. She doesn't like this either. I'm letting her down, but I don't think I'm cut out for a more official role. Leading chants or being a stabber would take away from my gardening time. I wouldn't be able to do it anymore and who would take care of my plants? The real reason behind my primary reaction is that I'm just not ready to be someone else. I try to show her that in a flash with just a pleading glance, but we're on a tight schedule, apparently.

So now there's arguing, and uh-oh, pointing at me. I can't understand everything, but I can understand the tone. They're *glerlming* pretty loud. (Intuitively, that's how I think of communicating: I glerlm, you glelrm, he/she glerlms, etc.) Some acolyte pulls from its robe a knife that's maybe just long enough to be considered a sword in some circles, something between a blade and a tentacle. (So many tentacles these days.) The knife seems to want something from me. Get in line, pal.

Not too soon, my wife inserts herself between me and the increasingly agitated crowd. She appears to be more chitinous than anyone or anything else here. We all realize that at the same time. She rears up in front of me, makes the absolute worst noises you've ever heard in your life (but who knows?—the night's not over), and brandishes appendages, some of which grow on the spot.

With a refreshingly humanesque arm, she points at me, and then to the way we came in. I do as the pointing suggests, muttering apologies and platitudes as I shuffle away. Russ's flaps part. I crouch-walk and try not to let any of the goo drip on me as we leave. It's a losing battle. But we leave early and no one gets murdered—my kind of party.

At home, I feel sheepish and don't really know what to do with myself, so I sit by the cauldron and look sad. She watches me for a bit, then she sits next to me. In silence, we watch the ebb and flow of the cauldron's goo.

After a while, she turns toward me and pushes her hair (looking more and more like a bundle of spider legs) out of her face. One of her mouths turns upward in what I could be forgiven for thinking is a smile. I extend my hand, and slowly, she reaches for mine and takes it with a raptorial appendage. Her eyes are all black with no distinction from pupil or iris or sclera. Are they still hers? Looking back at me

D. A. Salvatore

with love, adoration? Is she still in there somewhere?

But am I still me? I don't know. I was on the cusp of a change tonight, and I rejected it. I disappointed my wife, but she supported me when it counted. (The next meeting at the Wrights' is going to be super awkward, though.)

Maybe it doesn't matter. Growing old together doesn't have to mean growing the same way. I give her clasper a squeeze. Her return squeeze is gentle, but strong. I know she could pierce my hand through the bone at will, and I know something inside of her tells her to do it, to destroy me.

But she loves me, so she doesn't listen to it.

←♥→←♥→←♥→

D. A. Salvatore writes horror. You can find him lurking around the Pacific Northwest drinking too much coffee. Email him at SalTheTerror@gmail.com.

About the Editor

Gevera Bert Piedmont (Transformations by Obsidian Butterfly LLC) is a neurodivergent cyborg swamp witch living on the edge of a frog pond in Connecticut with her spouse, cats, and an impressive collection of rubber lizards. She is the author of *The Maw and Other Time-Traveling Lizard Tales* and the Mickey Crow paranormal series, and coauthor of *Airesford* (the other author is an actual zombie). She is the Amazon bestselling co-editor of *Horror Over the Handlebars,* an anthology of Connecticut horror.
Her next anthology, with co-editor Elizabeth Davis of Dead Fish books, will be *The Atlas of Deep Ones.*

Her short stories have been published in *Love Beyond Death, The Fellowship of the Old Ones, Heart of Farkness, Through a Scanner Farkly, Doomscrolling, Wicked Sick, Something Woked This Way Comes,* and others.

Bert has an MFA in creative writing and belongs to the Horror Writers Association, Connecticut Authors and Publishers Association, and New England Horror Writers. Connect at Facebook.com/geverabertpiedmont, geverabertpiedmont.com, or obsidianbutterfly.com.

About the Designer

Bridgette Rodrigues of Obsidian Butterfly Designs designed the cover and interior layout for *Necronomi-RomCom.* She is a graphic designer, artist, and book lover. She loves all things witchy and batty, and is obsessed with Halloween and steampunk. She lives with her husband and a great many Cthulhu stuffies in Connecticut. She has a BFA in graphic design from Rivier University of Nashua, NH. Bridgette can be reached at bdesigns13@gmail.com.

About the Illustrator

Karolina Mochniej (Arts from Cards) is an independent artist based in Krakow, Poland. In her work she explores the occult, mythological and archetypal tropes, tarot symbology, and relationships with animals and nature. Her artwork has been featured in various art and literary journals (*Diet Milk, Lovecraftiana: The Magazine of Eldritch Horror, Archive of the Odd, The Magazine of Eldritch Horror, New Reader Magazine*) and displayed in art exhibitions (*Ars Necronomica* at NecronomiCon 2022 in
Providence, RI, *Constructing Consciousness* exhibition at Brookfield Craft Center). View more of her work on Instagram @artsfromcards. Karolina can be contacted at arts.from.cards@gmail.com

www.ingramcontent.com/pod-product-compliance
Lightning Source LLC
Chambersburg PA
CBHW060648260626
47161CB00008B/3043